C000027611

SUMMER STORM

Season of the Lawman - Book One

MARIE HALL

Published by Blushing Books
An Imprint of
ABCD Graphics and Design, Inc.
A Virginia Corporation
977 Seminole Trail #233
Charlottesville, VA 22901

©2019
All rights reserved.

No part of the book may be reproduced or transmitted in any form or by any means, electronic or mechanical, including photocopying, recording, or by any information storage and retrieval system, without permission in writing from the publisher. The trademark Blushing Books is pending in the US Patent and Trademark Office.

Marie Hall
Summer Storm

EBook ISBN: 978-1-64563-133-0
Print ISBN: 978-1-64563-174-3
v2

Cover Art by ABCD Graphics & Design
This book contains fantasy themes appropriate for mature readers only.
Nothing in this book should be interpreted as Blushing Books' or the author's advocating any non-consensual sexual activity.

Chapter 1

Arizona Territory, 1887...

C *lack, clack, clack.*
Chase rolled his shoulders, trying to ignore the woman in the next cell. Her heavy sigh signaled she'd again turn and start banging the small tin cup along the bars.

Clack, clack, clack. The staccato ring echoed in the stone room.

With a sigh, he reached up and tugged the brim of his hat down more. It wasn't enough to block out the view from her waist down. And it was a view. Her denim pants didn't leave too much to the imagination. Normally, he didn't like women in britches, but on her, they weren't too terrible. That banging, though. His head was going to start hurting soon.

"Would you please stop? It's not helping," Chase said, pushing his hat back and leaning up on his forearms.

"No?" she asked and not like it was really a question. "You know what would've helped? Listening to me when I said don't bring that sorry ass Gracen's corpse to this rotten town. I told you—"

"Yeah, yeah," Chase grumbled, lying back and pulling his

1

hat over his eyes. He might have to give her this one. When they had ridden in with the body over the back of the horse, she'd warned him the sheriff and his deputy were no good. Sure enough, before they were dismounted, there were guns pointing at them.

Chase quickly identified himself as a U.S. Marshal and announced he'd a bill, a warrant, allowing him to bring Frank Gracen in, dead or alive. The woman did too, though hers was signed by a judge somewhere out of Kansas. Neither of those things prevented them both from being taken inside the only halfway sturdy looking building on the street and locked in the two cells.

Chase wasn't overly concerned. His identity could be confirmed with a telegraph, and he'd vouch for the woman he'd encountered when they both took aim at, killed, and then claimed the corpse. But she wasn't having it. The longer they stayed locked up waiting for the judge to act, the more irate she became. And for such a beautiful woman, she was a bit scary when she was spitting mad.

The banging started up again, and this time it seemed she put a bit more force in it. Maybe she'd dent the cup and have to stop. Before that hope could rise, the door between the cells and the office opened and the fat, sweating, deputy stepped in. His stench made Chase's eyes water.

"Knock off that noise," he shouted.

"Let me out of here; you've no legal reason to hold me," she shouted back, recoiling when he stepped closer.

"You don't shut your whoring mouth, it'll be more than holding done to ya," the man threatened.

"Now, wait a minute," Chase said, getting to his feet. "Ain't no reason to call names. The lady ain't done nothing wrong."

"Lady?" the man laughed then coughed, likely because the effort was too much for his hulking weight. "You must be blind; round here, we know whores when we see 'em. And around here, we don't tolerate 'em. We got nothing but good decent folk in this town and we aim to keep it that way."

"Then let me go, and you can have back your puritanical township," she snapped. Chase raised a brow at the word choice. If she was educated beyond what most women were, it certainly made her more interesting to him. She was certainly educated far above the deputy who looked not to understand the word.

"You think you can just throw insults?" he snarled, grabbing the keys from his belt and stepping toward her. "I'll teach you pur-tan-al," he said, jamming the key in the lock.

"Wait a minute," Chase shouted as the girl backed up as far as she could. "You need to stop," Chase warned as the door to her cell opened. "I'm a U.S. Marshal, and I'm ordering you to stop."

"I'll stop," the man said, dragging his arm over his mouth as he worked to back her into a corner, "after I teach this whore some manners."

She was clever enough not to get cornered, and when she stepped on the bench, she'd a slight advantage as she could perhaps kick him some place he'd feel it. "Only one here needing manners is you," she snarled and sent her foot into his jowls. He stumbled back and hit the door, which sent it swinging wide.

"I like 'em with a little fight," the deputy taunted and charged her.

"I order you to stop," Chase said, not willing to watch the woman get raped right in front of him. He reached out and grabbed the open cell door, pulled the key out, and used it to unlock his cell. He stepped into hers as the deputy moved from just pinning her down, to leaning in and licking her face.

Chase took hold of the man's collar and belt and threw him forward. His head bounced off the bars, but it wasn't enough to knock him out. Waiting until he turned to look at who'd interrupted his mating ritual, Chase sent his fist into the man's face. It took two more blows to knock him out.

When he looked sideways, he saw she'd managed to squirm out from under the pig, but she was breathless and unnaturally pale. Those big blue eyes, wide with fear, looked back and forth between him and the man unconscious on the floor.

Chase held out a hand to her. "Come on," he said. She took it, and he hauled her to her feet and backed out of the cell. He let her go long enough to pull the key from his door and use it to lock the cell now holding the deputy. "You all right?" he asked as the lock clicked in place.

"Yeah, sure," she said, still a little breathless. "Let's get out of here."

"Slow that pony," Chase said, hooking her by the back of her flannel shirt.

"Let's go; I'm not staying here." She tugged, trying to get free.

"And when we are duly set free, we'll go," Chase told her as he took hold of her arm and dragged her into the cell with him.

"No, we're free; we need to leave." She tried to shove past him, but he stood his ground, blocking her. She was a tiny thing, even with all her bristles up.

"No, we'll go when the sheriff clears us and when the money is handed over for Grungy Gracen." He held her back as he reached out and grabbed his cell door, swinging it closed and quickly locking them in.

"Are you crazy?" she screeched, going for the keys he held above his head. Even jumping, she couldn't reach them.

"No, I'm a sworn officer of the law, and I've a reputation I won't have tarnished with a hasty act." He set a hand on her shoulder to stop her efforts to grab the keys as she was already panting.

"Yeah, well, I'm just out for a bounty and not stupid enough to stick around where I'm not wanted." They looked over to where the deputy was now groaning and picking himself up off the floor. She made a grab for the keys as he'd lowered them, but he pulled them out of reach.

4

"We'll wait, be cleared, be paid—"

"That is my bounty. I found him, and if not for me, he'd have blown your head off," she snarled, crossing her arms over her ample enough chest.

Chase snorted; he wouldn't have this argument with her again. They'd, or rather she'd, made it an issue the entire ride to town. She'd gotten crabby enough over it, he had almost yanked her over his lap. A few good smacks to her pert bottom could still serve her well. And he was considering it when the door opened again.

"What the Sam Hill?" the sheriff yelled.

What the Sam Hill indeed? Chase would be asking him that question a lot now.

Chapter 2

"What the Sam Hill?" Summer was about to take a seat when Sheriff Broward walked in.

Marshal Storm took a step in front of her, like she needed protection or something. "Your deputy lacks manners," he said.

Summer snorted, only to get elbowed in the arm.

Broward didn't even raise a brow at the remark, just leaned in and unlocked the cell door. "You're free to go, Marshal Storm, and we sure are sorry for the delay. The bank'll have your money for Gracen by morning."

Summer watched the marshal collect his hat from the bench and prepared to follow him out. In the cell beside them, the deputy used the bars to get to his feet, weaving. Summer rather hoped he'd fall on his face again.

"You all right, Dewy?" the sheriff asked his man. The only response he got was a grumble.

Personally, Summer couldn't care less if he was all right or not. He was a pig. Stepping forward, she readied to push past the marshal and get out of the building, the town, the whole damn Arizona territory.

"Not you, sugar britches," the sheriff snapped, setting a hand in her chest and pushing her backward."

"What?" Summer shouted and righting herself, headed for the door which was slammed and locked close in her face.

"Why is she being held?" Marshal Storm inquired.

"Judge sentenced her to five years in Yuma," the sheriff said with a shrug. "Ol' Dewy gets to escort her there on Friday." The sick smile on the sheriff's face mirrored the one on the deputy's. Summer's knees weakened. "Should be a good eighteen, twenty days, there and back, I'll be without my deputy, but I think we'll manage. We've a good town here."

"What do you mean, the judge sentenced her to five years in prison? On what charge?" Marshal Storm asked, at least sounding somewhat outraged. "Without a trial?"

"Don't need no trial," the sheriff said with a shrug. "She is guilty; just look at her. Come on now. I'll get you your things, and you can take a room in the hotel until you get paid then be on your way. Though it sure is an honor to have a man with your fine reputation grace us here."

"She's guilty of what?" Marshal Storm asked, stepping to block the sheriff from unlocking the deputy's cell. "What was she charged with?"

The look the sheriff gave the marshal said he couldn't believe he was being asked. "Isn't it obvious, whoring, indecency in public, corruption of the people in this town?"

Summer listened to the charges, and when her legs couldn't hold her anymore, she sat down and put her head in her hands. Her stomach twisted. Five years in Yuma Prison? She turned to look at the deputy in the cell next to her. Ten or more days on the road with him? She'd never make it to the prison. She tried to blink back the tears, but damn it, they spilled out.

"Have you all lost your minds?" Marshal Storm shouted.

"Look, Marshal, we all know you've the finest record for upholding law and justice. Everyone west of the Mississippi read how Mr. Cleveland had you up in Washington and all, so why you fussing over this little tart, well, I don't right know."

The ringing in her ears drowned out most of what was said next, and not until something clanged against the bars did she look up. The marshal looked as stricken as she felt, but behind that, there was a determination in his face she couldn't bring to muster for herself.

"I'll fix this," he said to her before turning back to the sheriff. "Let's go speak with this judge." When the sheriff moved to release the deputy, Marshal Storm stepped in his way. "Nope, he stays locked up until we get back." When the sheriff looked to protest, he added, "I'm sure it won't be good for you, should I send a wire to the territorial governor about how prisoners in your custody are treated."

There was a hesitation, but the sheriff gave in. Whoever this Marshal Storm was, he had sway. Summer hoped it was enough to get her out of the mess he had gotten her into. Setting his hat on his head, he made to follow the sheriff out. "I'll be back," he said then closed the door, leaving her locked in a cell beside the man who'd get to spend at least ten days raping her if he didn't return.

"Judge Hooper ain't gonna change his mind," Deputy Dewy said with a sneer. "He can't stand little whores like you. One done killed his son, and now..." He reached through the bars, and Summer fell off the bench avoiding his touch. "Yeah, that's all right, me and yous gonna get real fine acquainted and all. Maybe even take our time getting down to Yuma." He practically licked his lips.

Summer picked herself up off the floor and took her seat on the bench, out of reach, "You do know, it's completely hypocritical of you to preach to me about the immorality of wearing pants while explaining how your covetous person will be raping me for two weeks."

The man was silent for a while, then taking a seat himself, he grinned at her. "You won't be so high and mighty, using all dem big words, once they close the doors behind you in Yuma. You make it out, it'll be you what's hip-a-crit-al and cover-ous."

Summer could only groan, lean her head back, and close her eyes, because as it grew later in the day, she began to think Marshal Storm wasn't *fixing* this or even coming back. It was his damn reputation he was protecting when he wouldn't let her escape, and it was that damn reputation that was going to take whatever life she might have from her. Damn men and their pride. Damn men and their unwillingness to listen to anyone without a pecker swinging between their legs. Damn men, just damn them.

SHADOWS STRETCHED out and the growling from Summer's stomach was starting to grow louder than the snoring from the cell next to her. That she could even think of food at this time was probably more because food was always something in her life that meant warmth, comfort, and love. Not so much eating it, but preparing it. If she was given a last meal, she'd likely opt to make it herself than to actually eat it. But as the darkness continued to sweep deeper into the room, she rather doubted she'd ever find herself elbow deep in flour again. Raising her hand, she brushed at the tears that rolled down her face. Her skin was chapped now from the constant battle to keep them off her skin. She hated to cry; it was a sign of weakness, but in the face of what loomed, she'd no care to be strong.

A loud bang from the office startled both prisoners, and when the door opened, the lantern glare blinded her for a moment.

"You," the marshal's voice boomed, "out and stay out," he said, unlocking the deputy's cell and all but kicking him in the ass as he stumbled out the room. "You," his voice softened greatly, "clean up and change into this." He unlocked the cell, setting a bucket of water on the floor and handing her some clothing. He then turned his back to her and folded his arms over his chest.

"What happened?" Summer asked, holding up the skirt, realizing it was hers. "What happened? Am I free?" Putting on a dress was all it was going to take? She didn't let the tremble in her hands slow her down from unfastening her belt. "Did the judge set me free too?"

"Not exactly. Just get dressed, and I'll explain it to you." She didn't like his tone. It didn't sound completely guilty, but it didn't sound relieved, either.

Summer made quick use of the water and the rag twisted over the bucket's handle. She took extra care to wash her face, erase the evidence she'd given in to the despair and fear. As she stepped into the skirt, she tucked her shirtwaist down so it was smooth then fastened the skirt and replaced her belt. "I'm dressed. Can we get out of here now?"

Marshal Storm turned and lifted the lantern to give her a once over then frowned. "Nope," he said. "The pants need to come off, not just be under the skirt."

"What the hell difference does it make?" Summer asked, not ready yet to lose the garment, both because it was easier to ride in them and because it was harder for men to get at her with them.

"It's gonna make all the difference. Get them off, and we'll get this over with."

"Get what over with?" God help her, was she going to the gallows? She sat to pull her boots off, stood, and lifted her skirts enough so she could shuck the sturdy denim. The marshal remained quiet until she stomped her foot into the second boot. He again turned, this time holding his hand out for the pants, which she handed over, before he stepped aside. "Well?"

"We're getting hitched."

Chapter 3

Chase sighed wearily as he stuck the key in the door of their hotel room. Even if he wanted to leave before he was paid, it was too dark to get far enough from this deplorable, corrupt, tumbleweed town.

As he let the door swing open, he stepped aside to let Summer Rain—no, Summer Storm, his new bride—pass. She did, her arms still crossed over her chest as they had been from the moment she'd stepped before Judge Hooper. Her heated glare burned like the desert sun as she walked in and stopped, making him pass around her to set their belongings down on the small, *too small*, bed. He made a trip back to close the door because she'd not even wanted to be that helpful.

Leaving might at least have gained a bit of cooperation from her, but given none of this was her choice or even her doing, he wasn't going to expect any from her for now. That she'd actually hesitated when told she had to choose between five years in the women's prison in Yuma, Arizona or marriage to him was concerning. Even his assurance his reputation was well obtained and he could support her didn't have her jumping at the option.

Still, in the end, she'd agreed, and with the judge's wife and the sheriff as witnesses, Judge Hooper had made them man and wife, not something Chase himself really expected to experience. Though, with the new position he'd accepted in Willow Springs, Colorado, it was as good a time as any. No more months on the plains hunting outlaws. He'd only be responsible for the area currently known as the San Miguel region. And though he'd not yet seen the place, Willow Springs was said to be a boom town, the extended railway shuttling cattle, coal, and even gold through the San Juan Mountain Range.

He was selected to run an office for the U.S. Marshal services, picking up where the Kansas City and Denver ones stopped, supporting the mining and rail companies who were, at the moment, being hit hard by bandits. He'd be given the authority to swear in men to pursue those outlaws west of the Rocky Mountains.

And while he'd not planned to show up with a wife, the house that came with the job should be enough for them to start life together if she didn't murder him right here in this dusty hotel room.

"Are you hungry? We can go down to the eatery, or I can go and bring something up if you don't—"

"As soon as the bank is open and I get my money, I'll be gone," Summer hissed at him. She dropped her arms, crossed to the bed, and sat down hard. "And this is your fault, so you sleep on the floor."

Chase drew in a long slow breath and let it out with the same ease. "Look, we'll need to talk about some things and—"

"No, we won't. Soon as that money's in my hand, you can forget I exist."

"Summer..." Dang, he liked that name on her. It perfectly suited her. Thick gold and coppery, sun streaked hair, big pale blue eyes, lips that were as full and looked as sweet as a cherry, warm peach skin. She was the embodiment of the season. And he was still amused that her taking his name changed nothing, really. She went from Summer Rain to Summer Storm, even Summer Rain Storm, as she'd declared no middle name and thus held her own when she signed the marriage certificate. If she was going to marry someone, at least marrying him didn't cripple the beauty of her name. But marrying him didn't keep that lightning out of her eyes. Now might not be the best time to try to speak about the deal struck and what it'd mean for them. That he'd no idea who she was, really, meant he'd taken a big risk by offering her this out. She could at least be thankful for that much. Right now, she wasn't thankful for anything. So maybe, over supper... "How about I get us some grub and we talk?" Her response was a shrug and a refolding of her arms over her chest. "All righty then, you wait here. I'll go see what I can scrounge up."

"Fine," she muttered.

"Stay in the room, Summer," he warned, knowing if he was her, he'd be out a window or down the backstairs before two shakes of a lamb's tail. "I'm more than sure we're being watched, and if it looks at all like you're not abiding by the terms..."

He let that hang out there as he opened the door and stepped out. He closed it firmly and turned the lock. Dang, he couldn't have started off worse with her. But then, that meant things could only get better.

Chase made his way down to the dining area of the hotel. It wasn't much but a couple of small tables and chairs next to an open cook stove and larger table.

"Can I help you again, Marshal?"

Chase turned to find the proprietor who'd checked him in standing behind him wiping his hands on his apron. "I was wondering if it was too late to get a meal?" He looked back at the pot on the stove.

"Chrissy?" the man who'd introduced himself as Clay Pennington yelled.

"Yes, Papa?" the young, rather beaten down woman asked as

she scrambled in from the back door, wiping her face on her shoulder, which she hunched forward, likely trying to hide the large, reddening mark on her neck.

"Get the marshal something to eat," Pennington snarled then turned and walked away grumbling that his own daughter was a no-good female like her mother.

For her part, as soon as the old man had his back turned, the girl breathed a sigh of relief and smiled weakly. "The stew is still warm enough, but I'm afraid the biscuits'll be cold."

"Anything is fine," Chase assured as she moved to pull a single bowl from the shelf and carry it to the table. "No, sorry. I need two meals, and I'll take them up to my room. My wife wasn't feeling up to eating in the dining room."

At the mention of a wife, the young woman's smile fled. That, in the space of two minutes, having just left the arms of someone else, she'd looked at him hoping to find her ticket out of here spoke to the desperate nature of females in this town.

He'd certainly not missed the way men shoved any woman who happened to be outside behind them when he passed on his way between the jail and the judge's house. Nor had he missed how, like this girl, every woman was dressed, neck buttoned to the top, in several layers. Even this late in the day, heat lingered. It'd be oppressive, even dangerous, any other time the sun was blazing down.

"I hope you and she enjoy," the woman said, handing him a tray with two bowls of stew and a small basket of biscuits.

Chase reached in his shirt pocket for the silver he kept there. He handed it to her and took the tray. "Keep that change," he told her, knowing the vast over payment might be the start of her escape from the prison this whole town seemed to be. He'd threatened to send a wire to the governor about how things were being run here. Climbing the stairs back to his room, he made it a promise; the very first wire office he came to, he'd put it out someone needed to come investigate. He set the tray down to unlock the door then called out, "Summer, it's just me," before opening the door.

He half expected to see she'd run, but she hadn't. She sat on the floor with everything pulled out of her saddle bags, angrily refolding, rewrapping, and replacing it. "I can't believe you went through my things," she said, not even looking up.

"I only got in them to see if you owned a dress. Otherwise, I'd have had to see if there was a dress shop to buy one. Didn't think you wanted to sleep in the jail tonight." He carried the tray to where she sat, and being as no table was in the room, he set it down and took a seat. "Eat something, and we—"

"Where's my guns and my rifle?"

"With the horses at the livery; we'll collect them tomorrow," Chase said and watched her frown but nod her head once. "Why, were you thinking of shooting me tonight?" he asked as a jest, but the sideways look she gave him made him wonder. "Look," he started.

"No, not you," she said, tracing her fingers around the edges of a worn bible. "The horse's ass sitting on the roof outside the window." She said then shoved the book into the pack with a bit too much force.

Chase chuckled. She had planned to run. "Told you." The look he got this time reminded him most guns held more than one bullet. "Summer, I know this isn't ideal, but if you'd just try to make the most of it." Nothing. "Maybe you can tell me something about yourself? Where you were born? Went to school? Where your family is?"

"My family is dead," she snapped, shoving the last of her things back in her packs and taking up one of the bowls cooling on the tray.

"Everyone?"

"Let me help you," she said with a heavy sigh. "I was born in Highfield, Kansas in 1865. I lived my whole life there until..." She scooped out a spoonful and shoved it in her mouth.

"Highfield," Chased echoed then swallowed. Highfield was burned off the map in '77. Raiders in the style of the old Quantrill gang swarmed the town and the entire surrounding area, burned every home and business, all crops, and murdered every man, most every woman, and even a number of children. Before anyone could even get to them from either Fort Leavenworth or Riley, they'd disappeared.

She swallowed hard. "This is horrendous," she said, reaching for a biscuit. "And these are cold and..." She tapped the bread on the side of the bowl. "Hard as a rock."

"I'm sorry," Chase whispered. What else could one say?

"Yeah, everyone's always sorry," she muttered, crumbling the biscuit into the stew. She mixed the crumbles in and took another bite. Chase picked up his bowl, and for a while, they ate in silence. And she was right; the stew was awful. But he'd eaten worse. He was ready to give up hope they'd spend the night learning about who'd they be spending the rest of their lives with.

"What's the 'D' stand for?" she asked, startling him.

"What?"

"The 'D'," she repeated. "When you signed your name, it was so much chicken scratch, I couldn't make out any of the letters but the first in each. C. D. S."

"Chicken scratch?" Chase grumbled then chuckled. His mother, sisters, and his aunts even complained about his penmanship. Said it took weeks to decipher any letter he sent them. "Chase Daniels Storm. Daniels is my mother's maiden name, so I never use it." Maybe she'd ask something else.

"Just the 'D'?" she asked, and he nodded. He heard her snicker, watched her shake her head and giggle. It was a sweet sound. "So you're Chase D. Storm? Chase *Dee*." She stretched that out. "Storm." Again, she snorted, head still shaking. "Couldn't have just been Joe Smith."

"Smith wouldn't have been a good last name for you." He

smiled when she glanced up at him. "And you're one to talk, Summer Rain."

"My mother was a romantic," she said with a shrug.

"I take it you're not?" Again, only a shrug. "Well, at least you've an excuse. I got both first and last names, because as fifth born, my parents were out of suggestions and picked out of a hat the first, and my brothers already used up surnames from my father's side."

"You have five brothers?" Summer sounded a bit in awe.

"Total, I have six and two sisters. I also have nine or ten nieces and nephews, maybe more by now. It's been a while since I got a letter. You married into a big family." He hoped that might cheer her. It always seemed people who didn't have a huge family liked the idea of them. But if anything, he sensed her pulling away again.

"Chase D, Summer Rain... Storm," she muttered. "That's gonna be a hard one to forget."

"I guess it will at that," he said, wondering why it felt like she was going to try.

They finished eating in silence. Chase didn't make any complaints about putting his bedroll on the floor. He waited until Summer wrapped up in her roll then blew out the lantern. It maybe wasn't how most wedding nights went, but, again, it could only get better from here.

He hoped.

Chapter 4

S ummer hadn't ever witnessed such ineptness in a kitchen in her entire life. The girl had more eggshell in the bowl than she had egg. Taking both from her hands, Summer proceeded to show her how it was done. "One firm hit," she said, cracking the egg and manipulating it to open enough to drop the contents from the shell. "It's all those little taps that cause the shell to break into the mix." She set the bowl down and moved back to slicing the two day old bread. By itself, it wouldn't be worth eating, but once she soaked it in egg and milk, it'd be just right for the *pain perdu*, one of many simple recipes she committed to memory for having made it so often.

"You sure this is gonna get ate? All soggy like that?" the girl, Chrissy, asked, looking on doubtful and perhaps fearful of the wrath of the men sitting at the table.

"Trust me," Summer said, and wetting the tip of her finger, she let a droplet hit the hot grease in the pan. The sizzle was about right, and using a fork, Summer whisked the eggs and milk together, dropped in a few slices of bread, made sure they were well soaked, and lifted the slices from the bowl to the pan. She let them cook until she could see the bottom edges getting brown and then flipped them in the pan.

"That smells really good, and it's so easy," Chrissy proclaimed.

"If you have any preserves or honey, better put it out now. These are best when they're hot," Summer told her as she added more bread slices to the bowl while the first batch finished frying. She plated them with more than a little resentment, knowing they'd be served to the sheriff and that pig of a deputy. And while she secretly hoped they'd choke and die, she was determined to do whatever was necessary to get paid and get gone from here without stirring up another hornets' nest. If it meant feeding the sheriff, deputy, and the banker a good breakfast, she'd do it and wait to laugh until she was riding hard east.

She plated the second batch and handed the plates to Chrissy, letting her decide who to serve first.

"Think to poison us, girl?" the deputy called out.

"If only," Summer muttered to herself. "I have a name, you imbecile." So much for no stirring beyond the eggs.

"Yes, she does."

Chase's deep voice turned her, and she found him leaning a shoulder against the wall. He looked all at once relieved and annoyed. "I didn't hear you get up and leave, Mrs. Storm." He stepped forward and placed a kiss on her cheek. His scent, which had plagued her the entire night, lingered when he pulled back. Like leather and maple, it reminded her of a tannery or even her aunt's house.

"Marshal Storm," the sheriff called, and Summer saw him close his eyes and take a breath. "How was that first night of wedded bliss?"

It was a taunt, but Chase didn't rise to it. "It was as perfect as I knew it'd be," he said, giving Summer a wink before turning to face the group at the tables. "What else, with a perfect lady as my wife."

That caused some looks to pass between the men, but without much else said, they went back to eating, even calling out for seconds when they scraped the last from their plates.

"Well, seems your new missus can at least cook," the banker called, holding up his plate so Chrissy could collect it for a refill. Summer dropped two more slices on the plate and then sliced more bread so there'd be some for Chase and herself. She also added eggs to the pan, frying them up slightly less than hard. She'd ask later how he liked them.

"So it seems," Chase said, stepping up behind her and looking over her shoulder. She could feel his body heat over the heat coming off the stove, and his build pressing against her back was more solid than the cast iron four-burner sitting in front of her. She felt his hands settle at her waist and pull her back a bit. "Don't wander again; who knows what it'll take for them to toss us back behind bars."

"I was hungry," Summer hissed as she put his meal on a plate. "Last night's stew wasn't even edible. I didn't want to wait and see what slop was served for breakfast."

"All right," he said, taking the plate and stepping back. "It's fine this time. But until we're clear of this town and county, stick close." He took the fork she held up for him and moved back against the wall.

"Sure." She was ready to agree to anything to get gone from Sheriff Broward and Deputy Dumbass. Turning back to the stove, she fixed herself the same meal she'd just made for Chase. Then, standing at the small table used to prepare meals, she ate hers.

"This is…" Chase stared, only to cover his mouth and swallow the rest of the way. "This is really good. What is it?"

"Has a lot of names, *aliter dulcia*. My mother called it *Arme Ritter*. I like *pain perdu*. All means the same, lost bread, soggy bread. Something to do when you let bread get stale."

"Never have I tasted stale bread this delicious," Chase said. He smiled too, and Summer felt her knees shake.

Damn, he was about the handsomest man she'd ever set eyes on. Dark brown hair, soft grey eyes, angular but not sharp features, and more than he had all his teeth, they were rather straight and white. His shoulders were broad, his arms thickly muscled, his stomach flat... she had to smile at that, because she knew any man who was loved well didn't have a flat stomach. She swallowed hard when the thought crossed her mind. She wasn't the woman who'd be loving him well. Not past the second they crossed the county line. Still, the way his waist narrowed just a bit and his legs stretched. He was tall. Way taller than she was. In fact, the top of her head landed between his elbow and his shoulder. She'd never seen a man so large who didn't also seem disproportioned. Everything on this man seemed perfectly measured. If he was a horse, he'd be a prized stallion for sure.

Heat crawled up her face then. Prized stallions had but one purpose in life, and given what she knew of men, this one probably had any number of mares rearing to get close to him. But Summer wasn't one of them. She'd plans. She was so close to achieving them, and not a single one included having a man in her life.

Just get the money and get out. She'd keep repeating the words until the sheriff, this town, and Chase Storm were lost in the dust behind her.

"If she's as good in bed as she is in the kitchen, you might be owin' us something for putting the two of you together," Deputy Jackass said, stepping too close to escape when Chase grabbed him by the neck and slammed him up against the wall.

"That's my wife you're speaking so freely about," he snarled, and the man went white. "If you don't want to get pummeled again, I suggest you start minding your manners, because, as of right now, you have no more chances to spare."

"All right now," the sheriff said, stepping up and then

between the men. "Dewy is harmless; he don't mean nothing by nothing. Let's just go get you paid that bounty and let you get on home with your bride."

"I'll go open the bank," the last of the trio said, almost running for the door.

"Mrs. Storm and I will be along shortly," Chase said, his voice never hinting at the fact he was ready to murder a man during breakfast.

Summer dropped her head to look at her plate as she ate, because being suddenly alone with this man had her wanting to reach out and run her hands over the stretched fabric of his shirt. Maybe up into that sable colored hair. Over his strong, square, freshly shaven jaw. And maybe just one time, she'd like to know what those lips would feel like on hers. Shifting, she tried to dispel the heat coiling through her. She shouldn't have worried. Chase did that for her with his very next words.

"We need some rules here," he said, and her head snapped up to find him glaring at her with narrowed eyes.

"Rules?"

He stepped up on the opposite side of the table, and setting his palms flat, leaned in closer. Again, that scent overwhelmed her. "Rules, yes. Rule one, we respect each other. Rule two, we tell each other where we'll be. Rule—"

Not being much for rules, Summer didn't care much for his. "I don't need any damn rules from you. You're not trail boss over me. Soon as we get the money and skedaddle, I—"

When he'd come around the table and spun her to face him, she didn't quite know. But he had her now pinned and bent backward as she tried to keep him at a distance.

"I'm not your trail boss. I'm your husband, and we'll have rules to keep our marriage from leaving the tracks."

"Our marriage?" Summer almost spat. "Our marriage ends as soon as we cross the county line."

"No," he said, putting his arm around her back and pulling her against him.

Summer did her best to lean back more, but his arm was an iron band. Her gaze dropped from those grey eyes which almost smoldered to his lips, which were almost where she most wanted them to be, on hers. She gave in and lifted her hands to that broad, solid chest and smoothed up. Exactly what she thought, nothing but well-defined muscle. His head bent closer, and her mouth dried up like the desert in July. Beneath her fingers, she could feel the strong steady beat of his heart. It seemed odd that his, too, would seem to be pounding like hers was.

He was almost there, his breath puffed out on her bottom lip, and when he spoke, his lips brushed softly against hers. "We'll have rules, Summer," he said in a hushed tone. "And we'll both stick to them."

She waited and held her breath until her lungs burned. When she couldn't wait any more, she opened eyes she didn't know had closed. He was still right there, looking at her, eyes no longer just smoldering but burning.

"This is that pesky rule one, darling," he said as she searched his face for clarification. "Respect. It means I'll never force you. Give me permission; show me you want this."

She didn't even know how to start, but it seemed all it took was for her to lift her head toward him.

His lips pressed down on hers, moving with the laziness of a deep river, each sweep becoming stronger, like a current driving her toward the rapids, and when his mouth covered hers completely, she knew what it would feel like to go over the falls.

Summer heard someone groan but wasn't sure if it was her or Chase. A moment later, his kiss became lighter, back to lazy river force and then down to the brush of the wind, light. When she lifted her lids, she found him staring down at her, the heat in his eyes more intense if it was possible.

"You're a beautiful thing to behold, Summer Storm," he said, his knuckles settled on her cheek. "Everything I might have hoped for."

Heat rose up from her chest, and her face felt like it burned. Exactly what had happened, she wasn't sure; it was like a spell took hold of her. She wasn't supposed to start liking this man. Certainly wasn't supposed to desire him the way women in story books did. She'd scoffed at the twittering females in those Jane Austin novels. Hadn't she learned enough about the foolish entanglements of following one's heart from *Wuthering Heights*? How many books did she read that brought her to the same conclusion each time? Solitude and independence were the better trail to follow.

Chase stepped back, and Summer readied to run. Before she could take a step, he took hold of her hand and, holding it firmly, gave her little choice but to trip along beside him as they walked from the hotel to the bank.

Stepping inside the squat, brick building, Summer took note that the party had grown. Now, not only the three from the hotel were there, but also the judge, someone she heard introduce himself as a pastor, and a lanky man she assumed was a bank clerk.

There were a few stiff pleasantries exchanged, none of which included her, but within minutes, the business of why they were here began.

"Gracen didn't do this world any favors by being born," Broward said. "But at least dead, someone will benefit."

"Reward for bringing him to justice is set at seven hundred and fifty dollars," the judge said. "That's a mighty fine bounty."

"The family of the man he shot is very wealthy; they put up the reward," Chase explained. "And they made sure it'd be tempting enough for anyone to go after it despite how dangerous it could be."

"Well, seems you beat the danger, Marshal," the sheriff said, and Summer glared at him as he took a bank draft from the clerk's hand and held it out to Chase.

"No, I want my money in cash," Summer announced.

"Mrs. Storm," Chase started in that grating tone that said he thought he knew best. "A bank draft will be fine. Small banks like this might not have that kind of money on hand. Seven hundred—"

"Three hundred seventy-five," Summer corrected. "If we split it evenly, which we shouldn't, because I'm the one who took him out, but if it gets me out of here that much faster."

"We can discuss all of this at a later point," Chase told her in that same tone. The same way he'd said they'd drop Gracen here rather than take him further east, and look where that had landed them.

"Best listen to your husband, missus; he knows best," the banker chimed in.

"Really? I disagree, and no one asked for your two cents," Summer almost snarled. If a single bank draft was all they were given, she'd have to stay with him until it was turned in and she could take her share."

"It'll be safer to travel without large sums of money," Chase said as he folded the note and stuck it in his pocket.

"Safer for whom?" Summer snapped. "Maybe you. No, I want my share of that reward, and I want it now." If she didn't hold ground now, she might have to walk away from this bounty empty handed. Three months wasted. She wasn't willing to do that. Large bounties like this were rare. It took ten times as long to track down enough twenty-five and fifty dollar bounties to make up for what this single one brought her, even if she did have to split it.

"See, told you that making an honest woman of her wouldn't help," Broward commented dryly. "I can still have Dewy run her down to Yuma."

"No," Chase said as he sat his hat on his head and took hold of her arm. "I am more than capable of dealing with my wife." His grip tightened, and he lifted two fingers to the brim of that black hat. "Good day, gentlemen. I can't say I hope we see you again, or that the stay was pleasant, but I am glad the dust settled as it did." With that, he turned them and headed straight out the door without a backward glance.

Summer tried several times to shake free, but his hold remained. "Listen, you stinking pole cat, if you think I'm just gonna let you ride off with my bounty, you're corned."

"You don't stop acting like a child, you'll be spanked," Chase told her, directing her back into the hotel and up the stairs.

Summer planted her feet and leaned back as he unlocked and opened the door. "You wouldn't dare." She was a grown woman. A grown woman who, most days, carried a gun and a knife.

With a jerk, he pulled her forward, stumbling into his body. "I promise you I will. You'll be respectful of me in public. If you want to disagree, we can do it privately." He pulled her through the door and followed up with a hard smack to her ass. "Get your things packed, so we can get out this hell hole."

"I want my money," she insisted, grabbing up her bedroll and hastily folding it to be tied to her gear. Noticing he wasn't doing anything, she looked around. His belongs were already packed.

"You'll get it when I give it to you. You keep harping on it, you'll ride out with a sore tail." He waited until she'd shouldered her bags before lifting his and stepping aside so she could pass back into the hall. She couldn't help turn a bit sideways as she went, either, and hearing him chuckle set her teeth on edge.

Preceding him down the stairs, she stepped up to the desk and rang the bell. It took a few minutes for the man to step out of the back. "Are you checking out then?"

"We are," Chase said before she could answer for herself. "You manage to get my list filled?"

"Oh, yes, Marshal. Chrissy was right on it after she cleaned up from breakfast," he said, bending down to take something from behind the desk. He set two rather full flour sacks on the counter, and given the thud they made, she knew they weren't filled with ground wheat.

"Then, my bill?" Chase asked, taking both sacks in one hand and lifting them to the ground at his feet.

"Well, the stay, and the meals—"

"I cooked one of those meals," Summer reminded him. Damn, she hated a cheat. Like nobody else valued money like they did.

"Mrs. Storm," Chase said again in that tone that wasn't clearly annoyance or supportive. "What's the total, then?"

The man took his pencil and scribbled on the pad a minute. "I think two dollars should cover everything," he finished like he was proud he could solve the simple calculations.

"Two dollars?" Summer shrieked. "Did we stay in a damn palace and no one told me?"

She watched Chase set a five-dollar silver piece on the counter. "That should cover it, and thank you for the hospitality," he said as he bent to retrieve the bags and turned to go.

Summer knew her mouth was hanging open, but before she could reach out and take back the coin, Chase managed to grab her wrist and, again, she went out tripping. "You paid that man two and a half times what he earned. And I cooked that meal this morning. *I* shouldn't have been charged."

"You weren't, *I* was," he said, not pausing in his stride.

"If you are so haphazard with money, maybe it's best if I carry the note," she said, letting her eyes adjust to the dark interior of the livery.

"Ha," was his only comment the entire time he packed the new supplies onto Sir Frank, *her* mule, saddled both their horses, gave her an unnecessary leg up, and rode out into the desert of the Arizona territory.

Chapter 5

Chase glanced sideways again. It was a few hours past noon, and like the last two days, Summer had out her map as well as several bills for wanted men. She seemed to be plotting ways to intercept them based on notes she took about their habits and movements.

Though he'd no intention of letting her keep trying to collect bounties now, there was no reason she couldn't keep working at it this way. She could sell the information to another hunter if she wanted. Money did seem to consume her.

He could guess it had something to do with growing up orphaned and poor. They still weren't really speaking, though she was more receptive to his questions and comments when she was either cooking, a chore she took over when she saw him about to dig into a can of cold beans and lectured him for the whole night on how disgusting it was, and when she was eating, though for someone who could make the most heavenly biscuits, she didn't eat a great deal herself. He'd gotten a few notable things from her.

She knew three languages fluently, French, Dutch, and Spanish and could get by in both Navajo and Cherokee. She said those were all spoken in her home and then in places she'd stayed when she had lost that home.

She'd traveled nearly coast to coast in the last ten years or so and been to Mexico and Canada, which she referred to as that place 'northways'. She didn't voice any kind of preference for where she might want to call home, so he had reason to think where he'd settle them would be good enough in her opinion.

Still, he wanted so much more than just a grudgingly given, one syllable response when he talked to her about anything other than food. They'd been married almost three days, and she was a complete mystery. One he wanted to reveal a little faster as he could still taste the sweetness on her lips from that first, *and last*, kiss.

Damn that kiss, too. The way it had made him feel was more akin to a foolish, young buck chasing his first doe in spring, than a man with enough general practice to no longer be driven to actively seek it out. Women came to him. And he didn't always take them up on any offer. But Summer heated his blood and made his head spin. All with just a kiss. He could hardly wait to know what she'd be like naked, sprawled out on his bed, breasts and pussy open to his mouth the way her lips had been. He could already see her hair wrapped around his fist as he took her from behind.

"We're still heading due north," she said, looking up at the sky, giving him time to shift and adjust himself before she might take notice of his stiff, aching cock.

"Yep," he said, reaching for his canteen and using the water to wet his bandana and wipe his face.

"Well, how far north are you going?"

"As far north as it takes to get to Colorado," Chase told her and watched her take her little spyglass from her pack and use it to sweep the landscape around them. The first day and a good part of the second day, they were followed. But he knew they would be, and he knew once they crossed the county line, the deputy would turn back.

She folded her bills and stuck them in her pack but she held on to the map. "Well, that's too north for me. We can make a stop at Flagstaff and cash that bill." He watched her find the place on her map. "At the very least, the rail conductor should be able to cash that." She folded the map and stuck it and her glass back in her pack. "Who's in Colorado?"

"Who?"

"Yes, who? I haven't seen any bills come out of there. Can't be much of a payout."

Chase laughed; damn, the woman was single minded. "Not who's in Colorado, *what's* in Colorado," he told her. "I took a position on the west side of the Rockies."

"Oh." She shrugged with no excitement at all. "Well, good for you."

"Good for me?" Chase echoed. "You mean good for us?"

She chuckled. "No, if you're still planning on keeping half my bounty for Gracen, then I need to make up the difference. Best bounties are coming out of cattle country lately. Still won't be many like Gracen. But if I can find a few fifty dollar ones…" She stopped and looked up. "Clouds rolling in, might be best to get higher up. If it rains…" She jerked her reins hard right, and Chase had little choice but to follow her to slightly higher ground.

"Summer," he called and nudged his horse forward as soon as the path widened enough to let him ride beside her. "Summer, we're going to Colorado."

"*You're* going," she said, not seeming concerned he was serious. "I need to—"

Reaching out, Chase grabbed hold of her bridle and pulled them to a stop. "Summer, you're going where I go. We're married. That's how it works."

She seemed completely surprised by that announcement.

"We're not married; we just did that to get out of that crazy town. As soon as you give me my money, this… marriage ends and we can part ways."

"It ends when 'death do us part'. We took vows, before God and witnesses, and we'll uphold them. *All* of them," Chase told her.

"Wait a minute," Summer shouted, dismounting and stomping back to the mule. "I didn't agree to that. That isn't what I agreed to." She began pulling the supply packs off. "That isn't what you presented me with when you told me the bargain you struck."

"It is exactly what I said," Chase said, getting off his horse and heading over to where she was already sorting through the packs to separate things according to some idea she had in her head. "I told you we were getting hitched, married. That is what we did; we got married."

"We got married to get out of there. I agreed, because if I hadn't, I'd be on my way to Yuma with a man who… But we're well out of that county, so they can't touch me now, I won't be going back. I didn't even want to go in the first place. You forced me to. But you're not forcing this on me, too. I have a life. I have a damn good life, and I have plans. And they don't include you." She bent down, snatched the pack with her things in it, and tossed it back over Sir. Chase grabbed her before she could get back to her horse.

"Summer," he said as calmly as possible. Given the look on her face, the storm brewing in her eyes, one of them needed to remain so. "It's completely true the reason we got married is because it was the only way to keep you from being sent to Yuma, and I admit it wasn't the best choice, but we needed to get rid of the body and that was the closest with a bank. But that doesn't change the fact we are married, and that didn't end when we crossed the county line."

"And what, I'm supposed to give up my life, my dreams, and

follow you like some stupid dog? I won't." She shook off his hold, but he grabbed her back again.

"No, you don't have to give up anything. No one has to give up anything. We combine our dreams, our goals. We work together to make them happen."

"Well, my dreams aren't in Colorado. I'm not giving up my life for—"

"What life, Summer? What life? Are you telling me that you want to spend the rest of your days chasing outlaws, sleeping on the ground, eating salt pork and dried beef? Until when? Until you're not fast enough on the draw, until someone gets wise a woman is chasing them and ambushes you, until another dishonest lawman takes advantage of you? Maybe until life just gets so hard, you die in your saddle in the middle of the godforsaken desert, to be picked apart by vultures? What life is that?"

"Mine," she screamed. "Mine, you judgmental bastard. It's mine." The way her voice broke, she wasn't convincing him that was the life she wanted.

"Not anymore, it ain't," Chase said and let her go. "It's not your life anymore. It's not mine, either. We're starting fresh. Get in the saddle; we're going home." He bent and made to lift the other supply bag back onto the mule.

"No," Summer yelled and yanked it out of his hands. "I'm not going any further with you. You just give me whatever cash you have on you now, and we'll go our separate ways. The whole seven hundred is yours."

"Summer," Chase said, grabbing the pack back from her and tossing it over the animal. She pulled it right back off. "That's enough of that. Stop acting like a child before I start treating you like one." For the third time, he lifted and placed the pack over the mule. She made a reach for it again, but he caught her hand and the struggle that ensued was short lived. She decided it more prudent to get free of him than get the pack down. What he didn't expect is she'd take up a stance with her feet apart and her right hand hovering over the gun at her hip. Years of habit made him turn to give her only a narrow profile as a target, and his own hand went to his gun. "You better be real sure, missy," he told her, voice low and strong. "You better be real sure you want to draw down on me."

Chase waited, watching her like he'd watch any man in the same situation. The difference he saw was there wasn't murder in her expression. There was anger and fear, but they weren't rising to the level of hot headed murder. She wasn't an outlaw. As a bounty hunter, she was as committed to keeping law and order as he was. She just went about it in a different way.

He swore he heard her swallow before he noted the movement in her shoulder that said she'd not be drawing. "Wise choice," he said before grabbing her arm, twisting it behind her back, and relieving her of her gun.

"You son of a bitch," she yelled, trying to twist away. "I'm not going with you. I'm not."

Chased sighed, tossed her gun to the ground, and then shifted his hold so he had her around the waist. He planted his feet and bent her over his hip. "Stop," he said, bringing his hand down on her ass. "Acting..." a second smack. "Like a child," he finished, punctuating each of those words with a blow from his hand.

"You dirty, stinking pole cat," she screeched, flaying her arms and legs. "Yellow bellied snake."

Chase was prepared to let her go after those first few swats, all she needed was to show a smidgen of contriteness. Rather, she continued to cuss him. With a shake of his head, he jostled her into a better position and put some force behind the next spank he landed. The gasp breaking up her stream of foul words said he'd made an impact, and without hesitation, he began a steady barrage of spanks, covering her entire ass with the same or a bit more force.

Her fight couldn't outlast his will, and after he was sure he'd covered the whole span of her seat at least three times, the curses changed to demands to stop and then to pleas of the same. He aimed the next few lower, knowing she'd feel them worse every time she used her legs to direct the horse.

"Stop," she choked out. "Stop, please. I'm sorry."

Two more pointed spanks and he dropped her to her feet. He took the time to steady her, but her knees buckled and she landed in the dirt. Standing there, he wasn't sure exactly what to do. She might have surrendered, but everything about her said she was still madder than a wet hen. The ache to gather her in his arms was superseded by the desire to hold on to his balls for a while longer. Chase stood there and waited. Sobs and gasps became sniffs and then silence. She wiped her nose on her shoulder then used the back of her hand to wipe the tears.

Chase knew the exact moment she set her focus on her gun. And given her proximity and angle, she'd likely win, as he'd either have to shoot through his holster or draw first. "Next time you think to draw on me, Summer, my belt comes off and your pants come down," he warned. "Think about it. Is that really how you want to start this off?"

She didn't move, didn't lift her focus from the revolver, didn't say anything.

"Go on," he said and not as a challenge. "Pick it up." She gave him a sideways look. "Go on; pick it up." She reached out, hesitated, then used her fingers to pull it close enough that she could take a grip on it. Her finger stayed well off the trigger as she shifted enough to expose the holster. "No," Chase said, keeping his voice soft. "Give it to me." He held out his hand, again waiting to see what choice she made. With a sigh, she gave it a little toss, catching it so the butt was toward him and held out. "Thank you," Chase said as he reached down and pulled her to her feet. "You can have it back after we talk." He turned and made his way to his horse, tucking it in his saddle bag. He knew she had both the repeater and a Derringer; it wasn't like he was leaving her defenseless.

When he turned back, he caught her rubbing at her ass, and he bit his cheek not to suggest he could rub it for her, though he couldn't stop his cock from straining at the idea. He bent and snatched up her hat, holding it out until she noticed he was.

She took it back, her expression a mix of so many things, he couldn't read her. But the urge to collect her against him was strong enough that the only way to deny it was to walk away. "Mount up," he said more sharply than he intended and saw her flinch.

In the distance, the sound of thunder rolling in turned them both westward. The dark clouds and rain bands told of what was coming. In the desert like this, these kinds of sudden storms could be deadly. Chase quickly made sure the supplies were secure on the mule and then stepped up to help Summer mount as she either struggled or just hesitated.

"We're gonna need to find some cover from that," he said, ignoring the way she was again wiping tears from her face as she settled in the saddle. Scanning the horizon, he could make out several jutting rock formations. "Let's head toward those. If nothing else, they might keep us from getting swept away in a gully washer."

The first drops of rain, carried on the wind, hit them as they reached the largest out cropping. The once warm desert turned cold. Summer located a spot where an overhang stretched out above a flat rise of rocks. It wasn't a cave but close enough, and it should allow them cover without trapping them if it flooded. Chase left her to lead the animals in and scrambled to collect enough kindling to keep a fire going through the storm. By the time he returned, Summer had the horses unsaddled and the packs off the mule. But as the rain started to come down in earnest, she made no move to settle in. Rather, she stood with her shoulder against the rocks, looking down at her feet.

Chase didn't abide pouting, but he wasn't sure if she was. He simply didn't know her well enough to say. And of course, that was their problem. They didn't know each other. And while her objection to being married to someone she didn't know was reasonable, her angry little tantrum wasn't. He left the fire, walking to where she stood. Not missing how she tightened up at his approach, he resolved to start fresh. Summer and he, though, had a hard time getting like-minded.

"Summer, look…" he started. "Look, I'm sorry th—"

"You will be if you ever lay a hand on me again," she snarled then tried to step away.

Chase set his hand on the rock wall to prevent her escape and pulled her around to look at him. "Let's get something clear," he said in a tone he used for more serious words. "I'm not sorry I spanked you. You deserved it, and if you deserve it again, I'll do it again, so get used to it. Your behavior was reckless and dangerous for both of us, completely out of character for you."

"You don't know that; you don't know anything about me," she snapped and tried to step away in the opposite direction.

He set his other hand on that side and trapped her between his hands, his body, and the rocks. "That's because you haven't told me anything about yourself. I'm trying to get to know you, but you won't let me. I do know, however, that no one makes a living hunting outlaws with a bad temper. No one lives long hunting them if they respond to things with emotions rather than brains. You and I do the same kind of work. And I'm guessing you've done it a good while, too, which means you think things through before you act. What you did back there, that wasn't thought, that was anger, temper, and recklessness. What do you think would have happened if you'd drawn? If you didn't kill me… what? And if you had? If you'd gunned down a U.S. Marshal… what? Eventually, you'd be the one someone was hunting, and you know it."

"We can't be married," she muttered. The only indication what he said got through to her, the change of subject.

"Well, we are," he said, shifting a bit closer. "And I'm very willing to give you... us, time to get used to the fact." A little closer now. With her back against the rocks but her legs out in front so her ass stayed clear, he was able to step close enough that he could hear her breathing. And it wasn't a smooth, relaxed sound.

"I'll never get used to being hit."

"I spanked you; there's a difference. Tell me you don't know that." She only shrugged. "I'm not going to hit you, beat you. I'll never raise my hand to you in anger. I don't need to blacken your eye to prove I'm a man. The very act would disprove it. But you behave childishly, you behave like you did back there, in a way that puts you in danger..." He put his fist under her chin and lifted. "Little girl, you won't sit for a month of Sundays next time. I won't have it. I expect my wife to be a woman with good sense, a woman capable in her own right of making the right choice and getting the work done. I don't need a child at my side. I need a partner, one I can trust to be responsible for things when I ride out. One who isn't going to collapse if things get hard. So far, though you've been a tad bit annoying in your ways, you've held up." He saw her brows draw down, but her lips also pursed to the side. It wasn't a complete insult. "I have a feeling, you're gonna continue to stay in the saddle no matter how much life tries to buck you, and that is exactly the kind of woman I want as my wife." Again, he moved a little closer.

She sniffed then lifted her eyes to search his face. "What you apologizing for, then?"

She did seem to make wide circles around a conversation. "I'm sorry that I ever let you think you were tying yourself to a man who didn't keep his word, one who made promises and then broke them. If I say I'm gonna do something, Summer, I do it. My word is good, and I'm not going to do anything that might change that. I've worked hard to build a reputation that gives people confidence that I'll honor any duty I take on, that I'll see my work finished before I walk away. I'm sorry you didn't know that first, before you made your decision to choose me over Yuma Prison. But it was because of my reputation, I was even able to strike that deal. I promised I'd see you made an honest woman and I'd keep you that way. I didn't then and still don't think you've ever been anything less than honorable." He paused when he noticed sadness and tears welling in her eyes, but he pressed on. "So my job should be easy enough."

"You don't know me," she repeated.

"Well, I'd like to, but you have to let me." The tears spilling over her lashes gave him concern. Did she have something in her past that might come back to haunt them? He didn't get that feeling from her, and he was a pretty sound judge of character.

"I... can't," she whispered.

"You haven't tried." He lowered his head. "And you haven't had me there to help." He waited, and like before, Summer raised her head to meet his eyes, let her own drift closed, and held for his kiss. He only brushed her lips this time. "This time, Summer Storm, you'll have me to help you with anything you need." He brushed his lips over hers again then leaned back, chuckling when she followed him.

She pulled back, opened her eyes, and licked her lips. It was fascinating to watch her eyes go from calm brilliant blue to storming as she set her palms against his chest. He was expecting some advancement of what he started, so when she shoved him back, he was off guard, tripping backward enough to allow her to slip past.

Summer marched over to her gear, lifted it, and, without a word as she passed, moved to the shelter opening. She dropped her stuff and then herself to the ground, back facing him, and refused to speak to him. She continued to refuse to speak to him the next three days.

He'd hoped she was only thinking over what he'd said to her. But when he woke that fourth morning, he knew she'd been thinking on something else entirely. And when he did have the next chance to speak to her, Chase was going to be saying a whole lot of what needed saying with his belt.

Chapter 6

Summer leaned her head back against the wall and sighed. Again, she was looking at a nice long stay in prison. She planned to cuss the day she ever heard the name Storm until her death. That man ruined everything. Life was never as difficult as it was, starting from the moment they both drew down on Gracen. At least for now, the lawmen here in Durango were respecting the badges they wore. She wasn't being treated like some whore. In fact, the sheriff went out of his way to make sure she was as comfortable as she might be, sitting in a jail cell.

She'd the suspicion that the name on the bank note was why. When she handed it over to be cashed, the clerk looked at her funny then waved over a man standing behind her in line. The man who stepped up was the sheriff, and every instinct told her to just run, but she needed the money to get started on her next bounty.

"Miss," the sheriff asked, holding the note out, but not over to her. "Can I ask how you came by this?"

Truth was always easier than lies. "Marshal Storm and I ended up chasing the same bounty, Frank Gracen." She waited as the sheriff took a look at the amount the note was for and nodded. Big bounties were well known to everyone. "I caught him, but the marshal insisted on riding in with me. Unfortunately..." And here was where Summer knew she was leaving a lot out of the story, "The sheriff wouldn't sign over such a large amount to me. He wouldn't even sign half the amount." She shrugged. "Marshal Storm is a good man, though, little that I got to know of him. He was honest and handed the note to me. Then we went our separate ways." Again, she shrugged. "I'd like it cashed out; I have a lead on Jay Sickle," she said, pulling out the bill from the small shoulder pack she carried. "I'd like to catch him, too."

"Bounty hunting ain't no proper work for a lady," the sheriff said, but his disapproval wasn't sharp.

"And if I can catch a few more before I'm too old, I can quit it and do something more proper," Summer told him. It was a common enough response from her. She'd said it more than a million times from the very first time she'd ever turned in someone for a reward.

"You say you got a lead on Sickle?" Summer nodded. "Marshal Storm didn't want to chase that one down, too?"

"Marshal said he was taking a new post, somewhere here in Colorado, of all places. He said he was expected there. I'm headed east, toward Missouri." She wasn't, but if Chase Storm bothered to try to track her down, that would be where he was sent. She hoped he'd not bother. But hearing him say he didn't break promises or vows...

"Well, Marshal Chase Storm is an honorable man, and I can't see why if you collected the bill on Gracen, he'd not see you receive what was due you," The sheriff turned, handed the note to the clerk, and asked, "Can this be cashed out now?"

"That amount is a bit large. The train is due in four days, though, and I can cash it in full then."

"Well, how much can you cash now?" Summer asked, stepping up. She'd rather have it all, though this little train station wouldn't have enough, but she didn't want to take a chance that after mentioning Flagstaff, Chase would track her there. "If you cash it in part and give me a note for the rest, I can get moving on Sickle's trail." She looked between the clerk and the sheriff now and hoped she read their expressions correctly. But then she added, for safety sake, "Besides, it's not smart to carry so much cash. I really only need about fifty dollars to resupply and…" she faded off and shrugged again.

"I think that is manageable," the sheriff said, and the clerk nodded. "Still don't think a woman ot' be out chasing bounties, but you don't strike me as dim. You get what you need, and then you remember to be safe."

The relief washed over her, and with a deep sigh, she nodded. "I will, thank you."

She stepped back up to the clerk, and the sheriff stepped back in his place in line. She only gave half a thought when the door opened and she heard some call for the sheriff. She didn't even turn around as she waited for the clerk to count out the money and write a new note, this one with her name on it. It was almost over when she felt someone step up close and put a gun in her back.

"It's not nice to lie to people," the sheriff said and reached around to hold a telegram in front of her.

Attention Sheriff of Durango County.

Look out for female. Blonde, blue eyes, small in stature.

Runaway. Took bank note. Hold if spotted.

"Larry, put that money up some place safe until we get this matter sorted out," the sheriff said, and then taking Summer by the arm, he turned her toward the door and marched her out.

She'd pleaded the entire walk over to the jailhouse, but though he remained polite, the man wouldn't budge. So, for the second time in just two weeks, she was once again behind bars, thanks to that damn Marshal Chase Storm.

She sat there for three days, too. Nothing to do but think

about him. And as much as she tried to only cuss him, every time she closed her eyes, she recalled his warm scent and the way he tasted. Not even recalling how sore her backside was for a few days could stop the questions in her head about what his arms might feel like wrapped around her or how it might be to have his body pressed against hers in the dark.

Chase Storm wasn't like any man she'd ever encountered before. His good looks aside, Summer couldn't deny that his even temper and quiet strength drew her. He hadn't yet become belligerent or demeaning toward anyone, even when she had. And, yes, he was correct; the way she made her living was much like the way he made his, and hot tempers usually meant short lives. He certainly held his better than she held hers.

Even his response to her going for her gun was far more measured. She'd not once ever hesitated to draw and fire on someone who had made the first move. All he did was spank her. Spank her. And, yes, she did know there was a difference between getting hit and getting spanked. She was never a spoiled child, allowed to get away with anything she wanted. Bad behavior earned a punishment and neither her mother nor her aunt ever let any of the children slip out if it was deserved.

But getting a spanking as an adult was a completely different experience, as was being spanked by a man. Especially a man she already felt a stirring of desire for. More shameful than painful, she should have wanted to run and hide. Rather, the urge to lean on him had struck her. And for a minute, she'd thought maybe he'd take her in his arms.

But he hadn't, and he hadn't because he wasn't with her by choice. any more than she was with him. Neither of them could really want this. Yes, he'd made a promise, but she was willing to excuse him from it. Even if what he offered was so very tempting.

That thought startled her. What in the world even made her think that a man, hell, anyone could be trusted so much? She'd learned fast enough, the world was filled with people who said things they didn't mean, only to open another up to be used. No, Summer would get what she wanted out of life on her own.

Voices from beyond the door made her look up just as the sheriff opened the door, stepped aside, and asked the person behind him, "That her?"

Summer cringed when Chase stepped up. "Yep, that's her," he said then stepped back.

"You want to press charges?" the sheriff asked as he pulled the door closed again. What was said past that she didn't know? And as she was left to sit in the cell most of the day, she did wonder if Chase Storm perhaps had pressed charges. Given what came next, she rather wished he had.

IT WAS NEARING sunset when Chase came back through the door. Summer sat up and swung her feet to the floor. "Well?" she asked when he stood there saying nothing at all.

Before he could respond, the sheriff stuck his head in the door. "Here's the board." Summer watched him hand over a small, thick, wooden paddle. much like one used to beat out a saddle blanket. Chase took it, gave it a good looking over, slapped it once on his palm, then nodded. "The key," sheriff said. handing that over. "We'll give the two of you some privacy. Just leave 'em both on the desk when you go."

"Thank you, Sheriff Turner," Chase said and waited until the door closed before turning back to look at her, shaking his head and palming that board.

"Look, Marshal," Summer tried, only to be silenced by his glare. Why she ever thought the man had little temper, she didn't know. She'd not really known him well enough to make that determination. Perhaps now, she was about to learn his true nature.

Chase stepped up to the bars, the paddle slapping down light and rhythmic on his hand. "You stole my horse," he said.

"I didn't," Summer denied. Had he charged her with horse theft? If he had, prison wasn't how she'd land. "I didn't," she insisted when his glare became more heated. "I only... I only moved him." She flinched when he struck his palm harder with the board and the crack rang out. "He wasn't even a mile away."

"You also took my boots," he said and snapped the board again. Summer swallowed hard and pressed back against the wall when he stepped forward.

"I left them with the horse," she said then regretted it. Making him walk a mile, barefoot, in the desert wasn't exactly harmless. "I left you half the supplies," she offered then scooted back into the corner as he stuck the key in the lock and opened the cell door. "Fine, just take the damn money. Take it all. I don't care," she offered as he stepped closer. He was now slapping that paddle against his thigh.

"I don't care about the money, Summer," Chase said, pulling her off the bench and against his body. "You're my wife, and you're gonna start behaving like it, or you're gonna be one sorry little miss."

Summer took a deep breath, inhaling that rich scent that was his alone. Pulled against him like she was, she felt every hard contour, all the warmth coming off him, and his slow, measured breathing. "You didn't... didn't press charges?"

"You're my wife; what's mine is yours," he said evenly.

"Then I can go?" She needed to go, because the longer she stayed standing this close to him, the more she wanted to stay standing that close to him.

"The law ain't gonna punish you, Summer, but I sure as heck am." He turned then, and sitting down hard on the bench, yanked her down so she was lying face down over his lap. "What you did was reckless, dangerous," he continued as she felt him lift her and adjust her forward.

"It wasn't even a mile," she screeched when he bent and grabbed the hem of her skirt. Damn, but if she'd not been concerned she'd run into another man who thought her wicked for wearing pants.

"I don't care about that, either," Chase growled and, despite her struggling, managed to get her dress up to her waist. "I'm talking about trying to cash out, alone, in front of so many witnesses. You don't think that amount of money would have attracted the wrong kind of attention?" he snarled as he captured both her hands at the wrists and pinned them to her back. "How far might you have made it before someone who knew you had that much money on you stopped you on the road? And you think the money would have been all they would have taken?"

"I wasn't going to cash it out in full; I wasn't," Summer pleaded. She would have, though, if it was possible, and she did know that kind of money would make her a target. She was shoved forward again, her face nearly hitting the floor and the weight of his legs over hers announcing she was pinned.

"Turner said that you tried," Chase said at the same time Summer felt the string on her bloomers get tugged. "You calling him a liar?"

"No," she yelled as the draft hit her bare skin. God help her, a man, a grown man, was looking right at her naked backside.

"So, you *were* gonna take it all in cash?" he asked, and her flesh prickled at the touch of his hand striking those globes.

"No." God, he needed to stop touching her because... because...

"So the sheriff lied?"

Because she liked it. "No." Summer had no idea at all at the moment what she was trying to deny.

"Well, someone is lying to me, little girl," Chase said, and his hand passed over the roundest part of her ass and settled on the back of her thigh. The heat coming off his palm set a flash of something akin to lightning right to her gut, and then that sensation shifted lower. God in Heaven, what was he doing to her? "I don't care for liars," he said, his fingers squeezing her flesh and making something pulse between her legs. "So let's have the truth, and maybe we won't have to discuss the sin of lying after we've discussed the recklessness of your actions."

"Stop," Summer yelled. It was all she could manage, given the wild mass of sensations she was feeling at the moment. Help her, why did she want him to slip his flingers a little higher up her leg. This was madness. She was crazy. "Stop," she begged.

"Answer the question. Did you intend to try to carry seven hundred and fifty dollars in cash with you?"

"Yes," she almost moaned, when his fingers pushed a bit between her legs.

"Thought so," he said, and she turned to see him lean back a bit and then reach for something. When he lifted the paddle, every heated feeling she was feeling turned completely cold.

"No, no, Chase. What are you doing? No." She tried her best to break free of his grasp, but it was like steel. And no amount of twisting or bucking got her off his knee.

"I told you, if you do reckless, dangerous things, I'd see to it you couldn't sit for a month of Sundays," he said as he laid that cool wood against her skin. "I did hope, though, I wouldn't have to spank you a second time before we've had a chance to get better acquainted. I thought I gave you enough of a warning. Maybe you just didn't believe me when I said I always keep my promises."

"Don't, Chase, please," she cried as she saw him draw his arm back and lift the paddle. "I'm sorry. Stop." She squeezed her eyes shut. There was simply no way to prepare for the hell fire Chase Storm rained down on her. And before it was done, she wasn't only swearing she'd cuss his name every day; she was swearing she'd be the most cautious woman ever born this side of the Mississippi.

Chapter 7

C hase raised his arm once more, cracking the paddle down on his wife's fine ass before letting it come to rest for the last time. He'd delivered the spanking in sets of four, each time stopping to scold her about running off, about taking stupid chances, about not believing he was a man of his word, and about taking his damn boots. And despite the unrelenting crying, choking, and coughing he heard and the limpness in the body over his lap, and especially given the deep red and already bruising ass under his eyes, that last thought made him smile.

She'd taken his boots. He'd have never thought of something so simple as a means to slow a man down. The hour he spent looking around the camp site and then the more than two hours it took for him to find his horse, get saddled, pull on his boots, and then start tracking her gave her all the time she needed. And as she likely predicted, he headed first to Flagstaff. Wasted almost a day there before deciding to send out several telegraphs alerting the nearest lawmen he was seeking her. He got his reply almost instantly and had to at least appreciate she'd headed where he was heading to start with.

No, this woman he was married to wasn't in any way stupid. Stubborn as hell but not stupid. And reddening her ass for being recklessly stubborn only strengthened his determination to keep her by his side. Marriage never really appealed to him because he really didn't care for all the simpering beauties who were paraded before him by either his own family or theirs. He didn't want a wife swayed by crowds or gossip, or worse, criticism given by people who didn't give a damn about her.

Chase Storm wanted a woman who could stand on her own, and he'd always known that would mean he'd have to be willing to let her. But he'd also have to know when to step in, when to draw a line and make her hold it. It wasn't ideal that he was having to do this with a woman who became his wife less willing than another might have, but if he could get her to understand, to believe, he'd no need, no want, to deprive her of whatever that dream she had was, he knew she'd be the most perfect woman for him.

What he already felt for her, be it lust, or love, or some violent mix of the two, was stronger than anything he'd felt for a woman before. Even the one he very nearly proposed to four years ago didn't affect him like this one did. And his effect on her didn't go unnoticed. What he saw when he'd looked at her over his knee said a great deal about what she might have really been protesting. Her response to him was the spark that rekindled his desire to achieve more than he'd already achieved. In the very short time he'd been in Summer's company, he'd become rejuvenated. He'd taken the offer in Colorado out of boredom, thinking if there was no thrill in life chasing outlaws across the plains, then what did it matter if he no longer actually chased them himself? Settling down and experiencing this next leg in life seemed logical. Now he'd have someone to share it with. But first, to convince her.

Looking down at her battered back end, though, it might not be quite as easy as he'd hoped. He'd certainly laid one on her.

His arm had fallen twenty times, and Summer wasn't a big woman in any way. From the first crack to the last, she'd screamed and sobbed. Oddly, though, she'd not begged him to stop once he began. She'd taken it. She'd submitted to at least his pronouncement she'd been in the wrong. It could bode well for them, as long as he was always careful to never haphazardly judge her so and to be completely fair in any sentence he handed down.

He heard her sniff and gasp, realizing she was through the worst of the crying. He let go of her hands and saw them slowly slip down so she could push herself away from the floor. Chase took hold of her waist and drew her back, setting her more to her own preference, but then he put his hands under her arms and forced her to sit on his right thigh. As soon as her seat connected with his leg, she cried out and the wailing started again. Chase quickly set about getting her legs over his left thigh, so he could roll her against him and give her some relief.

"All right now," he said, adjusting a bit so he could lean back and she could get more of her tender ass off his thigh. He lifted his hand and guided her head against his shoulder. On her own, she wrapped her arms around his neck. "All right. Rein it in a bit," he soothed, rubbing her back and nuzzling her hair. "Everything is going to be all right. Hush now." Again, a few sniffs and gasps from her. "Time to talk," he said and brushed the hair from her eyes when she lifted her head.

She pushed off him a bit, though not so much that her ass actually came in contact with anything. Using the heel of her hand, she vainly wiped at the tears still falling. Chase rolled to one side and pulled his kerchief out of his back pocket and offered it to her. He'd not known he'd held his breath until she took it from him and used it to blot at her eyes. Just as she looked to be done, he watched her expression crumple and a new fit of crying picked up.

"All right, all right," he soothed and again forced her head against his shoulder. Hooking his hand behind her knees, he pulled her closer, so she was curled in his lap. It felt odd that a full grown woman could fit so easily, but she did. She fit perfectly. "It's gonna be all right; we'll get it sorted and get this wagon rolling." He waited, rocking her gently until she dried up. "Ready to try again?" He felt her shrug her shoulders, but she didn't sit up. It could be the best he was going to get from her, and as she at least heard him out, he'd take it as a good sign. "Summer, I get how against this you are. I do, really. You've made it clear. And to be honest, it's not how I thought marriage would happen for me, either."

"Then why don't we just fold and leave the table?" she grumbled, still not lifting her head from his shoulder.

"Because, Summer, I only take a gamble when I believe it's a sure thing. I never bluff, and I am a man of my word."

"No one keeps their word," Summer said, lifting back a little. "Not really, anyway."

"I can't tell you how much I wish that wasn't what you've been made to think," Chase told her, knowing she had just given him insight as to what drove her. "There are a lot of people in this world who do keep their word. And I'll keep mine."

"Until it suits you not to," she countered, sitting up more but not looking at him.

"Look, you don't know me from Adam. I can see where you're coming from. I can. But I have built my life on my good word. It's not going to behoove me to start acting different now. If a man won't even treat his wife well, if he won't be faithful and true to the woman he swears to God he will be, he's not a man other men are going to trust. If you give me a chance, I can prove this to you."

"You just proved untrue now. Making it sound like I even have any choice in this. If you wanted what's good for me, you'd not have run me down. And what happens when you go back on your word? You have me arrested again? You throw me in the gutter?"

"Summer, if we honestly find we don't suit…" He had to be careful here, because it went against his personal creed. "If we can't find a way to shoot straight and hit the same target… Then we can part ways. But you have to give it an honest effort. You can't just let one buck throw you. You have to go heels down, spurs in, until the pony's broken."

"For how long?" She finally met his eyes.

For how long? What would be a duration long enough to convince her she could be happy with him, but not so long she'd refuse the challenge? "It's what, March?"

"Yep, maybe almost April," she confirmed, clearing her throat and using his kerchief to wipe her nose.

"Will you agree to try until the end of September, until the end of summer? If it don't work out, you'll still have time to get clear before the snows set in." That was nearly six months. If he couldn't convince her in six months, he'd have to admit he'd been wrong. Hell, it only took three months to discover the woman he thought he would marry was the wrong one.

"And then what, I still end up with nothing?"

"What do you mean?" He could toss in the bounty money if that was what she was getting at. It wasn't like he needed it. He could easily live comfortably just off his shares in his family's ranch.

"I mean, I've worked ten years to have what I have. Marriage means my husband gets everything I own and—"

"Hey now, rein that pony in," Chase warned. The bitterness in her voice might well tell him even more about her, but the condemnation wasn't earned. "It don't gotta be that way between us. I'm not looking to steal from you. I am more than situated, and I'll be earning a good wage at this new post. You can keep what you have, use it how you want, and if we end up on different trails, you can take it with you."

"So for six months, I'm just supposed to be domestic, not be able to add to what I've earned. I can't do that. I can't waste six months. It's already taken ten years."

This time he heard a bit of desperation. "Ten years to what?" She looked away without answering. She wasn't ready to tell him what that dream she had was. "Wives get allowances and—"

She shoved off his lap hard, stepping back and letting her hand hover at her hip. Not that she was armed this time. Clearly, it was more a habit than a threat. "I'm no child to be taking an allowance for doing stupid chores."

Chase used a finger to rub at the twitch in his eye. "That wasn't want I meant, I on—"

"So what, you think to pay me for being in your bed like some whore? Because if that's what you think, I—"

"That's uncalled for, missy," he said, surging to his feet. "That never crossed my mind. And you stop being so prickly, or you'll be back over my knee getting those stickers burned off you."

"I'm not a child, and I'm not a whore, and I won't be treated like either," she yelled at him.

"You'll be treated how you behave," Chase said, lowering his voice and returning her glare. She flinched first, her eyes darting to the side before coming back to hold his. "Now, I wasn't suggesting anything like either of those things. A *household* allowance will let you save any money you have for things you want to do. And clearly, you want to do something; you have some plan for after you're done hunting bounties." She dropped her eyes to the floor then dropped her chin a bit and, finally, her hand flexed, then fisted and settled on her hip. "Yep, thought so," Chase said, easing his tone back to a less authoritative one. "I can guess that maybe what you want to do can be done in whole or part once we're settled?" Again, she wouldn't clue him in on what it was she wanted to do. Her response was a shrug. "And if not... It's a new town. I'm sure there will be honest work you can find to do for fair pay." Again, she shrugged. "What bills do you still have?"

"What?" she asked, her head coming up so she was again looking at him.

"What bills do you still have? Or better, how much are they all worth in total?" Maybe he could convince her this way.

"Why?" she asked. But when he continued to look at her, she said, "I mean, I'm not sure. I have about six, maybe two hundred."

"If you happen to get them all?" Those would be pretty average rewards. Twenty-five, maybe fifty dollars.

"Yeah, but even if I didn't, I'd pick up others. Sheriff out of Kansas City don't care who picks up the bounties."

She said that more like she knew he saved them for her. Chase would find out who the sheriff was and see what he might learn about Summer from him. "Okay, you give me six months, you do what you can on your own to earn some damn money, and if you can't stand it at the end of September, I'll give you the whole of the seven fifty for Gracen and the two hundred you *might* have earned tracking down those warrants."

Summer pulled back and looked at him with a slack jaw. "You can cover that?"

Chase nodded. Hell, he could cover that right now with what he carried.

"How do I know you'll be able to when it's time for me to go?"

"When we get to Alamosa, I'll take you to the bank, and you can put the money in an account under your name, with the stipulation the funds don't come out until October. That way, neither of us can touch them. Or if you want, you can wait until we get to Willow Creek, so it's even closer." He could see her considering it. Money drove her. Or at least it drove her as a means to get what it was she really wanted. "Six months, Summer. Couldn't you at least use the rest?"

She used his kerchief again to wipe her nose then stuck out her right hand and he took it in his. "Fine, but you go back on your word, and it'll be me on one of those posters, wanted for your murder."

Chase had to work to keep his face straight. As serious as she sounded, she didn't strike him as the kind who could commit a murder. "Deal," he said and shook on it.

Chapter 8

Summer reached back as discreetly as she could and rubbed her seat. She hated the way Chase smirked every time he caught her doing it. She hated more that something in his eyes said he'd be more than glad to take over the chore, and that simple look made her stomach twist around like a tornado.

She dropped her hand as soon as she heard the lock in the door click. If she expected Chase to go ahead of her into the hotel room, she was mistaken. He actually opened the door, stepped aside, and motioned her to go in first. Gentlemanly behavior straight from a book. She never thought she'd live to see it.

Though, if she thought about it, Chase Storm might be more in the habit of such things than she wanted to admit. He'd not said a single word as she'd adjusted her clothes. Her bloomers were down around her ankles still when they shook hands. He'd even turned his back as she did. Then he'd put a lid on the deputies who snickered and whispered while Chase handed back the paddle with a word of thanks and collected the little bit of gear he had with him at the time. All it took to get those men to hush was a hard look. They walked out the door, hearing Turner chewing the men out for being rude and disrespectful. He did it differently this time, but like when he turned Sheriff Broward's lude remarks into a compliment, he didn't need anything more than his reputation and a glare to defend her honor and pride.

"I don't suppose you're feeling up to sitting in the dining room," he asked, and she turned to answer and caught his lips twitching upward. "I mean, with the hard chairs and all." He couldn't quite hold in the snicker.

But it was that snicker that made her realize she was again rubbing her ass. Balling her fists at her sides, she sent him her dirtiest look. "Just when I was starting to think you might be a gentleman."

If she'd thought his looks or scent could do crazy things to her, when he threw his head back and laughed, her knees weakened and that hot, spinning feeling dropped from her stomach much lower. She was frozen in place by the sound, and when he stepped up and put his arms around her, she fancied she felt the way butter left in the sun felt.

"I'm sorry," he said, still chuckling. "I'll be nothing but a gentleman if that's what you insist on." He pulled her a little closer and leaned down to whisper in her ear, "But the just plain man in me would really like to help with what ails ya." He let his hand drift down her back, stopping just shy of the top of her ass.

She'd no ability to answer, afraid if she opened her mouth, she might consent to exactly what he was offering. And here again, she was figuring out exactly the kind of man he was. Because as he'd said before he kissed her the first time, he'd wait until she did consent. As her husband, he didn't really need to. His fingers brushed back the hair near her ear and his lips pressed against her temple. She was a breath away from telling him he should do it, when he stepped back and dropped his arms.

"Maybe next time," he said with a wink before turning

around and heading to the door. "I'll go down and put in an order, have it brought to the room. I already paid for you to have a bath, and there should be a towel; I paid for one. Clerk said the bath is located at the end of the hall, and if they started filling it when we checked in, it should be almost ready. Go enjoy it, and then we'll eat." He opened the door and stepped out then looked back over his shoulder. "Remember we have a deal, Summer."

As soon as the door shut, Summer reached back with both hands and rubbed furiously at her bottom. She also crossed her ankles and tried to squeeze her legs together to stop whatever the throbbing between them was. Darn him. Why couldn't he be a braying jackass like every other man she'd crossed paths with? She certainly didn't plan to stay, but he certainly wasn't giving her a whole lot of chances to pick a fight and prove it wouldn't work out.

Perhaps in a few days, after the new rubbed off a bit, she'd have the opportunity. For now, she might as well take advantage of what was being offered. A quick search of the room revealed her packs and saddle bags were already here. Grabbing up the largest one, she dug through and came up with a fresh pair of pants and a shirt. In the smaller bag, she pulled out clean bloomers and camisole. She felt her checks heat a bit when she realized Chase didn't go through this bag when he was searching her belongings for a skirt.

She didn't have much with her in the way of ladies' things. Most everything she owned, she'd left with Mrs. Larks in Kansas City. Maybe if it looked like she'd really be staying the entire six months, she'd send for some more of her belongings. But for now, she had enough with her, and she could just wash what she had more often if need be. Maybe if he saw she couldn't dress to the status of wife of a respected U.S. Marshal, he'd send her on her way. And she'd be sure to take that nine hundred and fifty dollars and get.

Wadding her clothes up in a bundle, she hurried out the door and down the hall to where that reported bath waited. She nearly knocked over the older woman coming out with two empty buckets.

"Sorry," she muttered. "Is someone already in there?"

"Are you Mrs. Storm?" the woman asked.

"Yes, ma'am," Summer said and rolled her eyes when she heard herself say it.

"Well, I'm Helga, and I just put the last bucket of water in for you."

"Thank you so much," Summer said and sighed. She couldn't remember the last time she'd bathed in an actual tub. Rivers, lakes, and ponds were her usual wash place.

"Don't thank me. That fine-looking man of yours insisted. Paid me but good for hot water, too."

"Hot water?"

"Yes, indeed," Helga said with a sharp nod. "You got yourself one fine man." She nudged Summer with her elbow as she passed. "Fine in a good many more ways than one, I think."

Summer wasn't sure what that meant, but she only gave it a minute of thought before she pushed into the small room, shut and locked the door behind her, and started stripping out of her dirty clothes. A hot bath, what a luxury. That he even thought of such a thing made her head spin. As she stepped in with a sigh, she eased herself down, hissing a little when her sore ass touched the water. But she wasn't going to let any of the discomfort distract her from the complete pleasure she felt as the water folded in around her. She splashed a bit over her face then slid down so she was completely submerged. She had to sit back up and unravel the braid, and using her fingers to shake her hair loose, she slid back under.

She'd just resurfaced and set her head back on the rim when a knock at the door had her reaching for her gun, only to realize she didn't have one. Damn it. She'd not grabbed her guns when she left the jail. Where had her mind been?

"Summer, you in there?" Chase called through the door.

Inhaling, she let out a heavy sigh. "Yes?"

"Just checking. Its gonna take about a half hour for dinner. Will that be enough time, or should I tell them to hold it a while more?"

"No, no," she said, even as she tried to rationalize his attitude toward her. Why such considerations? "Thirty minutes is more than plenty."

"All right, if you have all you need…"

"I do," she said, reaching for some soap and the bath brush. "Thank you," she added.

"Holler if you need anything else," he said, and she heard him step back from the door. "Like maybe some help washing your back."

The brush clattered to the floor, and she heard his rich laughter again as he headed back down the hall. Gritting her teeth, she resolved to just wash and get out. Her resolve held for about five minutes, and after some violent scrubbing, she gave in and leaned back, letting the water ease her body and mind.

Summer was just smoothing her shirt tails down her pants when he knocked again. "Food's in the room," he called through the door.

She quickly fastened the Levi's and reached for the door. "I'm finished," she said, taken aback by his clean and fresh appearance. "Did you want to use the…" She pointed over her shoulder to the tub. "The water is still warm."

"You should have said something. I'd have held the food until it was too cold for you to soak in," he said, offering to take the bundle she lifted from the chair but not insisting when she didn't hand it over. "And I used the other tub on the next floor up."

"You paid for two baths?" Summer almost shrieked, grinding her teeth when he just laughed. "I think you need to go make your way back over to the bank here and get a deposit note for that money you say you're gonna put in the bank in Alamosa. The way you spend, we're gonna be broke before we get there."

He laughed, shook his head, and pushed open their room door. "Not likely, Summer, not likely."

She wanted to ask him what he meant, but the words stuck when she saw the way the room was set up. A small table, with a cloth, two chairs, a lantern in the center creating a warm glow, and two plates, each with a good size steak and a pile of potatoes. A bowl of gravy sat to the side as did a small basket of biscuits.

"I was real tempted to wait for you to get done with your bath and then try to talk you into making that bread thing you made before," Chase said as he ushered her in and closed the door. "But then I thought, for the next six months, if I supply you with all the stale bread I can find, I might get a chance to eat enough that I'll be satisfied for a while."

He might have been teasing, but it was sweet and the words sent a little warm tingle down her spine. "Soggy bread really is the least of my talents," she told him.

"I know, those biscuits you made on the trail were some of the best I've eaten," he said, holding out the chair for her.

"Those were hardly biscuits, grease and flour is all. Let me get ahold of some fresh buttermilk, and I'll make you a biscuit," she told him and then hoped she could remember the exact recipe without her books. It'd been so long since she'd had a chance to actually cook anything more than campfire food.

"You like to cook?" he asked, taking his seat

"My second favorite thing to do after baking," Summer said and hesitated to take his hands when he set them out to say grace.

"Aren't they the same thing?"

"Oh, no, sir," she said and tried to sound offended. He only smiled at her, bowed his head, and after a few words of thanks, he squeezed her fingers then pulled his hands back.

"Well, I can't wait for you to demonstrate the difference to me."

"Hope you're ready to get fat," she teased.

"Do your worst," he shot back and winked then lifted his knife and cut into his overcooked steak.

The conversation stayed fairly focused on the meal before them, and Summer took some joy in having someone to talk food and cooking with again. It'd been something that had dominated every conversation when she was a child, before she'd lost her family and found herself tossed around by happenstance like a tumbleweed. She didn't realize at all until he shoved his plate away that they'd talked so much about it. A heat crept up her neck and she busied herself eating the last of the potatoes that were as undercooked as the steak was overcooked.

She set her fork down and used the napkin to wipe her mouth. "Will we being staying in a tent then when we get to where we're going?" she asked, wondering if she'd gotten ahead of herself thinking she might have a real kitchen with an actual cook stove.

"No," Chase said, reaching for the canteen he'd set up in the table when he realized no drinks had been brought with the meal. "Job offer came with housing, but it wasn't specific other than it wasn't a tent. I sent word ahead about meeting with someone to buy some land and get a house built."

"A house? A real house?" She'd never lived in one. She and her mother had shared rooms over the eatery they worked in. Eight people in just three rooms, and the outhouse was almost two hundred paces out the side door.

"This is where I'm settling, Summer. I've been a rover long enough. Time to put down roots, build a house, a home, a family." The way his eyes swept up and down her body as he said the last made the heat flare.

"This place…"

"Willow Creek," he supplied

"Isn't it just getting started? I mean, it could be a bust in no time." How many times had she passed through a place that when she was there a year before was thriving, and the next was full of dust and ghosts.

"Place's been steady growing for a while. Some kin of Kit Carson was farming up that way back in forty and place been drawing them in hard like for a good fifteen years. Even if the silver runs out, its rich farm land, and with the D&RG rail in there, I don't think it's going anywhere."

"The rail is in?" That could be a real benefit if she gave staying a thought.

"Of course, that's what we'll be taking in." He stood and held her chair, forcing her to get to her feet. "As long as the snow is cleared off the tracks, it should be an easy trip."

"On a train?" She'd never been on one. She'd almost purchased a ticket in hopes of catching a man whose warrant had him valued at two hundred and fifty dollars, but when she understood she couldn't take her horse or... "I can't go on a train, my horse and Sir."

"My horse, too." He laughed, holding the door open as a couple of boys and a girl came in, collected the dishes and table, and carried them out. "Though, that mule of yours..." He reached in his shirt pocket and pulled out a silver coin, handed it to the girl, then stepped back in and closed the door. "That mule has bitten me twice now."

"Because you didn't call him Sir, probably," Summer said, trying to hide her grin.

"Yeah, well, *Sir* better mind himself. I can always push him off a moving train if I have to," Chase said then motioned for her to take a seat on the little stool in front of the vanity while he sat on the bed. "Yes, the animals will get on, too," he said with a shake of his head.

Rising to his feet suddenly, he moved to the window and pulled back the curtains. "Something happening?" Summer asked, finally remembering she needed to ask for her guns back.

"No, but it's not too late if you want to take a stroll," he said, sounding a little edgy.

"Not really, my hair is still wet, and I don't care to get arrested again for wearing pants in public." Although she wasn't the only female in this town doing so.

"If it's all right with you, I think I will have a look around," he said, stepping in front of her and taking a gentle hold of her chin. "Finish drying out and maybe get some sleep. Train pulls out at sunup." He bent down and again stopped before his lips actually touched hers, making her close the distance. "Lock the door, and don't wait up."

Before she even opened her eyes, he was gone. He closed the door and left everything behind. Right now, she could gather her things, rifle through his for what could be useful, and vanish. It did sound like he'd be gone a while. She could again be on her way east, and this time he would have to let her go, because he was due to head north. Getting up, she crossed the room to her pile of belongings. She could go, but lifting her hand and touching her fingers to her lips, she didn't. Maybe he was a man of his word, maybe he wasn't. But she always did what she could to keep hers, and where he was taking her didn't sound terrible. And then there was that almost one thousand dollars that she'd have by the end of summer just for sticking it out.

Bending down, she snatched up her bedroll and carried it to the bed. What could it really hurt to see this Willow Creek, Colorado and what it had to offer? As long as she left with more money in her pocket, she'd take the time away from the trail.

She could at least wish, though, that it would be someplace not so cold.

Chapter 9

"Summer, stand inside," Chase said again to the woman shivering beside him. The train was still offloading the passengers whose destination was Durango or at least those who wouldn't be heading further east on the narrow railway through the San Juan Mountains.

"Not with those three wild Stavelys tearing about," Summer said and shuffled closer to the steam coming up from under the train cars.

Chase hooked her by the collar and pulled her back again. "Steam is dangerous, I told you."

"Steam is warm," she countered but stepped back.

"Go inside the station house," he said again but then turned when a shout from a man and a loud crash rang out.

"I'll wait until this coup d'etat is finished," Summer grumbled then groaned when a few flakes of snow caught the lantern lights on the boarding platform. "Besides, I want to see this. I've never seen this."

Chase ground his teeth but then smiled and stepped up behind her, wrapping his arms and his far thicker, far finer coat around her. She snuggled back just as she did when he'd crawled up on the bed with her the first night in the hotel. He'd come in to find her curled under her blanket, shivering so much, her teeth clacked together. Just covering her with his blanket didn't help. Once she was cold, she was cold.

He taken the chance, hoping he'd not lose that ground he'd gained and got in beside her. She'd protested, but as soon as the heat from his body started to sink in, she hushed. With word of a delay, they'd stayed a second night, and this time she openly invited him to share the bed... for warmth, of course.

Some quiet talk in the dark, and he learned she'd no tolerance for cold, always traveling further south as the weather turned cold. He hoped it was only a matter of getting accustomed to it, as the area of Willow Creek sat well up in the mountains. Heavy snows came as early as mid-October and lasted until late May.

"Oh, look," she cried and pointed down the platform. "They are loading the horses." Chase looked down, and sure enough, his buck gelding and her bald face roan mare were being led up a ramp into one of the stock cars. "Where's Sir?" she asked, pulling away from the pocket of warmth he'd just gotten around her.

Chase grabbed her back and folded his coat around her. "I'm sure they're bringing him." A moment later, a few shouted profanities, and Chase watched the mule run up the ramp on his own, stop at the door, turn and bray loudly at the man just now making it to the bottom of the ramp. The animal actually looked to be laughing. The man, however, wasn't sharing the amusement, and several more unpleasant words were said before he pulled the ramp down, stranding the beast in the car. "There, you see, all loaded."

"I told them to call him Sir," Summer said and then giggled. "Ever since we had that copy of Lord Tennyson's work..." She trailed off.

"Thinks he's king, does he?" That was perhaps the most surprising thing about her. Her formal education was completely lacking, but she was actually very smart. Self-taught, through reading, which did seem to be a vice of hers. He'd a devil of a time getting her to put down a paper she'd found on an abandoned table in the dining room so they could walk over to the mercantile and make sure they had what they would need for the first leg of the train trip. He'd bought a few extra blankets. By now, his belongings had already shipped and likely awaited him inside whatever housing he'd be given temporarily. But Summer wasn't exactly coming to him with a well fitted dowry. She likely didn't have trunks of lovingly made quilts and a set of her grandmother's dishes. For all he knew, all she had was what she carried with her. And as miserly as she was about money, she refused to buy or allow him to buy anything she deemed absolutely unnecessary. And in Summer's mind, everything was unnecessary.

"I think he thinks he's Sir Lancelot," she said then turned to him with sparkling eyes. "You know who that is, right?" Before he could answer. "Oh, that's right, you had that fancy education back east."

Chase laughed. "Yes, I had that fancy education, so, yes, I know of Lancelot of the Lake." He laughed again and shook his head. That fancy education his mother bemoaned every day he'd wasted by not taking his law degree and following his brothers into politics. How his mother prayed everyday at least one of her children would make it into the governor's house, either through election or marriage, she didn't care which.

"I wish I could have gone to a real school," she said, almost to herself.

"You've done well enough without it," Chase praised. Truly, given her extensive vocabulary, her ability to do sums in her head quickly, and her broad knowledge of the law, he was completely surprised to hear all she'd had was what her mother could teach her at home. There'd been no school in Highfield, and then there just was no Highfield. She only shrugged and went back to watching the train being outfitted.

Again, there was yelling, and this time a lady screamed. When they turned to look, the old woman who tried her best to get the three rambunctious boys to settle was being ushered out of the warm station house, and the three boys were dragged or shoved out. And the lack of care they took for the old woman now shivering in the cold didn't set well. Chase was about to shrug out of his coat and leave Summer to go set them right, but the train attendant called out over the whistle.

"All aboard, next stop Pagosa Junction."

"That's us," Summer said with almost childlike joy.

"Yes, it is," Chase said, letting her go to bend down and retrieve their bags. He handed her the smallest one then nudged her toward the rail car. He'd reserved a berth but suspected Summer might want to sit at a window and watch the scenery fly by. A last look back, and he saw the boys push past the woman to board the train. He waited, making sure they were all getting on. Not that the woman had the least bit of control, but there needed to be someone to hold to account if they didn't settle down.

"Are you coming, Marshal?" Summer asked as the conductor helped her step up.

"I'm coming," Chase said and followed her up and in.

"Where do we sit?" she asked, moving down the aisle.

"Wherever looks good to you."

She took a seat not quite midway down, and even as she shoved her pack under the bench, she didn't stop looking around. As he stowed their things, he wondered if he might have enhanced her experience a bit by taking the offered opening in another passenger's private car. The man said he was out of Denver and knew his family. Chase politely declined but asked him to give his best to his family and let them know he was back in Colorado. Perhaps if there was time, he'd write a letter and hand it to the man to deliver. Then he noticed her noticing that others were gawking at her and watched her pull into herself.

No, Summer wasn't from his world. And of course, that's what made her so appealing. Maybe someday, he'd take her home to the family ranch and introduce her to his father. But he'd worked hard to distance himself from their influence. He couldn't lose the family name, but he'd done his damnedest to insure it was his merits and his only that made his name what it was.

He pulled free one of the blankets, and with a smile, he took a seat across from his wife and draped it over her. "It should warm up. Once we're moving, someone will light the stove."

She gave him a quick smile before turning to look out the window. He took the opportunity to adjust his crotch. Despite the cold, standing with her tucked close had heated his desire all the more. It was an odd kind of shift for her. She'd gone from completely standoffish to far more open, though she held much back still. If it was the deal, the prospect of getting gone and gone with a good deal of money, then he was glad he'd made it. He only needed a little time to convince her.

The train cars filled up, and the conductors began making sure everyone seated had tickets. When one stopped in front of him, he didn't miss the worried, pensive expression on Summer's face. Giving her a quizzical look, he pulled the tickets from his coat pocket and handed them over.

"You've a bunk in the sleeping car," the conductor said as he handed them back. "Its two cars back through the dining car. Enjoy your trip and call if you need anything."

"Thank you," Chase said, returning the tickets to his pocket.

"A sleeping car?" Summer asked in a hushed voice. "Don't we just..." She turned a bit and pointed at a man sitting across but two rows back. He'd already pulled his hat down over his eyes and started snoring.

Chase laughed. "Only if you want to wake up with your neck permanently twisted."

"Isn't that expensive?"

"I'll let you in on a secret." He leaned forward and crooked his finger at her until she did the same. He got very close to her ear before speaking. "I'm a rich man, Summer."

"I'm a rich woman," she whispered back.

"No, you have money," Chase corrected.

"Yes, because I don't spend it like a fool," she said, and he chuckled again at her admonishment.

"You have money; I'm rich," Chase said, leaning back and getting comfortable.

"U.S. Marshals don't make that much," Summer said, eyeing him suspiciously. "And bounties…"

"Family money, investments," Chase said casually. He'd have thought the announcement would cheer her or at least help her relax, but that nervous, pensive look crossed her face again, and he could have sworn before she turned back toward the window, tears were welling in her eyes. "Summer?"

"Your family is not going to approve of me," she said, lifting a finger to draw a little picture in the condensation her breath left on the cold glass. "Are you going to tell them it's only for six months?"

She was still set to go, leave him, sure it wouldn't work out. But it was only March; he had a good long while to change her mind. "Summer." He waited until her eyes flicked his way. "My family doesn't approve of me."

She was quiet a while, then the corner of her mouth lifted. "Maybe we'll get along then after all," she said and turned to face him, a wicked little smile on her lips and in her eyes.

"Why, you little…" Chase gasped, feigning outrage as he lifted out of his seat and loomed over her. "That is not at all a proper way to support a husband."

"No?" she said, lifting her face and stretching a bit toward him as she did every time he intended to kiss her.

"No," he said and felt his lips brush hers. "You need a lesson I think in—" To his compete surprise, Summer made the move to close the distance.

Her first touch wasn't even hesitant. She pressed her mouth against his, pulled back a bit, then pressed in again. Her fingers gripped his arm through the coat as he lifted his hand to set it against her cheek. She pulled back again, and it became obvious she didn't know what she was doing. Chase leaned in more and used his tongue to trace her bottom lip. The act startled her and she gasped enough, his tongue could slip inside her sweet mouth.

Somewhere in the back of his mind, he heard the train whistle blow, and as he readied to deepen the kiss, maybe take her back to the sleeping car now, the train lurched forward, throwing him off balance and nearly to the floor. He righted himself, but the moment was lost and he sat back in his seat, adjusting the bulge in his pants.

Summer caught his eye for a second, color high on her cheeks, then dropped her eyes to her lap. "Sorry," she grumbled.

"Uh-uh," Chase warned, again trying to get his cock to stop throbbing. "Don't be sorry. Don't ever be sorry for that."

"I…" she started, glancing up then back down.

"We respect each other, Summer. First rule, remember."

"I suppose you have the right to—"

"I have the right to support you, protect you, and provide for you." He waited until she looked up at him. "Spank you when you're naughty." Her flush increased, and she shifted uncomfortably. "Those are the rights I have. Those are the things I'll do."

"You don't want to…" He didn't think it possible, but she colored even more.

"Yes, a great deal," he said, moving to take a seat next to her. He lifted her hand and placed it over his straining prick then covered it so she couldn't pull back and miss how it twitched and jumped. "Yes, I want to. Do you?" He knew the answer before she shook her head. Lifting her hand, he brought it to his lips and placed a kiss on her knuckles. "Then I, we, won't."

She nodded, and when he put his arm around her, she leaned against him. The sunrise gradually filled the car with a soft light and Summer remained leaning against him. "I'm sorry," she whispered.

"For what?"

"Taking your boots."

His laughter rang out, disturbing the man sleeping across from them.

Chapter 10

"Not again," Summer moaned, seeing the first of the three boys who'd been running up and down the cars for hours. They pushed and shoved and knocked into people. Each time, the conductor would demand they return to their car and take a seat.

She'd heard whispers that there were threats to put the family off the train. But apparently, they were a family of prominence. She wished they would get off the train; they reminded her way too much of the boys who'd tormented her back in Highfield. The same boys who'd said after the raid, they'd take care of the survivors, all children between the ages of four and fifteen. They did for a few days, but as days went by and the army didn't come to help, they got tired of having to feed and comfort a couple dozen scared kids. The day they disappeared and didn't come back, Summer had actually felt some relief. At twelve-years-old, she didn't miss the way they sometimes looked at her and the other two girls who were slightly older. If only they'd stayed gone. They hadn't, and like this time when the boys ran through the train car, the return was disastrous.

She saw Chase turn in his chair and took the moment to

again study his profile. He was a damn fine looking man. The distracting thought was enough so she missed how it happened, but shouts, yelling, a scream, and then the wailing of a baby knocked out of its mother's arms and nearly stepped on.

Two conductors were on the boys, but Summer had no hope they'd put an end to their activities. She heard one actually taunt the uniformed man about not having the power to remove them from the train.

"Summer?" Chase's voice called her attention back to him. "Are you all right, honey? You look like you've seen a ghost."

She dropped her head and cleared her throat, doing what she could to push those memories down. When she thought that she had it under control, she looked up, gave him the best smile she could, and said, "I'm fine." And she might have been if one of the boys hadn't broken free and rushed past her as she reached for her canteen. He hit her shoulder, sent her spinning to the floor where her ass hit hard right in a spot Chase had paddled particularly well. She howled and reached back to rub the spot, but Chase's attempt to assist her back into her seat interrupted.

"I'm sorry, sir, madam," the conductor managed as he left his partner with the two still struggling boys and went after the third.

"Not as sorry as those boys are going to be," Chase muttered, stopping Summer with his words as she was leaning up to rub her ass. She watched in awe as he unbuttoned and removed his coat, folded it neatly, laid it over the back of his seat then removed his jacket and did the same. He was rolling up the second sleeve of his shirt when the boy who ran was dragged back to join his brothers. Chase let them pass then stepped into the aisle and followed the group out of the car.

It took more than an hour before he returned, and as he walked toward her, his wide, thick belt was slapping against his thigh. He paused to say something to the mother, whose baby was still whimpering. Whatever it was, it lit up her face and made her nod enthusiastically.

Summer watched as he folded that belt over his coat and jacket and easily took his seat. He smiled when she caught his eye. "What happened?"

"Nothing, I just took care of the problem," he said, leaning his head back and closing his eyes.

"Chase," Summer called as she looked between him and the belt lying right there in plain view. "What did you do?" He'd lifted his head to look at her.

"I told you I took care of a problem," he said, laying his hand over the leather a minute before giving her a lazy smile and a wink.

Summer sat back and huffed, but before she could question him further, she saw the conductor escorting the youngest of the group back into the car. "Did you?" Her question made Chase turn in his seat.

"Again? Already?" he said, getting to his feet to meet the boy.

"No, Marshal," the conductor assured. "Boy just wants to say something to you."

"Well?" Chase said, his tone much like the one he'd used when he was waiting for her to concede she'd been wrong in her actions.

The boy shifted. Twisting his hands together and sniffing, he didn't look up when he spoke. "I'm real sorry, Marshal," he said then glanced quickly at Summer. "Ma'am. I didn't mean nobody to get hurt." Summer suspected anyone listening did like the boy and glanced back at the woman holding the baby and glaring at the boy. "I'm real sorry is all," he finished and sniffed again.

Chase took a seat on the edge of the bench, and taking the boy's chin, he lifted his eyes to him. "That's very manly of you," he said, his tone softer now. "Just because you're hurting doesn't mean you get to behave badly. But you took your licks and admitted you were wrong, apologized, like a man should. If we don't have no more trouble out of you, we can all just move on." He slid back in his seat. "If we do, though..." Summer saw the boy look at the belt then shake his head furiously. "Good boy," Chase praised and patted the boy's shoulder. "Go on back with your grandmother. She needs your support."

"Yes, sir," the boy muttered and sniffed.

"Thank you, Marshal," the conductor said and held out his hand. "Don't know what we'd have done without you."

Chase was just about to take it when the boy turned and flung himself against him. "Hey, it's gonna be all right," he said, holding the boy against him. "It's gonna be all right, and even if it's not, you'll get through it. You got your grandma and brothers."

"He's gonna die; I know it," the boy said.

"You don't know it, and you putting all this worrying ahead of all the hoping and praying doesn't help," Chase said, sitting forward again and holding the boy away from him. "You hang on to hope as long as you can. It'll keep you strong, no matter what happens." He stood, offered his hand to the conductor and then watched them walk back down the length of the car and out the door.

"He gotta sick parent?" Summer asked, rather amazed at how wonderfully Chase dealt with the boy.

"A sick brother, his twin, if I understood the grandmother correctly. Boy was in a bad way, so his parents took him up to Denver to see a doctor. They got a letter telling them they should come visit, but I guess the letter didn't say if things were better or worse. Boys have been acting up now for a while. This trip made it worse." Summer leaned over to make sure the boy was gone. "Summer?" She sat up. "You all right? You looked upset even before you got knocked down."

She tried twice to smile but couldn't hold it. "They just reminded me of someone," she said vaguely. "Maybe we should eat," she said to change the subject.

To her relief, Chase let it drop, and maybe if she'd been a little quieter as they lay together in bed, it would have remained that way. But at the third sniff, she found herself flat on her back and Chase lying over her, his hips settled between her splayed legs, his bare, broad, smooth chest brushing against the thin chemise she wore. She could feel the pull in her breasts as his warmth enveloped her.

Resting on his forearms, he cupped her face in his hands. "Tell me what's wrong?" he said, keeping his voice low as others slept around them.

"Nothing," she whispered, shaking her head.

"My belt is still in reach, Summer, don't lie to me." He shifted forward, putting their lips a little closer. Like this morning, all she could do was try to resist kissing him. Even with the threat ringing in her ears, she wanted to know a little bit more about what she didn't really want to know about.

"Nothing's wrong, honest," she insisted, taking the chance and lifting her hand to his chest. It was as hard as that part of him she'd felt when he'd set her hand on his crotch.

"Something is eating at you," he said, and his arms went under her, and just like that, she was rolled on top of him. He adjusted the blankets and then their bodies so her hips were lined up with his. This put her head center on his chest. "Something's been bothering you all day." His hands flattened against her back then slid down further until he was holding her bottom. "Tell me what it is; I'll fix it."

She bit back the moan that rose up when his hold tightened, but then she wanted to squirm away when it tightened more than was pleasant. "Chase," she complained.

"Tell me; let me fix it." His grip eased a bit, but the feeling it left behind again had her wondering at what she felt between her thighs.

"There's nothing to fix. It can't be fixed. It's the past. I just want to let it lie." She shifted again and this time felt that hard ridge of his shaft. Even through the clothes they both wore, it was enough to make her want a little more.

"Tell me about it, Summer," he said, his hands now holding her in place against his cock. "Who'd those boys remind you of?" She shook her head then yelped when his fingers squeezed hard. She flexed her hips down trying to get away, only to feel him flex up against her. Her skin prickled, even with the heat she felt rolling through her body. "Tell me."

"After the raid..." she started then stopped to swallow. "There wasn't anyone left but children."

"You included," he said, and his palm started rubbing and squeezing her flesh gently.

"Yes, but I was older, almost twelve and—" She stopped when he snorted. "Anyway, we all ended up in a group together, Lizbeth said the Army out of Riley would be coming for us. She was the oldest, so we believed her. We just waited." She stopped again and took a deep breath. "But it wasn't just girls, you know. There were some boys. Mostly real little but a few... a few, they were older."

"They hurt you?" He stopped rubbing and wrapped his arms around her. It was comforting, but she'd rather him rub her more.

"They... They didn't hurt me directly, really. They just didn't help the situation and..." It was odd to her still how sometimes, when she'd believed fully she had put the past behind her, it'd sneak up and knock her down. "They didn't help is all. I don't want to talk about it anymore." She lifted up, breaking his hold, and shifted to lie back down.

"When you're ready, Summer," he said, and rolling toward her, he set his hand on her back. She'd almost fallen asleep to his light touches when she remembered what she'd meant to tell him for days.

"Chase, I want my guns back."

"Get some sleep, Summer."

Chapter 11

Chase shook his head again at the looks his wife was getting as they walked into the dining car. She was again dressed in pants, and this time with a revolver at her hip. If the men weren't looking at her with admiration for the fine curves of her body, they were looking at her with trepidation.

She certainly carried herself differently when she was armed. But maybe everyone did a little. It made little difference to him how she dressed or if she was armed, other than it took that wary look off her face. She still remained open and friendly toward him during the day, chatting about things seen as the train moved along, asking questions about Colorado and what it was like living here when it was given statehood in '76 and joined the union. Her interest really seemed to peak when he mentioned going skiing and sledding as a kid. And that conversation drew in a few others who talked about the best places to do both activities.

Summer expressed some doubts about trying it until a much older couple said they still go every year and ski. Still, she made no promises she'd try it and he knew it was because she was still only looking at being here until September.

But that was during the day. At night, when he'd get in next to her, still wearing his jeans, and pulled her against him, her hands and lips told a different story. One where she desired him, wanted him closer, and not just through the night.

When he returned each touch, each kiss, in kind, she opened more, allowed more. He could not only see and feel her passions building, he could smell them. The sweat scent that wafted off her skin as her body warmed and the slightly muskier scent of arousal kept him hard and aching through the entire night.

And he pushed those limits, gained her consent for a little more each night. She no longer stopped him if he reached under her camisole to stroke her breasts and tease her nipples. He could draw his hand up and down her bare legs, clutch her thighs and ass. And she didn't pull back anymore when he'd press his stiff shaft against her mons.

Why, exactly, she was holding back, he wasn't sure, but he also wasn't going to push. She'd come to his bed as a wife completely on her own accord. Otherwise, they'd both regret it, especially if something happened and she really did walk away at the end of six months. Though at this point, he knew if she did, he'd follow.

Summer Rain Storm simply was a part of him he didn't know was missing. Everything about her felt right. Even those things he'd correct by putting his hand down on her ass didn't feel mismatched. He liked her spunk, he liked how she tried to glare at him, liked how she pursed her lips when she was frustrated or doubtful, and he loved the way she smiled and laughed.

Of course, she still held back. What person in their line of work didn't? He wasn't exactly offering up his life story, though if she asked about something, he told her everything truthfully. And he was sure the answers she gave, what she told him about her life, were also truthful.

"Did we slow down?" she asked, pulling him out of his musings.

"Probably climbing a bit," Chase said. "Did you want to take a stroll, stretch your legs?"

"No, I..." She stopped midsentence and leaned over to look down the aisle, and of course, he turned to see what she was looking at.

"Marshal." One of the conductors hurried in.

At first, Chase thought the boys were acting up again. Even he couldn't expect three boys to remain still on the slow ride with frequent stops. Getting to his feet, he waited to hear what they'd done now.

"Marshal." The man lowered his voice and leaned in. "Something's been laid on the tracks, and we're not just carrying mail."

"Gold?"

The man nodded. "Two full boxes, plus payroll for the Holy Moses."

"All in the mail car?" Chase asked, already trying to form a plan. Things didn't just get laid on the tracks. And they were between Chama and Antonito, the two biggest sites. Given the number of passengers, if this was a robbery plan, it could be best to just surrender it and chase them afterward. "Did the rail or mine set anyone onboard for security?"

"Chase?" Summer asked, getting to her feet and stepping closer.

"The last three attempts all came after Antonito Station. We're supposed to pick men up there."

"What's happening?" Summer asked and shifted to put her hand on the butt of her gun.

"Looks like we're about to be robbed," Chase said. No reason to either lie or even discourage her help. Though he'd set her to keeping passengers safe.

"Who else is on the train who can help?" she asked, knowing just the right question.

"There are a few men, armed. I think one or two might be former Cavalry."

The train was definitely slowing. "Get any man who'll volunteer to the mail coach. I'll meet you there," Chase said and turned to tell Summer what he needed her to do. She'd already moved away. He stepped closer and heard her instructing a group of ladies to hide their money and valuables.

"Not on your person or in a bag," she was saying. "Put them in the cushions. Leave enough on you that you don't look like a pauper, and when asked, hand it over. Don't beg, don't resist. Your life's worth more than a watch or a ring."

"You have this?" Chase asked as she turned and almost crashed into him. Damn, she'd just acted exactly as he needed her to without instruction. She nodded, moving past him to the woman with the baby.

"Get up," she instructed and helped the woman move herself and the baby. She kicked the woman's bag further under the seat then dropped a pillow on the ground to conceal it. "Sit with them and say hello to Junior's new grandparents. Get rid of that jewelry unless you want to hand it over." She left that group and stepped back up to him. "You better go; I have this," she said, reaching under where he'd stored his gear and pulling out her second gun and his rifle, before pulling his holster from under the seat. "You want the rifle?"

"No," he said, strapping on the heavy belt with two holsters and checking the number of loads he had. "They should have a few in the mail car." He stepped away as she stood up and checked the rifle. "Summer."

"Yeah?" She bent again and fished out a handful of cartridges.

"Don't be reckless," he said, giving her a quick peck on the cheek before heading to what should be the main target.

The train came to a complete stop just as the first of the bandits stepped aboard. The mail car sat second behind the engine and the dining car sat behind it, so no passengers were in danger of getting hit when bullets started to fly. Chase had situated four men, all former army, inside the mail car with the clerks and conductor. The reinforced car and the safes bolted to the floor meant the bandits needed to blow their way in. Four bandits laid down cover fire against Chase and the three men he was with as one man did his best to get the stick of dynamite wedged in the door and the fuse lit.

Everyone took cover when the fuse shortened. Smoke hadn't even cleared when shots rang out again. Pinned between Chase's group and the group inside the mail car, the bandits fell rather quickly.

Pulling down the bandanas they wore, Chase shook his head at the wasted youths dead or dying on the tracks. He helped drag the first body clear and turned to get the second. They could send someone back to collect them when they reached the next stop. It wasn't a well thought out robbery. Even if Chase and the others hadn't been on board, the conductor and the others could have held them off. He passed by the men carrying the second body, ready to help with a third, when a scream and gunshots from the passenger cars rang out.

Chase lit out down the tracks. Stepping on the bar under the car, he rose up and peered in the first window. All the passengers where there, crouched down, looking toward the end of the train. He was almost to the middle of the second car when a shot broke out the glass over his head. Ducking, he turned back and climbed the steps to the door and carefully looked inside.

"Now, I knows y'all got more than what you're giving up," a man with his back to Chase yelled and waved his gun around wildly. Chase reached for the door handle. "Nows tells me where it's all hid, and I won't shoot the infant."

Chase froze as a second scream echoed. Another shot and another broken window. Doing his best to stay out of sight, he peered in again. It looked like Summer had everyone behind her and was facing off against the man holding the baby. She didn't look to be armed, though.

"Only a yellow dog coward holds a baby as a hostage," he heard her say and gritted his teeth; she didn't need to provoke him.

"Yellow dog?" the man snarled back, waved his gun in the air and then fired, hitting the wall lamp to the right of Summer's head. "You better take that back, bitch."

"Or what?"

Damn her.

Another shot, this one not revealing where it went. "Or I'll shoot this crying brat."

"You will?" he heard Summer taunt as he reached for the door again. "With what?"

Chased pushed through the door just as Summer twisted and pulled the rifle from where she must have hidden it. She had it leveled on the man who'd twisted around to see what happened behind him, but when he put the barrel to the baby's chest, Chase stopped, showing his hands.

"I swear I'll shoot this yawling pup," the man threatened.

"You can't," Summer said, and the distinct sound of the hammer being cocked reached Chase.

"Course, I can."

"Nope, that Colt you're holding," Summer said, stepping closer, "five shots." Chase took a closer look at the pistol. "One," she said, swinging the barrel of the rifle to the ceiling of the car. "Two." She swung toward the first window. "Three." The second window, then she leveled the rifle again and took aim at the man. "Your fourth went in the lamp and, well, number five, I'm sure we'll find it and dig it out. Give it to the baby as a souvenir."

The man looked at his gun, looked back at Summer, and slumped his shoulders. "Well, I guess yous got me."

"Give the baby to that man behind you, easy like," Summer said. Chase didn't wait for easy; he snatched the gun first then the baby, turning to put both on the nearest seat. He saw it, the man going for a second gun at his waist, but he could do nothing but shout his warning, "Summer," her name drowned out by the crack of rifle fire.

"Charlie?" Chase turned back to the door as another man wearing a mask came through, gun drawn. "Bitch," he screamed, taking aim at Summer when he saw Charlie wasn't going to be answering. Chase's foot took out his knee, and as he fell, he turned his gun toward Chase, who could only try to shield the baby. A second crack of rifle fire, and then a hot, wet splattering across his neck and side of his face.

"Chase?" Summer yelled, stumbling as she stepped over the body of Charlie. She put herself between him and the second man, leveling her rifle. But even from his position on the ground behind her, he could see half the man's head was missing.

"I'm all right," Chase said, getting to his feet and lifting the baby. "So is this little guy."

"Tyrus," the mother cried out, and crawling over the seats, she took the baby from him.

"He's all right, Amanda," Summer assured, ducking her head out the door, probably to check and see if any more bandits were going to try to surprise them.

"Everyone else all right?" Chase asked, reaching out to force Summer to lower the barrel of her Yellow Boy. He saw heads nodding and heard murmurs of affirmation. The passengers were helping each other retake seats.

"These two came up from the back," Summer said before he could ask. And for the first time, Chase noticed the third dead body between the seats. "I guess they took what they could from those people and came in here looking for what we had. But that one pulled a knife on..." she had to look around, but Chase spotted the old man holding a cloth of some sort to his neck. "I got him, but then that one grabbed up the baby. I had to drop my gun, but then he started firing and yelling. I just backed up to where this was." She lifted the rifle and waited.

"Yeah, you waited," Chase grumbled. He was ready to

strangle her or maybe hug her, or even better, just make love to her. "You taunted him. I told you not to take any risks." She had the nerve to shrug at him.

"She was so brave, Marshal," the baby's mother said in her deep southern accent. "I sure didn't think I'd be getting back to Georgia, everyone safe without a scratch even." She reached for Summer's hand and squeezed it. "Thank you, Summer, I can't ever repay you."

Chase didn't miss the discomfort that caused his wife. But he didn't get to address it or her actions for a few hours, as men came in and carried out the bodies and the conductors helped people move from the shot up, blood splattered car into a cleaner one. Belongings were returned, and as the train started rolling again, Chase sat facing Summer across the aisle where she'd sat to give a second recount of what happened to the conductor. Neither of them thought any of the men involved were wanted; they'd not had control of the situation from the start, so even though she asked and reminded the man several times that any reward was hers, she knew there wasn't going to be one.

He wiped the damp rag over his neck once more, still feeling like that man's noggin parts were there. With a sigh, he tossed the rag down and leaned back to level a look he hoped she'd take seriously. "You took a big chance, Summer."

"Yep, but it paid off," she said with yet another shrug.

"Damn it," Chase said, surging to his feet and yanking her to hers. "You can't take those kinds of risks." He jerked her hard against him. He'd every intent of laying down the law to her, right up until she practically melted against him, her palms flattened on his chest and smoothed upward across his shoulders and then around his neck.

"Did it make you nervous, Marshal?" she almost purred.

Chase swallowed hard and nodded. "Don't do it again."

"Or what?" She pressed closer, lifted up on her toes and nipped his chin.

"Or I'll… paddle you so you can't sit for two months of Sundays," he said, claiming her lips and quickly deepening the kiss as his hands smacked down sharply on each side of her sweet ass. She moaned as he took hold and lifted her up.

Her hold around his neck tightened and she held nothing back, returning his kiss with as much heat as he gave it. Their kiss was a wild duel of lips, tongue, and teeth, and which of them was making what sounds, he didn't know or care. Chase did everything he could to breathe through his nose so he could keep going. Feeling her fingers comb through his hair and pull him closer still, like perhaps she was as desperate to have more, started a fire raging in his gut. Damn, if she'd gotten shot.

A loud bang had them jumping apart. Chase had already shoved her behind him as he turned to see it was only the door, left unsecured when the train started moving. Instinct made him shift to block her as he insured it was nothing more than the loose hinges. Summer was having none of that, though. She shoved past him and then turned to glare.

"Don't step in front of me like that. I can't see what's happening," she snapped.

"I'll step in front of you when I think it's necessary, missy," Chase countered, reaching for her and pulling her against him again. "It's my duty to protect you and—"

"I protect me," she almost snarled, jerking free and taking several steps back. "And being this is the second time I've saved your hide, maybe—"

"If you hadn't been provoking that bastard—"

"I knew what I was doing."

"Did you? Because it didn't look like it to me," Chase ground out and stalked her as she stepped back again. "I told you not to be reckless, and I told you that it's my right to protect you."

"I protect me. And you have no idea what reckless is if you think I ever am." Summer took one more step back, set her rifle off to the side and reached for something in the seat to her left.

"I'm not the jackass who keeps insisting he knows what's best. That town, this train," she yelled, lifting her belt and holster and wrapping it around her narrow waist. "We should have ridden our horses into Willow Creek." He watched her get down on her knees and reach under the same seat for something. When she got back up, it was with her revolver, which she slammed into the holster. "Better yet, I should have kept going east without you." She took up her rifle again. "Seems to me, following you is the only reckless thing I've done of late."

Chase let her push back past him and turned as she made her way to the seats they'd occupied the whole trip. She had to yank hard to get her gear out from under the seat and he wanted to help, but this sudden want of independence she had needed to wane. Something had set her off, and he suspected it was his criticism of how she'd handled the situation. But then, she'd not really been upset until he made the more outright move to protect her. What was it about that act that had set her off?

"Move," she snarled, trying to get past him with everything she'd brought on board.

Rather than move back, he blocked her more. "No, we're gonna talk."

"I ain't got nothing to say to you, other than we're done."

"We're not done," Chase told her, thinking he'd made it clear there wasn't going to be any debate on the matter.

"We are. When the train stops at Antonito, you can go north clear to Canada for all I care, but I'm going east. Before you get me killed."

"No, you're not. We made a deal, and you'll stick to it." He snatched her packs away from her and carried them with him as he gathered up his own. "We're partners for the next six months," he said, crowding her toward the door. "And you better damn well know, if you don't want to end up over my knee with your pants around your ankles, you'll start working with me, like a partner, a wife." He pushed her out the door, reached around her, and opened the next. "Because, like it or not, right now, that is exactly what you are."

With a jerk of his head, he indicated she should go inside. The crowded car's only two open seats were clear down the other end, and Chase said nothing else as they claimed them and stowed their gear. Summer also remained silent, though he could see her fuming. He finished putting away his things and then without a word turned and left the car.

What the hell had changed? The last few days and that brief moment just now. She went from committed to cutting out, with barely more than a breath of wind. There had to be more to it, and he'd have to figure it out, because he couldn't lose her.

Chapter 12

Summer picked at her food. She'd no appetite at all. Hadn't had one for the last day and a half. Even the mostly decent food offered at the eatery in Antonito didn't stir her stomach. Though she wanted it to be because she was still mad, she knew it wasn't. She didn't feel like eating because of the man sitting across from her.

For that split second when she thought she'd see him shot down trying to protect that baby, all she'd felt was terror. The same as when she'd watched her mother and aunt dragged into a separate room by the raiders. Her mother screaming for her to run, to hide. She'd been sure when the ringing in her ears caused by gunfire finally stopped, she'd again find someone who actually meant something to her dead. Seeing Chase get back to his feet, none of the blood on him his own, her knees had gone weak. Then after hearing herself recount exactly what had happened, she knew she was if not completely to blame, at least partially to blame for him being in that dangerous situation. She could have done things differently. Little things like have the baby placed on the floor rather than handed to Chase, who then wasn't able to defend himself. She could have tried to see first if there was anyone else working with him, been ready when that second man stepped through the door. A hundred little things she could have done differently so that Chase didn't have to be left vulnerable. So she didn't have to be left doubting his survival.

And damn, when that doubt lifted, when she knew for sure Chase was unharmed, the relief hadn't calmed her. Rather, the complete opposite happened. A wild need to just touch him, to smell him, feel his heartbeat, his touch, know another of his kisses almost consumed her. And he made it worse with his more teasing than threatening tone as he promised to make her atone. He lifted her passion and spirits higher with every move of his mouth, each squeeze of his hands.

She'd been so ready at that moment to know what else he could offer her. Five more minutes, and she might have had them both naked. She would have learned what it was that a woman endured for the sake of having a man stand beside her. But then, that door slammed, and like that, she hit the ground again, hard.

That wasn't her way, her life. Hadn't she learned, over and over, not to trust people... men. Not to depend on anyone to do the right thing when it most needed to be done. Standing behind him as that door banged in the wind, realizing he'd again willingly sacrifice himself and this time not for a baby, but for her. Then insisting that was what he was supposed to do.

Well, it wasn't. She wasn't wrong; she could protect herself. She *had* to protect herself. Because leaving the job to anyone else either left her needing to get out of a worse situation or left that other person dead. And this time, with Chase, it was more than just his life he could have been robbed of.

When the train pulled in to the station and the marshal and his group started questioning everyone, it was clear the disapproval they had for how he'd involved her. And to rub dirt in it more, they scolded him for letting his wife wear pants. Saying a man with his reputation should give more consideration to proprieties. Chase didn't seem to care about their opinion. But she knew his reputation was everything to him. If he lost that, because of her, what kind of man would he become? One around whom she'd have to watch her back? And what might happen, too, if he learned about the kind of person she really was?

"Are you still not gonna eat something?" Chase asked, the worry in his tone making her need to blink back tears.

She shook her head and laid her fork aside. "I'm not hungry," she said when she continued to feel his stare.

"All right," he said a bit sharply and, pulling out his kerchief, spread it out on the table and started piling her uneaten meal in it. He added the remaining biscuits from his own plate then pushed back from the table as he tied it all up. "Enough of this," he said, reaching to hold her chair, even though she was half out of it by the time he did. As he took her elbow, he directed her out the door, across the street, and into the rooming house where they were waiting until the train was once again ready to depart.

She'd made half an attempt to get her animals pulled off, but Chase wouldn't permit it, and as her husband, everyone did what he said. But it was only a half attempt, because even now, the thought of really going their separate ways didn't appeal to her. So she didn't resist as he guided her down the hall to their room. She didn't resist when he unlocked the door and ushered her in, pulled out a chair and forced her in it, and she didn't resist the shame that welled up when he crouched down in front of her and gently took her hands in his.

"You need to talk to me, Summer," he said, the pad of his thumb stroking the back of her hand, causing little sparks to flick up her arm. "You need to tell me why you're so melancholy."

What could she say? She could tell him the truth. Tell him who she was when she wasn't working as a bounty hunter. Maybe even telling him that trying to have her as a partner, to have her as someone to depend on was a mistake that could one day really cost him his life, would gain her her freedom. But damn it, right now she still didn't think she wanted it. And damn it more, without that money he was holding away from her, she couldn't even start back on the trail.

She heard his deep inhalation and saw him slowly rise to his feet and make his way to the washstand. He grumbled something then lifted the pitcher. "Why don't you get ready for bed. I'll be back; they didn't refill the pitcher like I asked."

She waited until he was out the room before she muttered, "Like you paid for." She was in bed when he returned. She'd taken the initiative to lay out his bedroll even if she was again ready to feel him against her back as she slept, because he was the one who'd laid it out last night.

He didn't say much when he came back in. Dimming the lamp, he stripped out of his shirt, shoes, and socks, put the light out, and lay down on the floor beside the bed. She heard the clink of his buckle and squeezed her legs together to stop the pulse that caused. Listening more, she could hear him moving around but couldn't quite determine what it was he did, and then he was still and she couldn't hear anything more than the sounds coming off the street outside.

He was right there. She could reach down and touch him, but he might as well be clear in Boston for how far away he felt. She lay awake for what seemed the whole night, letting silent tears drip from the corners of her eyes into her hair. She needed to stop this. She needed to stop wanting him. She needed to go before she really couldn't.

"All right," he said, startling her and making her grab for the bed frame as he caused the mattress to dip. "I will allow your sulking to keep you from not eating. When you're hungry enough, that will stop. And I'll even allow it to keep you awake half the night. When you're tired, you'll fall asleep." The blankets lifted and his leg passed over hers before his weight settled down completely and the blankets covered them both. "What I won't allow is your wallowing in whatever misery you think is so much yours that you need to cry about it." He settled more firmly over her, pulling his legs together so hers were pressed together holding most of his weight. He rested the weight of his upper body on his forearms which were pinning her on either side, and his hands, free for the most part, settled on her face. His fingers brushing at the tears that flowed a little more freely as she realized this was what she wanted most. "You need to tell me what's ailing you, sweetheart. You need to tell me so if I can, I can help."

She opened her mouth, prepared to tell him it wasn't anything, or at least anything he could help with, but all that came out was a sob and then another and another until she had to gasp for breath. And the whole while, Chase held her tight and whispered soft words meant to sooth.

"Better now?" he asked when she dammed up the break. He rolled to his side, finally letting her lift her arm.

Dropping it over her eyes, she shook her head. "We can't do this, Chase. We can't do this."

"Do what?"

"We can't be partners. I can't be your partner. I can't be anyone's partner."

"Why not?"

His tone confused her. He actually sounded curious, like he really couldn't see any problem with having her help hold the reins. "Because I'm not right for you."

"You really don't get to decide that. All you get to decide is if I'm right for you. As far as I think now, you're about as right for me as I may ever get. And you're supposed to be giving me time to prove I am the right man for you."

"And I want to, but," she told him, then not believing she'd said that out loud moved so she was holding her hand over her eyes as hard as she could.

"But?"

"What happens to you when it doesn't work out? When I'm gone and you're…"

"I'm what? What do you think is going to happen to me if I can't convince you to stay?"

"Chase, I can't stay."

"Why? You have someone else you need to get back to?" His voice actually pitched a little high for a second.

"No, no." She shook her head. She didn't have a soul in the world she needed to get back to, who wanted her to come back to them.

"Then, what? What has you chomping at the bit to ride off, alone, into the sunset?"

"I'm a bad person," she whispered. "I'm a bad person. A coward if you have to know it. I'm a bad person, and I'll ruin your reputation if I stick around. Hell, already, people are questioning your judgment. That marshal thinks you less a man because I was wearing pants again."

"You wearing pants made him feel like less a man, not me. So what he thinks about me couldn't matter in the least. If a woman in denim makes him uncomfortable, that's his problem. And even if what he said mattered, that is for me to decide how much it might matter. My reputation is mine. And no one but me can ruin it. Do you understand that?"

"No," she said, and she didn't.

"My reputation is based on what I do, say, how I act or respond. Same as yours is. How you act is your reputation. How I respond is mine. If I really believe you're doing something that I need to respond to in a way to make you change what you're doing, I will. I think you even know how I will." She nodded. "If I don't respond or if I don't respond how someone else thinks I should, that is not my problem. I'm going to do what I believe is right for me. I always have. And I will do my best to always do what's best for you. If you'll let me." He stopped a minute, and she felt the top of his head come to rest on her shoulder. But then he lifted it and took a breath that pressed her more into the bed. "I didn't mean to make you think I thought you incapable of defending yourself. And I should have told you right away how damn proud I was you kept your head and held off those men, how thankful I am, you're a damn fine shot. We don't handle tough situations the same, I know, it doesn't mean I can't wish we did."

All she could do was nod. Was he really proud of how she'd acted? Why would he say he was if he wasn't?

"Summer, tell me now, right now, why you think you're a bad person."

"Will you let me go, walk away, if I do?" She'd never told a soul. She didn't think she could look another human in the eyes if she did.

"Tell me," he said, making no promises.

"Those boys," she started. "The ones who survived the raid with the rest of us." She stopped, gave her head a shake, and welcomed the feel of Chase's arms tightening around her a bit. "They got real tired, real fast of acting like men. A few weeks after, when the army still hadn't come for us, they lit out. They took the few horses we'd rounded up and left us. The oldest girls said we couldn't stay there, no one was coming and that we should try to make it to the next town." She had to laugh now at the stupidity of it all. "We didn't even know what direction to go, though. None of us had ever been away from Highfield. Not for anything. Best we could figure was we should head northeast. We knew Solomon River was that way and we should find a larger town, and that Fort Riley was just beyond that if we didn't." She felt it when he nodded his head, but he remained silent. "Guess we'd been going about six days; it was slow when everyone was small. Spent a lot of time carrying the real little one, and that meant stopping early each day to get something to use in a fire and try to hunt. We had one rifle with us but not a lot of cartridges and... Anyway, 'bout midday that seventh day, those boys rode up on us. They had several other men with them and a few women. Said they'd come back for us." Again, she had to laugh at all their stupidity. "Should have known just by their looks, ain't a one of 'em any good. But we were tired and hungry and… scared. They separated us. Put us older girls in one wagon, along with two of the smaller boys. The rest of us, they put in a little cart. I don't know when it happened exactly. But one day, we were all traveling together, then we weren't. We asked what happened to the other kids. Asked if we could wait until they caught up when we heard they fell behind, broken wheel or something. No one stopped. We somehow ended up outside Wilson Lake. Some unholy town named Breaker. A few shops, a mercantile, but mostly dominated by a saloon and broth-el." She stopped again, pushing her hand up her forehead. "Weren't no lawman or church folks come to take us in. We got shoved inside the saloon, and after the owner or whoever he was and the madam looked us over, they handed those boys a wad of money and dragged us upstairs. I knew, I knew right away what just happened. I knew it. I'd heard my aunt talking with my mother about how something needed to be done to stop men from selling their female kin off to be whores so they had whiskey money. But before I even said a word, we were shoved into a few different rooms, just two, three of us each and locked in. I told Hazel and Janet we had to get out of there. I told them we had to go, but the door was locked, and they wouldn't help me get it open. The window was open, but we were three stories up. They wouldn't follow me. I begged them to come. To help get the others so we could run, but…" Somewhere in her mind, she could still hear the shouts and cheers, the auctioneer calling out bids. "I went out the window, along the ledge to the rain pipe. But I couldn't go down. I had to go up. There were men every-where below and outside. No one was on the roof, though. I thought I could just wait until nightfall, go down, sneak back in, and get the others out of the rooms. We could run then. But more men actually came in. Just after sundown, I heard the screaming start. I don't know when it stopped. I don't know how long I sat on that roof. Might have been a few days. The town had emptied out by the time I took a look over the ledge down to the street. I could see a flatbed pull up to the saloon, someone carrying something out. Didn't know it was Hazel until the second body tossed in caused hers to roll. I think, in all, it was two of the girls and one of the small boys. And then I saw someone with a body over his shoulder. He just tossed that body, one of the older boys who'd sold us out, on top the others like a log. Wagon moved out, and everything was still. Was about midday, I climbed down off the roof, made it over to where that dead boy's horse was tied up. I stepped in the stirrup and dug in. I didn't go back for any of them. I didn't even think to. I just gave that pony its head and ran it until it was full lather and stumbling. I left them. I left them like a coward. I didn't do anything to help them."

"Summer," Chase whispered her name.

"I ran." She again covered her eyes with her hand. "I ran and didn't stop until I made Fort Dodge. The place was hardly anything. I guess Seventh Cavalry was still..." She shrugged. "Anyway, there was still a small group of Army men, but... I told them what had happened to us. I told them there were others who needed help. No one went after them. I was taken to Sergeant Dexter's house. He was old, needed help getting things done. I worked, and in between, the soldiers taught me to shoot and scout. I accidently took my first bounty while with them. Took the second a little more on purpose. I stayed almost three years. But after he passed..." Again, she could only shrug. That old man had been mean as hell, but he'd given her shelter and food and the chance to find the means to support herself. "I found a sheriff in Missouri, willing to give me a bill. Then another. He tried to warn me off when another bounty hunter asked to team with me to go after a larger reward. I didn't listen, thought the man was like me, wanted to uphold justice. He was a snake. I brought his body back, though. Sheriff told me keep what of his I wanted. I took his mule."

"Sir," Chase confirmed.

"Yep." She sniffed. "I went back. Back to Highfield. Before we walked away we all buried what things we couldn't carry. It was all there. Odd things, all if it. I packed it all out. Made my way toward Breaker. Found a few small skulls with bullet holes in 'em, nothing else, though. But I knew who they were, what happened after the youngest kids got separated. Breaker was cleaned up a bit. Saloon was still there, the brothel. Of the nine of us sold there... three were still there. I wanted to go up to them, to tell them I was sorry, that I had their things from Highfield. But I could see, when I looked at Lizbeth, she had died already. She might have been smiling and laughing at the men in the saloon, might have bent over so they could stick their hands up her skirts, but her soul... Maybe if I hadn't been a coward. Maybe if I'd stood by them. I didn't. I ran. I ran and left everyone else to die."

"Gawd," Chase breathed. He shifted forward and surprised her by kissing her softly. "You ran, Summer, because you were a child, not because you were a coward. You were a child." He kissed her again. "And running for that doesn't make you a bad person; it makes you an intelligent one."

"I left everyone behind," she repeated. Maybe he missed that part.

"They didn't follow you; that isn't your fault." More of his weight settled over her, and when it became too much, he shifted so she could spread her legs and he could lie between them.

"But I didn't own up, didn't say anything when I went back. I didn't even return their things."

"What'd you do with it?" he asked, and she let his warmth seep into her. He seemed a bit warmer than normal, lower down.

"Went back to Highfield and reburied it. Just the stuff that wasn't mine." Maybe she would send a letter, ask Sheriff Green to send her things. All her mother's recipes, the lace table cover, the candlesticks, and the few other things that had survived the raid and the fire.

"You're not a bad person, Summer. You're very lucky you survived everything that happened. And you shouldn't feel responsible for those who didn't or who maybe did but found a worse kind of life than you." The back of his knuckles brushed down her cheek. "None of that is going to ever be reason enough for me not to want to be your partner. Nothing you did, between when you lost your home and family and when you became what you are now, makes me want to be your husband less. I think about it, and I think I might be the really lucky one."

She sniffed, using what she could of the moonlight to try to make out his features, his expression. "How?"

"Well, I got me an intelligent, beautiful woman. One who's a crack shot and one who I don't think could ever be a bad person. I got me someone I can depend on. I may not always like how you do things, Summer, but you get things done. That's the important part."

"If people find out what I did—" Summer tried again, though she felt much less like denying his words, the more his lips nibbled up her neck.

"People should damn well good and know about what you did, what you survived. You were a child, Summer, what, twelve at the time?" He paused in his distraction to look down on her.

"Almost," she said, taking in everything when his face passed through the moonbeam. He looked serious, sounded honest. But she'd been taken in before.

"People should know that about you, that you're a survivor. Anyone who'd try and blame you for those losses, shame you for saving your own hide aren't good enough to lick your boots. And if I hear someone trying to do either, they'll get my boot right up their ass."

"Because it's your right to protect me?" she asked with a snort as she shifted her hips and felt more of his body than she expected to feel.

"It is," he said and used his weight to hold her hips still.

"I could still be bad for your reputation. I could still ruin it. Might not get us thrown in jail again, but not every place cares for women who wear pants and a gun."

"That's my problem to deal with, and did you think for a moment that maybe once you are settled, you might not have to wear those things? At least not every day. I certainly don't mind looking at your backside in denim, but I could think you'd look mighty pretty in a nice calico dress. Maybe one that's blue like your eyes."

She snorted and did her best to shrug with him lying on top of her more now. Damn, but there was something very different about him tonight. One more shift of her hips, and she knew what it was. "Are you naked?"

"Yes, ma'am," he said, and the humor in his tone heated her more than his body did.

"Why are you naked?" Damn, would it be terrible if she lifted the covers and looked down his body? She'd seen a few men naked before, but none whose physique matched Chase's. And though she couldn't speak to it for sure, she could almost be certain none of them had what she could feel pressing against her thigh.

"I sleep naked, Summer. Only reason I've kept my pants on and been uncomfortable every night was because I'd rather be uncomfortable close to you than comfortable out of my pants. I thought I'd be on the floor again so..." he trailed off.

"Sleeping in pants is uncomfortable?" she asked and bit her lip when he again pressed his hard shaft against her thigh.

"When I have this thing," he said and again pushed it against her. Through the gown she wore, she felt its heat, and when he pulled back, it left a small wet spot. "When I have this thing pushing and throbbing to get out, yep, it's uncomfortable."

"Sorry, I didn't know."

"Do you want to know?"

She knew what he was asking and she wanted to say yes, but the idea scared her still. So far, with the exception of Chase, she'd not had any good experiences with men. And the thought of it always brought to mind the screaming from that night. "I-I don't know, maybe?"

Chase leaned in and kissed her once more, softly, then rolled to her side and pulled her close to him. "When you're more certain, let me know. I can wait, and I can wait more comfortably now." He flexed his hip and pressed that long, hard thing against her ass. "Get some sleep, sweetheart. We've got a train to catch in the morning." He snuggled in, dropped his arm to her waist, and within minutes, his snores were filling her ear.

Damn, but she liked this. There was no better way to sleep. And if she did nothing else before she left him, she'd find out what else was better with him.

Chapter 13

Chase stepped off the train onto the narrow platform and dropped his gear. Before turning to help Summer step down, he adjusted his work jacket around himself. He'd forgone the formalities of a suit given they'd arrived on Saturday rather than Wednesday and given he'd gotten off the train twice on this short route to help remove something from the tracks. At least all the aid he'd given landed him and Summer in a private car with all the well-known Pullman luxuries.

When he turned, he couldn't help but smile as Summer stepped down on the last step and held out her gear. The last three nights had been amazing, even if he'd not really gotten much further with her. After they'd spoken, after she'd revealed more of why she held back so much, Summer opened and gave him her interest and willingness to touch and be touched more. She wasn't bold, but she was curious. And nothing made his cock harden like catching her looking at him as he got dressed or undressed.

The way her skin flushed like the sky at sunrise, or how her eyes sparked like a mica laden mountain, there wasn't any way she wasn't going to be a passionate spitfire once she gave in. And the wait was almost killing him, very much like the cold wind whipping around.

He tugged his coat down and checked to make sure it was buttoned then held his hand out so Summer would actually step down. Given the amount of snow piled up to the sides of the tracks, he thought for a minute she might try to get back on and ride back to the lower elevations. He hadn't missed the worried look in her eyes as they passed through areas where it was snowing but nothing lay on the ground, then into places where snow remained but only in shady spots. Still further up, snow covered most of the ground, and then it covered the ground in deeper and deeper drifts. He stopped listening when she complained for the hundredth time that she hated the cold. But he took as many opportunities as he could find to show her how he'd help keep her warm.

As she stepped onto the platform, she took a moment to look around, but that was all as the wind whipped by again and she became like a turtle, tucking her head and arms back down inside his heavy duster so her hat appeared to be sitting on the collar. With a laugh, he picked up all the gear and, jerking his head toward the station house, said, "Come on, before you turn into a snowman."

"Chase, it's nearly May. This snow won't be gone until July as much as there is," she said, trotting up behind him.

"I've seen snow in Kansas," Chase teased.

"Yes, and it's the worst thing there too," Summer griped, making him toss his head back and laugh out loud.

"Well, at least we don't get twisters up here in Colorado." He nudged open the door and then stepped aside.

"Cellars can be cozy," she said, stepping around him and inside the small building. Again, he laughed.

"I could get cozy anywhere with you, even in a cellar," he teased and watched in awe as she colored up all pretty like.

"Shh," she said. "There are people." She gave him a look that told him to just look around.

"So what?" he said, stepping a little closer, ready to kiss her right there in the station.

"Marshal Storm?" a deep voice disrupted his intent.

"That's me," he said, straightening and then stepping around Summer to greet the older man coming at him.

"Sure glad you made it, Marshal," the man said, holding out his hand in greeting. "Sheriff Buckley. Welcome to Willow Creek."

"Chase Storm, and I'm glad to be here," he said, ready to introduce Summer. The man, though, didn't seem to take notice of her.

"And we're glad to have you. As you saw, whole region been having trouble. And not all the trouble is as bumbling as the ones you took care of," he went on. "But we should get you settled. Day's just starting, and you can take some time, I'll show you 'round. Mayor wants to introduce you at services tomorrow."

"I need to check if my belongings have arrived, and—" Again, Chase tried to introduce Summer, who was still stuffed down in his coat.

"Sure 'nuff did. Last week, already moved them to your place. Everything's waiting for you if you'll follow me." He turned then touched the brim of his hat and nodded at Summer. "Ma'am, you waiting on someone?"

"No, Sheriff," Chase said before Summer could take a bite of the man. "She's with me. Sheriff Buckley, Summer Storm, my wife."

"Didn't no one say yous was coming with a wife," the sheriff sputtered, and with that, he ruined any chance that Summer might try to be nice to him.

"IT'S ONLY TEMPORARY, Summer. I promise," Chase said again as he struck a match and set the kindling on fire in the potbelly stove that would keep their living space above the jail warm. "I sent word a while back that I'd be looking to buy land and build. We'll pick a spot and get started as soon as we can."

"Chase," Summer chided, stepping closer as the logs he added to the fire caught and the heavy iron started to waft a warmth out over the room. "It's fine. It's a good home. Better than most I've had."

He watched her make her way to the front windows that overlooked the street. The large single room apartment didn't have a lot of luxury, but it had most everything they might need for now. He'd be sending for more of his things, furnishings and the like, once building started on their permanent home. Closing the grate on the stove, he stood and stepped up behind her. As he wrapped his arms around her, he pulled her closer and rested his chin on her shoulder. "Set this place up how it suits you, and if you need anything, we'll get it."

She turned into his arms and put hers around his waist before resting her head on his chest. "It has a cook stove and a good view of the street, what more could I want?"

"Ah, yes, my best biscuits making, sharp shooting wife." He chuckled when she pinched him. "I can forget how simple your needs are."

"Well, my needs might be simple, but if you want biscuits, then your needs will mean some shopping will need to be done. We'll need to stock up on staples."

"Buckley said most all the shops and services are open until two on Saturday, so we can at least get enough to hold us over until Monday. It's not," he paused to pull out his watch, "not even nine, and it will be warmer outside closer to noon, so let's unpack and do a little setting up, then we can go see what's to see."

Summer nodded and lifted her head to look up at him. As it often did, anticipation filled her eyes, pulling him in like a fish on a line. Lowering his head, he brushed his lips over hers, rewarded instantly by a soft moan from her. He went back for a second small taste, feeling her lift up on her toes and tighten her arms. He deepened the kiss a bit, pressing his mouth firmly against hers, and heard the gasp when his tongue traced the line of her full, pouty, bottom lip. She opened for him and—

The banging on the door made Summer leap back and spin away. Sure, she was open with him, but only in private. Though he'd not really had the chance yet to see if she'd walk the boardwalk holding his hand, he was going to try to insist she did. More banging, and he couldn't keep wishing whoever it was would go away.

Crossing the room, he pulled open the door, which sent Summer scurrying to stand closer to the stove. "Yes?"

"Hi, y'all," the younger man said, touching the brim of his hat. "Deputy Brown, Sheriff said I should run this up to ya," he added, holding out a stack of documents, "and tell you the boarding house serves supper at five sharp. It's the only place to grab grub 'round here, and its only once a day. The sooner you get there, the bigger the portions."

"Really?" Summer said, catching Chase by surprise with her tone. "Is the food good?"

"Well, ma'am," Brown started, pulling off his hat as Chase stepped aside and motioned him so he could close the door and keep Summer warm. "Its edible."

"Meaning?" she asked. It was the most interest she'd taken in anything he'd seen, other than her little stash of wanted posters.

"Meaning?" Brown said, maybe not understanding what she wanted to know about the food.

"Well, what is served?" Summer elaborated.

"Oh," Brown said, and Chase balled his fists at his side as the man's eyes widened in appreciation of his wife who was finally taking off his coat. She'd dressed again in her only skirt, but she'd traded the durable heavy cotton shirt for a far more feminine shirtwaist, one she kept carefully wrapped in sack cloth at the bottom of her bags. The dress didn't reveal the fine curves of her body the way jeans did, but she could have worn the sack cloth and still been beautiful. Chase cleared his throat when the man went on staring long past polite. It actually took Brown two looks away from Summer to realize Chase was about to punch him. He flinched then twisted his hat in his hands. "Um, um, most days, it's chicken stew, ma'am, but some days, it might be beef and gravy on bread."

"That's it?" Summer asked, and an odd smile curled her lips up in the corners.

"Yes, ma'am, and when the miners come in, its best to be first in line, bring your own plate, and carry the meal out to your own place. They run out of food right fast."

"Really," Summer said, and her smile grew. "Thank you, deputy Brown. That's quite helpful."

Chase didn't really see how it was helpful, but if it made Summer a little happier about being here, he'd take it. "Was there anything else?" he asked, reaching for the door before he gave in and reached for the man's neck.

"Ah…" the deputy stammered again, not able to keep his eyes off Chase's wife.

Chase jerked open the door and grabbed the man's arm. "Well then, we have a lot of settling in to get done," he said as he had to drag the man a few steps to get him moving. "Thanks for bringing these papers by and for the information."

"Oh, yes, sir, Marshal," Brown said, setting his crumpled hat on his head and stepping out the door. "Welcome to Willow Creek; enjoy your day." He touched his brim again. "Marshal, ma—"

Chase slammed the door before he could finish as he was

leaning in to try to look again at Summer. Behind him, he heard her giggle. "Damn puppy," he grumbled. Summer giggled again then pressed her lips together in a vain effort to keep from smiling. "I hope the other deputy here isn't a fool too." He crossed back to Summer and pulled her into his arms. "Be a damn shame if this place becomes a ghost town because of you."

"You gonna shoot every man who looks at me, Marshal Storm?" she asked and, setting her hand on his thigh, began to slowly draw it up toward his crotch.

"Yep," he said and tried to shift to accommodate his hardening member.

"Then you might need to stock up on bullets," she said as her hand settled at the bulge in his pants. Her fingers squeezed him through the fabric. "Damn, that's a big gun you have, sir."

Chase almost groaned. The first time she made the remark, it was with more fear than awe, but here he was, only a few days since then, and she was growing braver. "This one's for you," he said, covering her hand and pressing down. "This one..." He lifted his hand and brought it to rest on the hilt of his gun. "This one is for any man who looks at you."

She squeezed him again but snorted. "Men always look at me, Chase."

"It doesn't bother you?" He wasn't typically a jealous man, but the urge to protect Summer from anything unpleasant was strong.

She shrugged. "As long as all they do is look," she said and shrugged again. "Don't mean nothing."

"Well then, as long as all they do is look." He bent down and kissed her. Short and quick, because anything more, and they might not make it to the mercantile. "Guess we best be making something of this place."

"I think something can be made of this place," Summer said, but Chase didn't think she was talking about the apartment.

They worked hard until nearly noon, unpacking and moving

furniture around so the wide-open space had determinable areas. Chase's belongings consisted a great deal of those comforts he always missed when on the trail. Thick bedding, dishes and utensils, and clothes. Between them, their packs contained two fry pans, two coffee pots, more utensils, along with a couple of good cutting knives. They used the ropes they carried to string up the blankets of their bedrolls, blocking off their bed from the common area. And while Chase made use of a hammer and nails they'd found in a crate beside the stove to hang up their clothes, Summer sat at the small table and made a list of things she thought they should get immediately. At his insistence, Summer put her pants on under her skirts and changed her frilly shirtwaist for one of his thick flannel shirts. He was disappointed she stepped behind the makeshift curtain to do that, but he laughed as he rolled the sleeves of his shirt back several times just so her hands were out. Hats and coats donned, they stepped out the door, Chase laughing again when the cold hit her and she told him he could fill the list alone.

He gave his word it would get better as they walked, and he didn't lie. The sun shone bright along the street and the boardwalk, and the wind quit blowing. He tucked Summer's hand in the crook of his arm and encouraged her to lean into him for more warmth, which she did. And she stayed tucked against him even as people passed or stopped to have a more formal greeting.

They made several stops along the way. Chase had their purchases held until they had finished looking around town. They'd pick everything up on the way back. Summer made several inquiries at a few of the shops, the butcher she took quite a while with, and he saw when she was handed something to write on and with. She made several notes, shook the man's hand, and walked away with a smile on her lips. But she didn't tell him what she had asked about.

They took note of where the bank was, where the doctor could be found, the barber, too. They talked about if they'd prefer to take one of the still open plots in town to build or if something a little bit out would suit them better, but Summer didn't commit on her preferences, so Chase dropped the subject. She did pull him to a stop several times, though, to look at the few new but empty store fronts. And she didn't just seem to be taking note of the space. She paid attention to what was close by and the distance between the shop and some other things up and down the street. Again, she didn't say why she was looking, and Chase didn't ask at the moment, thinking maybe she'd tell him on her own, or something would give it away.

They made their way into the mercantile, which sat closer to the train station than any of the other businesses, and while Chase took the list to the clerk, Summer wandered around surveying the shelves of canned goods with great interest.

"Will you be opening credit here?" the clerk asked, taking a look at the list.

"I'll pay upfront today, but we're here for a while I think, so I'd like a line of credit for my wife to access at will," he said, looking back just as Summer popped up between the shelves. He turned back in time to see the man staring at his U.S. Marshal's badge behind his open coat. "Chase Storm," he gave the man his name. "My wife, Summer."

"Mr. Nelson will have to approve you, but if you're the new marshal everyone was talking about, I'm sure it will be no problem." The man moved away to start filling the order as Summer stepped up to the counter.

"What will be no problem?" she asked, and again, she took great interest in the items stored behind the counter.

"Setting up credit here so you can purchase what you need," Chase said then almost jumped back when she swung around on him.

"I'll pay for my needs, I don't want—" she snarled, a complete change from how she'd been at all the other shops.

"You're my wife," Chase said, taking hold of her arm and

pulling her close enough only she could hear what he said. "You'll put your purchases in my name."

"I can buy my own—" she said a bit too loudly for his liking.

"If you need to buy something, buy it on my credit, am I understood?" She narrowed her eyes at him but gave him a sharp nod. "Don't argue with me in public, missy, understand?" he said right next to her ear before pressing his lips against her temple. She nodded again, this time without the sharpness. But he could sense her pulling away.

"You sure know your wares," the clerk said, coming back with several of the items Summer had requested on her list. "We don't normally carry C&M baking soda, but we have a small supply of Arm & Hammer. You can put in a request if you prefer C&M. We get fresh supplies the fifteenth of each month and make changes and add special orders once a quarter."

"Arm & Hammer is fine," Summer said, glaring at Chase but putting a nice smile back on her face for the clerk. "You don't carry much in canned goods or preserves? And I don't see any fresh or canned fruits or vegetables."

"No, ma'am, sorry. The train will start to bring those things in 'bout next month, but we're so far down the line here, there's not much left to pick from," the man said as he continued to carry items to the counter. "Once the snows are gone, there are plenty of berries and such growing wild all about. And one of the farmers a bit back has a good orchard you can buy from if you don't mind riding out." He set the last items on the counter and wiped his hands on his apron. "I think that's it. Oh, and just a warning, when those things do come in, you're gonna want to be here when the shop opens, else those miners will swarm in and snatch it all up."

"Really," she said, moving back down the aisle as the clerk added up the total for what they'd just bought. Again, he heard the interest in her voice. "Exactly how many miners are we talking about that they come in like a herd of grazing sheep and strip every place they touch?"

"Well, the lot of them together could be close to two thousand or more, but we mostly only get the men working the gold and silver, them coal diggers get stuck spending their pay at the company's store."

"Hmm, interesting," Summer said but sounded more than like she'd had her curiosity satisfied. "Tell me, is it possible to get messages out to the suppliers who send up the fruits and vegetables? Perhaps make a request that certain items be put on board and held aside?"

"I don't rightly know, ma'am, I don't see why not."

"The farmers, they send a representative?"

"Yes, ma'am."

"And you say they start coming in next month?" Again, Summer walked over to the shelf with the limited supply of canned goods.

"Yes, ma'am."

"Do you carry Mason's jars here?"

"Just a few," the clerk said, stepping back to a shelf behind the counter to pull down the small glass container with its dull, metal lid. He handed it over when Summer returned to the counter.

"Paraffin wax?" she asked, looking over the jar intently before handing it back.

"We've ordered it before but not in a while."

She nodded her head, made a disinterested sound and then, with a smile, started collecting their purchases. "You said the proprietor will be here Monday?"

"Yes, ma'am. Nine on the dot," the clerk said as Chase fished in his pocket for the money to pay the man.

"Good. Marshal," she said, turning to face him, a smile on her face but not in her eyes. "We'd better start back, or we won't be able to collect our other purchases." She turned and headed to the door without another word.

Chase scrambled to collect the rest and catch up, giving the man a hasty thanks and goodbye. He was about to lecture her about her behavior until she turned, looked him dead in the eye, and said, "I think I could get used to the cold."

Chapter 14

"Guess we'll need some shelves," Chase said, and Summer gritted her teeth and added another log to the cook stove. The extra warmth would help take the chill out as the sun moved further west and dipped behind the jagged peaks of the San Juan Mountains.

Using the rag, she lifted the top plate to help the vent and get the stove hot faster. The single shelf at the back of the stove wouldn't hold much, but she'd rather have a long, narrow table than shelves, given it would serve as a place to both prepare and serve. Chase's shuffling around behind her was getting on her nerves, though, and she wanted to get supper cooked so he'd sit down.

"What's the difference between the baking soda you got and the one you wanted?" he asked, and she saw him lift the small canister.

She crossed to the table, snatched it from his hand, set it back, and glared at him. "Nothing." This was why she would buy what she needed for what she planned alone, so she wouldn't have to explain those purchases, and she wouldn't have to let anyone else touch them. Wiping her hand on a rag, she reached for the other items she'd need to mix up a decent batch of biscuits. Not just the grease and flour ones she'd been eating for months or the day-old ones the train and eatery folks tried to pass off as fresh baked. Measuring mostly by feel and using the recipe she'd had memorized since she was four, she made quick work of mixing and rolling out the dough.

"Still not talking to me?" Chase asked, making her realize he was in the room at all.

"What's to say?" she asked, crossing back to the stove to close the vent and put the plate back in place. The fire would burn slower and steadier, heating the stove enough to get a good bake on the biscuits and still hot enough to sear the steak and potatoes in the pan, which she set on the plate now to heat. She put the coffee pot on the other burner. This small stove was wonderful, but if she could, she'd get a double with six plates and two ovens. She'd seen them in a catalog once.

She worked without distraction, the way she'd been taught. Her mother and aunt could cook for and feed a hundred people and never drop an egg or burn a crust. That little bakery in Highfield had been their dream. Everything that had been perfect in her life happened in that bakery. She'd always thought she'd take it over one day. Mother had even spoken of sending her to a special school to learn how to make more fancy dishes and cakes that rich people would want served at the weddings of their daughters.

If she had anything at all to be thankful for, it was that every recipe she was ever taught—and many she wasn't but had seen worked—had been stored in a metal lockbox. Mother had said, that way, if the kitchen ever caught fire, they wouldn't be lost. Even when the building was left in smoldering ruins, those pieces of paper, some frail from age or use, survived. She'd have to send for them before she could really form a serious plan. But this place was an excellent stop to open her own bakery and eatery. No real competition, a dedicated patronage with just the miners, access to supplies and various foods brought in on the train at least once a week. And most importantly, several buildings completed and waiting for renters and more being built up.

She just needed to figure out how much it would all cost. She'd almost sixty-five hundred dollars stashed away. Ten years of working every day at anything that built that amount up. Even when she wasn't able to find a bounty, she had found some kind of work.

"Summer?"

But she wouldn't share it. Not with Chase or anyone. She wouldn't see it lost to an incompetent or dishonest partner. So, until Chase agreed that she'd buy her things with her money, and it would be hers, she wouldn't put a plan in motion.

Scraping the potatoes off the pan, she opened the oven door and slid in the biscuits then added the meat to the pan. She always felt efficient in the kitchen, always felt safe, the order of it, the way it made sense and she could predict everything, even the cost of her mistakes. She used the fork and flipped the meat over.

"Summer…"

A quick check on the biscuits, and she started packing up everything she'd used. They'd carried it home it two sturdy crates, and she used those to keep things orderly. She paused to scrape the potatoes and flip the meat, then she dunked a rag in the bucket of water next to the stove and wiped down the table. It was all so familiar.

"Summer," Chase shouted, startling her. Her first instinct was to check the food to make sure it wasn't burning. Not even a hint of over brown.

"What?" She turned back to face the man giving her a look more heated than the oven.

"What is the matter with you?"

"Nothing," she snapped.

"Well, something put a bee in your bonnet," Chase said then

slapped his hand down over hers so she couldn't finish wiping the table.

"I don't have a bee in my bonnet, I just have nothing to say to you," she said, pulling her hand free and stepping over to the stove, more to get away from him than because the food needed tending.

"Well, you must, because I've been watching it brewing in everything you do, so speak up."

"I have nothing to say," she said and tightened the grip on the fork to keep what she wanted to say from coming out.

"Summer, you can either talk to me standing up, or you can talk to me laid out over my knee, but—"

He didn't just threaten her, not after he was the one who decided she'd no say in the matter. "I have nothing to say to you," she said, barely refraining from yelling. "And don't threaten me when you're the one who laid down the law and told me how things would be. Told me I had no say in any of it." She bent, opened the oven door, and pulled out the biscuits, hardly able to take joy in the fact they were perfect. She pulled each one out the pan and dropped them on the cloth she'd laid on the table as quickly as she could so as not to burn her fingers.

"What did I tell you that you had no say in?" he asked, even as he reached for the hot offering. She gritted her teeth not to smack his hand, but given his tone and her dissatisfaction, it might be his head she slapped.

Taking one of the plates, she filled it with the meat and potatoes, all but dropping it in front of him on the table. She filled hers but rather than set it next to him, she set it across and then moved to drag the chair to the other side of the table. "Does it matter? You said I can't argue with you about it."

She saw him stop, fork almost to his mouth, and look at her. "I won't argue things with you, but we can discuss them." He took a bite, chewed, swallowed, and stabbed more with his fork. "But we will not discuss things in public; we certainly won't argue them." He finished that bite and went for another. "I'm not going to garner a reputation for putting our affairs on the streets so everyone with a wagging tongue can be entertained. If you want to discuss something, we will. In private," he said, reaching now for his third biscuit. If she didn't grab one, she wouldn't get one.

"I'll use my own money to buy my own things," she said, almost hopeful he'd concede.

"You're my wife; I'll support you. You will buy things on my credit, or I will give you the money."

"I don't want your money. I don't need your money," she yelled, pushing back from the table and getting to her feet. So much for hoping he'd be reasonable.

"You'll use my money, because that is how it is done. Husbands support their wives. And I'll not have anyone say I don't. I'm more than capable of providing you with anything you need and likely anything you want."

"I'll buy my own things, or I won't buy anything," Summer yelled and, snatching up a biscuit, headed for the door. "If everything has to be yours, then you figure it out and buy it." Yanking open the door, she stepped out and slammed it shut.

Instant regret settled on her as the frigid air quickly chilled her. Damn, if she'd not taken off her pants when they got back. Without her coat, she couldn't stay out, and the way he yelled after her to get back inside made her ass clench. But she couldn't stand out on the steps in the wind. Lifting her skirts, she hurried down them and swung under. The back door to the jail house was there, and she sent a little prayer up as she tried the handle. The door opened just as she heard the one above her open. Stepping in and shutting it quietly, she listened as Chase's heavy footfalls rushed down the steps then faded. She might give in to praying more if it helped her out like this.

The jailhouse was empty, and Summer left it dark as she moved toward the front to see where Chase went. She had to stand on a small bench to look out the high windows, but she saw him. He'd taken the time to put on his coat and had hers over his arm as he stood on the boardwalk looking up and down at all the other dark and closed buildings. She watched him cross the street and look up and down from there. For a moment, he seemed to look right at her, and then he lifted his gaze to their place above. He dropped his head, gave it a shake, and crossed the street again. Summer ducked back and waited, holding her breath. His treads sounded again on the stairs and then above her as he moved about in the room.

Stepping down, she took a seat on the bench, wrapping her arms around her in the chill. She was out of the wind, but without a fire, the brick walls were icy. Her stomach rumbled, reminding her that while Chase all but finished his meal, she'd not even taken a single bite. Rolling the biscuit in her hand, she lifted it and took a bite. Even cold, it was wonderful. Just the kind of biscuit her mother would have made, the kind she'd have been praised for.

Damn, she just wanted her own shop. Hers, not half hers. And here would be a good spot to have it. If only Chase would step aside and let her do it. Though she did suppose that if she could get through until September, she could try to set it up then. But could she? Could she stay here after they parted ways? Would he even let her? Of course, he could always be the one to go.

No, if one of them should go, it should be her. This place was what Chase wanted. There were a number of places she'd seen along the tracks as they rode here that would suit her needs. She just needed to get through until September. And she also needed to find a way to keep adding to her savings. But she couldn't do that if she couldn't do it on her own. Using Chase's money meant he'd have a say and he'd get a take. And he'd already shown her when the take was only partially his, he still kept it all.

She drew her feet up and tried to huddle for warmth, but it

was no good. As she listened, she waited to hear if she could tell what he was doing above her. The silence stretched. Maybe he'd gone to bed. Tears welled, burning as they fell down her cold skin. Was that how much he cared? Was he hoping she'd freeze to death while he was snuggled in a warm bed in a warm room? Her teeth began to chatter, and no matter how she rubbed at her arms, she couldn't generate any heat. She moved to search the building for a stove and found it quickly enough, but there wasn't any wood and, moreover, no matches. She couldn't stay here. She braced for the blast of cold and pulled open the back door and stepped out. She might have made it back up the stairs faster than she made it down them. But had she known what awaited her inside, with Chase, she might have chosen freezing to death.

Chapter 15

Chase took another deep breath and willed himself to stay right where he was. Summer couldn't stay downstairs much longer, but she'd already been out in the cold longer than he wanted. Maybe he should have marched in the jail when he spotted her peeking through the window. But what would it have accomplished? She'd be back and warm, but she'd not be back of her own will.

What he didn't understand was why she was so upset about his willingness, his ability to provide for her. She'd not protested any other time he'd paid for their needs. Now, all of a sudden, she wanted to buy everything? Wasn't she still trying to save up for something important? He didn't think he had misunderstood her. There was something she wanted, needed to earn money to have, lived more miserly than that character from Dickens' tale for. So what was it she was trying to convey in her stand against his attempt to help her achieve that?

He pulled his watch out again. He'd give her two more minutes; any longer, and he risked having her frozen solid before he got her back. As he watched the hand tick down the time, he again found himself holding his breath. It came out heavy when the door opened and Summer slipped in.

He wasn't surprised when her eyes went first to the kitchen area. Near that stove, she became a different person. Confident in every single move, talented enough, she hardly seemed to be concentrating on what she did. The kitchen was where Summer was Summer. He'd already told himself he'd make sure it was the center of whatever home design they chose And he'd outfit it to be exactly what she wanted.

As soon as her eyes settled on him, he stood and stepped to the side of the chair. "Get over here," he snapped and pointed to the vacated seat. When she hesitated, he added, "You don't want me to come get you." She tucked her chin down and crossed the room. He could hear her teeth rattling together. "Sit down there." When she hesitated again, he took her by the arm and forced her down. The cold of her skin, he could feel through the shirt she wore. He bent and, placing his hands on either side of the seat, slid the chair even closer to the regular heating stove. "Were you trying to freeze to death?" he scolded, crossing to the bed, and taking the quilt folded neatly over the end, he brought it back and wrapped it around her. "Are you hungry?" She sniffed and nodded. He'd cleaned up while he'd waited for her, but he'd left her plate on the cook stove knowing if it cooled too much, it could be reheated on the other stove. He crossed to the kitchen area, struck by an odd sense he shouldn't carry his anger with him into this spot. Shaking it off, he took her plate and the fork and brought it back to her. He let her get started eating before he knelt down and reached for her foot.

He pulled each boot off and rubbed her feet until they no longer felt like little blocks of ice. He'd have to get her warmer clothing. The weather would be warming soon, but she'd need them for next year. If he couldn't get her what she'd need here, a trip to Denver might prove fruitful or even just a wish book she could order from. Shifting to put his weight on his toes, he caught her eye. "You will not ever walk out on me like that again. I'm going to make sure of that." He waited until she swallowed the food in her mouth. "Do you want to talk now?" When she shook her head, he said, "Then you can listen. As long as it is completely in my capacity and even if it means I go without, I will support you. That is a promise I made to you when we got hitched, and I won't be breaking it. You will buy what you need, when you need it, and you will do so using my earnings. If need be, for larger things, we will use money from my investments. But I will be responsible for paying for things."

"But I want it to be mine. I worked for it. I should have it. It should be mine," Summer nearly wailed.

"Summer, it *will* be yours." How did she think this worked?

"No, it won't, not if you buy it, not even if you only pay for some of it. I want it to be mine. I don't want a partner. I want to do it. I want to do it on my own; that is what I've worked for. I shouldn't have to share half or any of it. It should be mine. I did the work. Me." Her voice cracked, and dropping the plate on the floor, she shoved off the blanket and tried to stand.

Chase jerked her back down, holding her there until she stopped struggling. What the hell was she talking about? What the hell *was* he talking about? Not the same thing. She was talking about something entirely different. "What won't be yours?"

"The bakery," she said with a sniff and a gasp. "It should be mine. I worked for it."

"Bakery?" He had to grab the chair not to fall back on his ass. "You want to buy… open a bake shop?" Was that her dream? Given how she looked to be in heaven when she cooked, in the kitchen or on the range, he might have guessed it before now.

"And an eatery too." She sniffed again.

"How does using my money stop you from doing that?" All her questions from today, all the observations he watched her make. She'd been scouting the town for a place to set up shop.

And given the question and answers he did pay attention to, this would be a great location. The town was large and growing, and it clearly had no such establishment yet. The single meal served at the boarding house wasn't much, and if Deputy Brown spoke correctly, it wasn't even good. Summer would have no competition.

"Because if I take your money, and use it, then I have to include you, get permission from you in running it. I'll owe what is made to you. And if I can't do, if... if it fails, I'll still owe you. I don't want to owe you or anyone. I don't want to check with someone before I do something. I want to run my own shop, not be run by someone else and—"

"Slow that pony, missy," Chase yelled before she worked herself up into hysterics. "I don't want to get in the way of you having anything. A bakery, that's a wonderful idea. And given what's here now, I don't see you failing if you open it. But I think we are talking about two completely different things." He knew they were. And the fix was far easier than getting her out of jail that first time.

"Different things?" she said again with a gasp and a sniff. "No? What?"

Chase took a breath and blew it out slowly. He was going to have to work more to get his wife to talk to him. If they spent the whole next six months miscommunicating, he'd never convince her to stay past September. "Different things. Yes, Summer. Completely different." He set his hand on her cheek and forced her eyes back to his. "I get you want all the control for your business. You're right; you worked for it, and you should have that. Though, I think it's a brilliant idea, and if you want an investor, I will invest in it with you," he said, raising his hand to hush her protest. "In a hands-off way. I can already tell what your basic plan is. The questions you've asked today... Yes, this place would be an excellent place to start that kind of business. But if you don't want me to partner you in any way, I can stay out of it. You want to use your own blood, sweat and tears, do it all on your own, I'll support that."

"You said—"

"I said you'd use my money to buy what you needed. Not what your business needed. And I should have been clearer. You use my money, *our* money, to buy those things that benefit both of us. Things for our home, food we eat... you use *our* money for that. I told you I would give you an allowance just for such things. If you can't abide mixing our money with your money, I will respect that."

"You will?"

"I will, even if it means not getting in on something that will probably make any investor rich. If it's for your business, in any way, it will be with your money; it will be your responsibility and in your complete control. If it's for us, our home, and..." He stopped before he said children. Hell he'd not even slept with her yet. "If both of us gain something, then use mi...our money. I'll even go back to the shops and make sure they know we'll have two different accounts."

"You'd do that?"

"Summer, all you had to do was tell me what you wanted. So far, nothing that's come out of your mouth has been unreasonable. And if I think it is, we can discuss it." He brushed his thumb across her cheek, gave her a nod, and saw her return it. "Is there anything else, right now that you can think of, any... rule you want me to keep in mind, other than keeping my nose out of your business?"

"Don't... don't mess with anything in the kitchen," she said, sounding like she was testing the waters.

"This kitchen? Our kitchen?"

"My kitchen."

"But the kitchen in our home?" She nodded, and he chuckled. "Why not?"

"I don't want you to."

He didn't need a reason. The kitchen was where she wanted to rule. It was an odd choice, given she was capable of holding her own anywhere if she wanted to. He picked up her discarded plate. "You gonna cook like this for us all the time?" he asked, and she nodded. She'd cook better once he got her more supplies and better outfitted. "Then I'll stay out your kitchen, Mrs. Storm."

He stood up and carried the plate back to the very place he'd be hence forbidden in. She might let him in to help with dishes after all. But then, looking around, he doubted it as all that was left after all that cooking was dishes. Even the cooks and staff at his family home hadn't maintained order like Summer could. He set her plate next to his then walked back to her. Now the hard part.

"Are you all warmed up?" He offered his hand then pulled her out the chair.

"Yes, thank you," she said, moving to step into his arms.

He sidestepped, but keeping a hold on her hand, picked up the chair and turned it to face the wall. He shoved it up close, making sure it sat flat, folded the quilt and lay it over the backrest then pulled Summer closer. "Don't thank me yet. You're about to learn how much I disapprove of someone running out in the middle of a situation." He saw her eyes flare, felt her draw back, but it took only a little tug, and he was able to turn her, lift her at the waist, and drop her over the chair back. "Give me your hands," Chase said, already working the buckle of his belt.

"Chase, no. Don't. Please. I'm sorry," she pleaded.

"Hands, don't make me tell you again," he said, pulling the leather through the loops of his jeans and folding it in half as she slowly offered first her left then her right hand back to him.

"Chase," she whined. "I'm sorry. I was mad. I didn't think you were listening to me."

"I wasn't, because you weren't saying anything. If you'd have stayed and we'd had this conversation then, you wouldn't be here now, about to get a whoopin'." He placed her hands at the small of her back, wrists crossed so he could hold them both at once. Then he reached down and lifted her skirts. He almost smiled thinking how convenient it was she always landed in this position wearing a dress and not thick jeans, though the thought of ordering her to take them down and getting to watch her wiggle out of them could be worth the inconvenience.

"Chase, please stop." She kicked her legs, and the chair legs scraped, but he had her well enough over, it wouldn't tip. Her pleas became a long wail when he pulled the string on her bloomers and, with a sharp tug, sent them down her legs to catch on her feet.

"You will not walk away from me like that. You're not a coward, and running isn't acceptable for a grown woman, the way it is for a child. You behave like a child, and I'll punish you like one." He tightened his grip on the belt ends and drew back his arm.

The first crack echoed like gunfire, and he delivered the second before her scream could bring the sheriff running. Two red streaks bloomed across her flanks. She bucked up with the third stroke, but he delivered the fourth before dropping his arm. "You won't step outside that door again without wearing what is appropriate for the weather. You could have frozen to death if you'd not taken shelter in the jail."

Her wailing increased substantially with his words, and he lifted his arm and brought the belt down across the fullest part of her ass.

"Chase," she screeched, arching back and bending her knees.

He knocked them down then landed three more blows in quick session.

"We won't discuss or argue things in public, but we will privately, until we get as much mutual satisfaction as we can. And you will stay until that is achieved." This time, he took aim at the place ass met thigh. Over the chair like she was, it was exposed to receive each of the next four lashes. Her keening wail ended on choking sobs. The last four strokes landed more randomly but held more force than the first twelve.

Summer lay limp over the back of the chair, sobbing, the skin on her ass nearly as red as the sunset. Tossing the belt over his shoulder, he worked an arm around her and used his weight to tip the chair enough that her feet touched the ground. She remained bent in half but stumbled back before he tightened his hold and steadied her.

"All right now, pull up, rein it in," he soothed, turning her against him. Flipping the chair back around, he swept her up then took a seat, careful to spread his legs so her ass fell in the space between. "You can't get all riled up and let that make you behave recklessly. You know this. It's a first rule for anyone who carries a gun as a means to make a living." He rubbed her back and let her sobbing ease. "Unless this is how you're gonna tell me that being a business owner will make you less cool headed." She still cried softly, but he felt her head shake against his shoulder. "Yep, didn't think so." He nudged her up then caught her chin. "Cooler heads from now on?" She nodded again then sniffed and wiped her eyes on her sleeve. Lifting his hip, he pulled a kerchief out of his pocket and handed it over. A hand on her head guided it back down to his shoulder. "Yep, cooler heads."

Chapter 16

S ummer eased down in the church pew and tried not to gasp when her ass settled on the hard wood. Chase hadn't made not coming an option. And as she was still trying to put order to what happened yesterday and restore what she'd had with him prior to her acting the fool, assuming things that weren't true, things Chase in no way gave her reason to think might be true, she didn't want to push him further away.

She'd almost cried more when she woke up, alone in bed, in a very dark room. For a moment, thinking Chase had left her until his soft snores called to her from the floor, she felt a little panic. If she'd insulted him enough, he could.

"No, we settled in right fast," Chase was saying as he stepped up next to the pew with the sheriff beside him. "Summer cooked one of her amazing meals for me, so there was no need." He said, holding his hand out to her. She took it, not wanting to further embarrass him publically.

"Did she now?" Sheriff Buckley said, looking her up and down.

"Yep, still trying to decide if she's better with a frying pan or with a gun. It might be too hard to pick one." Chase squeezed her hand.

"Well, then," the man said, disapproval in his tone. "Preacher plans to introduce you at the end of service. But I think a few folks will still be missing today. A group went up Silverton way a week or so 'bout. Not due back till late this afternoon. You'll still have to introduce yourself to them. Or at least to the ones who matter."

"The ones who matter," Summer said under her breath, but maybe not under enough as Chase squeezed her hand again.

"Shouldn't be a problem, not like I was planning on leaving town," Chase said, dropping her hand to shake the sheriff's.

The door at the back of the little church, which also acted as a schoolhouse during the week and a place where the people came if they needed to discuss town matters with the mayor or the like, opened and a plump little old woman was escorted in by an equally plump little old man. She watched the old man help the woman to her seat before stepping up to the podium. Chase slid in next to her, but he crowded, and she bit her tongue trying not to yip like a dog that's been stepped on when she had to slide over.

Chase took her hand in his lap, and as the preacher announced he'd be reading from the Book of Mathew, Summer opened her old, worn Bible. Several times as the preacher interrupted the scripture to give his own interpretation, Summer let her eyes drift to the writing along the margins. Her mother had given her own interpretations to the scriptures, too. The one that caught her eye today was written next to 1:5, the story of Ruth and Boaz.

Be strong in your own right, know your weaknesses, and know it takes strength to let others help you.

Was that her problem? Was that why she didn't know how to deal with Chase? Because she was too weak to submit to him? Summer couldn't remember her father. He'd come back from war injured and hadn't lived through her first year. But she knew her mother loved him. She saw the longing in her eyes every time she reached up and touched the ring that hung on a chain at her neck. Loving the man hadn't made her weak, and even when he was gone, she stayed strong. Strong enough to save her daughter when hell tried to take them all.

The crowd shifted, and Chase helped her to her feet for the final hymn. "Did you pay attention at all to the sermon?" he whispered to her.

She escaped answering by joining in the singing, and after a chuckle, Chase's deep voice joined in. As she listened to it ring in her ears, she was struck by how much it made her want to kiss him. Heat climbed up her face; what an inappropriate thought for church.

Better was how she'd thought to kick him when he chuckled again as she tried to sit without making her ass hurt more.

"Still sore?" he leaned in to ask.

"Yes," she pouted.

"Maybe I'll make it better when we get home," he said, smiling as he stood and Summer realized he'd been introduced.

How in heaven's name could he possibly do that? she wanted to ask, might have if, at that moment, the preacher hadn't announced his arrival and asked him to stand up. She continued to ponder the answer as the preacher announced the end of service but asked Chase to stay and answer questions.

She couldn't see what the hell anyone needed to know. A U.S. Marshal had taken up a post. Seemed pretty simple to her. An extra gun in town, backed by a badge. But as people stepped up, it was instantly known they wanted to be busybodies. Where was he from, how long he'd been a marshal, what experiences did he have, education, family ties? His answers gave her as much insight as it gave them, and she listened right up until the preacher's wife asked who the lovely young lady with him was.

"My wife," Chase said, and the pride and joy she heard in his voice startled her. After yesterday, how could he say the words without choking? "Summer Storm," he said, placing his arm around her waist, drawing her close. The act gave her some courage as she'd have preferred not to become too personal with anyone. "Reverend Wickfield and his beautiful, young wife, Mrs. Mary Wickfield."

"What a pleasure to meet you," Mrs. Wickfield said, her face so flushed, Summer wondered if she wouldn't faint dead away. Honestly, she knew Chase could be charming, but he was laying it on at the moment.

"Been married long?" another woman standing close asked.

Chase actually started at the question, and when he answered, he seemed a bit in awe. "No, not at all. It hasn't been—"

"Twenty-five days," Summer answered and then realized she too was surprised by the answer. How was it only twenty-five days? How? Time had flown by and yet seemed to drag its feet.

"Oh how sweet, newlyweds," Mrs. Wickfield cooed, reaching out to set her hand on Summer's arm. "Where'd you meet? How long was the engagement?"

Summer's stomach twisted. Standing in this crowd of totally respectable people, how was she supposed to explain they'd been forced to wed to keep her out of prison? That her past wasn't exactly a model example for young girls everywhere. This was exactly why she liked to keep to herself. She didn't have to explain herself when she was alone. "Chase," she said with a gasp. "I left the bread rising." Thank God she had.

"I'll take you home in a few minutes," he said, his tone a bit disapproving.

"No, no, it's fine. You stay as long as they need. It's you they want to get to know, they need to get to know." She pulled away and stepped back enough that he couldn't grab her without causing a scene, and she knew he wouldn't do that. "It was very nice meeting you. I'm sure we'll see each other around." She made a hasty exit toward the doors where coats were hung.

"Takes her bread seriously?" she heard some man in the crowd ask.

"She takes cooking seriously," Chase responded with a laugh that sounded forced. "But if she's not the best cook in the whole nation, she's the best this side of the Mississippi."

"Talented in the kitchen?" The reverend asked as Summer tried to push through the crowd of old biddies blocking the door."

"One of her many talents," Chase said. "I'm still trying to decide if she's better with a spoon or with a gun. Because she's a crack shot, too."

His words made her smile a bit, but it didn't last when he was again asked about how they'd met. She didn't wait to hear what he might say. He could tell her the lie he spun later; she'd go along with it. Holding the coat around herself, he hurried back down the street.

"Best cook this side of the Mississippi." The words made her smile as she worked the dough and waited for Chase to get back. Did he really think so? Even if he didn't, it was nice of him to say. She waited by the window overlooking the street, hoping to see him walking up. But it took quite a while for him to step through the door. She'd just put the second loaf in when the door opened and the wind did its best to chill the room.

"Have mercy, that smells like heaven," Chase said, removing his hat and coat and stepping over to the table where she'd set the bread to cool a bit. "Did you only make one?"

"No." She laughed at the sound of his complete disappointment. "I just put the second loaf in the oven."

"So only two, then?" He still sounded disappointed.

"Two should be plenty," she told him then felt her gut twist again. "Unless you invited someone to supper?"

"I didn't. I wouldn't without asking you first," he said with a frown but stepped up behind her and again wrapped her in his arms. This time, he leaned down and started kissing her neck.

Maybe this was how he thought to ease the ache in her ass, by creating one someplace else in her body. She took as much of his nuzzling as she could before she turned in his arms and lifted up for a real kiss. Chase didn't disappoint. His mouth claimed hers, and as she breathed him in, he pushed his tongue past her lips and teeth to twist with hers.

Damn, but she enjoyed his kisses. And as the hand at the small of her back pulled her harder against him, she knew he enjoyed them, too. His other hand slid slowly up her side then under her breast, and when he cupped her flesh, a rolling heat stole her breath. A more familiar wetness formed between her legs. If she wasn't ready before, she was now. What the hell could it hurt to try this? They were married, and it might well be her only chance to find out. She just needed to let him know.

Only when she rubbed against him, something wasn't right. He was angled oddly and seemed a little distracted. She leaned back, only to be slammed against his body. "Nope, stay," Chase said, but he didn't bring his lips back to hers and he was leaning her backward a bit too much. She heard him hiss and then swear. "Damn, that's hot." Again, when she tried to move, he held her. He hissed again, and his arm jerked.

"Marshal Storm," Summer shouted and broke free of his hold. "Get your fingers off my bread." She grabbed for his hand, and a brief struggle ensued. "It's not even cooled enough yet, you fool." She slapped his hand when he reached again this time, though he managed to tear a chunk off.

"Oh, ah," he cried and hissed, tossing the bread in the air and blowing on it a few times before shoving it in his mouth. "I know," he said, his eyes closing as he chewed. "But it smelt so good and it tastes—"

Summer pressed her lips together not to smile at his antics.

"It tastes like your last meal," she said, again slapping his hand away. "If you don't sit down over there and stop picking."

"You're a mean woman," he grumbled then smiled as he took a seat. She lifted a knife then turned to grab a plate.

"Touch that bread again, Marshal," she said, seeing him reaching before she'd set her hands on the plate. "And you'll be eating a barrel."

She heard him huff, but he sat back. "If I'd have known you were so mean..." he grumbled again.

"What?" she asked, raising a brow as she cut off the end of the loaf then cut him a piece larger than she might have cut anyone else. She held the plate away, though. "What? If you'd known I was so mean? What?" She came around the table, the plate high in the air. Though given how much taller he was, she suspected he could still reach, even from his sitting position.

"I'd have brushed up on my begging skills," he said, grabbing her around the waist and pulling her down in his lap. "Please give me the bread," he said with his lips against her cheek.

She did, more because she hoped to get her ass off his lap than because he asked so nicely, but he didn't let her up. "Chase," she whined, squirming.

His eyebrow did raise, but he didn't let her up as he took a huge bite, chewed, swallowed, and opened for a second. "Still sore, sweetheart?" His second bite left barely half.

"Yes, let me up," she told him, and he took only two more bites to finish.

"Maybe I can still help with that," he said between chews and swallowing

She stilled at his words and didn't resist as he turned her, back against his chest, legs apart over his. His fingers working up her skirts. Damn, she wanted this, but it was broad daylight, and Sunday. They were both still dressed for church.

"Yep, I think I can fix that," he whispered next to her ear as his arm went across her chest and drew her back. His other hand brushed up the inside of her thigh, and as she did whenever he touched or kissed her, she heated up like a well-vented stove. His hand moved higher, over the hem of her bloomer, up to the juncture where her thighs met, then over until they found the opening. But they didn't stop there. Chase pushed through the folds of fabric and then the folds of flesh.

Summer gasped at the shocking pleasure of it, moaning as his lips found her neck then crying out when he found a particular spot between her legs. That little nub sent sparks through her every time he touched it in any way.

Beads of sweat formed and rolled down between her breasts. Breasts he was kneading and squeezing. She couldn't get any hotter, and then she did as he shifted so her head dropped back and his lips claimed hers. His mouth, tongue, and fingers all worked at her so she could feel something building. Some tremendous storm that threatened to lift her into the air, toss her about and then slam her back to the ground. It was a storm she was helpless to stop, if she even wanted to, and she didn't want to.

One more touch, it was only going to take one more and she'd...

Bang, bang, bang. "Marshal Storm?"

Summer's cry was muffled by a hand over her mouth. The ecstasy she'd thought would be hers wasn't just muted, it was doused, as if someone had pushed her through the ice into a pond.

Bang, bang, bang. "Marshal Storm? Are you in there?"

"Yes, just a minute," Chase snarled. "Damn, this better be life or death, or it will be," he said, setting Summer on her feet and standing. He took a moment to steady her then adjusted the bulge in his pants before crossing to the door. He didn't open it all the way, though, and he stayed behind it. "What is it?" he snarled with even more heat.

"You Marshal Storm?" someone outside asked.

"I answered the door, didn't I?" Despite the feeling she'd just been denied something amazing, Summer snorted and smiled. She wasn't the only one disappointed with the interruption.

"Sheriff sent me," the man at the door said. "Men took the train out at Wheel Crossing, 'bout ten of 'em. They're pinned down, but Sheriff is out numbered. Needs some help."

"Damn," Chase swore, stepping back and opening the door so the man could step in. "I need a minute." He cast an apologetic look at Summer but then glared at the man before knocking his hat off his head. "My wife," was all he said as he stepped behind the curtain, presumably to change clothes.

"Ma'am," the man, or rather, the youth said as he bent to pick up his hat. "Doc Riot, Mr. Winter, and Mr. Anders are already on the way. They're former army. But Sheriff said you might not know where exactly to come."

"I know," Chase growled.

"This gonna take long?" Summer asked, though she knew it might. Even with more men, it would be ten to seven if the outlaws were hunkered in. "I could help?"

"No," Chase snapped, coming out from behind the curtain still buttoning his shirt.

Summer frowned at his all too quick denial, but she'd not been surprised by it. She saw him eye the bread as he passed by to grab his boots from where he'd left them at the door and take a seat on the stool to pull them on. "You haven't eaten," she said and quickly began assembling something he could carry with him from what'd she'd planned to serve him for supper. He was pulling on his coat and headed toward her just as she finished tying the meal up in a rag.

"I'm sorry, sweetheart," he whispered, pulling her close. "I'll make it up to you when I come back." He bent down and kissed her cheek.

"Just come back," Summer said, realizing only then that his

job didn't get any less dangerous because he worked in a town. She held out the bundle and stepped back.

"I will," he promised and headed to the door which the other man had opened in anticipation of stepping out. "I hope you cut this thick."

"I did," Summer said, and she had.

"Make more bread," Chase told her.

"Two loaves are enough, Chase," she said, giving him a smile, though it was forced.

"Nope, it aint." Then he was gone.

Summer rushed to the window, and seeing someone had already brought his horse from the livery, she watched him mount and set his spurs, driving his horse toward whatever waited in Wheel Crossing. She waited there until the smell of bread burning in the oven pulled her away. She managed to salvage it, but with nothing else to do, she started on two more loaves.

Chapter 17

C hase slipped back into the apartment as quietly as he could. He was cold, tired, and despite the quick meal Summer had put together for him, he was hungry. Breaking though the barricade hadn't been the hard part. No, that was tracking the bandits up into the hills and rocks and trying not to let them get so much of the high ground, it turned the lawmen into easy targets.

Sunset, turned out to be Chase's best ally. The outlaws climbed a west facing slope and the sun going down blinded them, allowing Chase, Sheriff Buckley, his two deputies, Brown and Zander, Mr. Anders, the blacksmith, Mr. Winter, a rancher, and Doc Riot, who was the actual town doctor, to get up on them. There was no surrender, and the last of the ten fell into a ravine after being shot. It was likely what killed him. The lock box was recovered, train passengers settled down, and Chase spoke with a few men who showed interest in working with him under a marshal's badge.

He hung his hat on the peg by the door, shrugged out of his coat, then sat and pulled off his boots. It was then he noticed the low burning lantern on the table with a plate covered with a napkin. Yes, he was hungry, but not just for food.

He assumed, though, Summer had gone to bed, as late as the hour was. He might as well eat. Maybe in the morning, he'd have time to make up to her for what she was denied when they were interrupted. Damn, just the memory made his cock stiffen and throb.

She'd responded so perfectly to his manipulation of her body. She had turned and pushed into every touch, opened to him like a morning glory at dawn. He'd planned to make her orgasm then bend her over the table and make her do it again, only this time with his cock.

He'd have gotten her to ask for it at that moment; he knew it. He'd seen it in her expression before he decided to slow it down a little by stealing some bread. Because, yes, she wanted it, but he'd wanted to know first why she had fled the church when questions about their marriage started. She wanted it; he wanted it so bad he hurt. But he'd not have her take it and then regret it.

That resolve went out the window, though, when she had started her teasing. As soon as she was in his lap, he was hard as granite. He'd still ask her, but it was much less important than giving her what they were both denied this afternoon.

A slip of paper under the plate caught his eyes, and he pulled it free and put it close to the light. A smile touched his lips. Damn, but she never stopped surprising him. His eyes flashed to the stove in the corner. The soft glow from the low fire burning cast out only a bit of light, but enough he could see the bucket and the two coffee pots she'd left. The note said they all held fresh water so he could clean up.

Taking the last bite, he made use of the warm water, an unusual luxury any other day he finished working so late, stocked the stove, added another log, and stripped from his shirt and jeans before pushing past the curtain.

Summer slept, hands folded under her cheek, long braid

sweeping the floor, knees slightly drawn up, with four blankets piled on top. He was ready to join her when he noticed the rest of the bedding piled on the floor. Damn, was she mad about something? Maybe pouting still, being he'd spanked her?

Unless he woke her, he wouldn't know, and he didn't want to wake her, given he mostly wanted to know only so he could claim her. With a sigh, he got on his knees, arranged the blankets, and lay down.

More tired than he thought, he was actually startled awake by the sound of weeping. As he listened, he determined it came from the bed. "Summer?" he called, sitting up. She might be crying in her sleep. She did; she also talked a bit. He set a hand on her, felt her shrink away, knew she was awake. "Hey, sweetheart. Why you crying?" As soon as she lifted her face from the pillow, the weeping became more pronounced. "Summer, what's wrong? Something happen while I was gone?" She shook her head. "Then, what?"

"I can't do this," she said, her voice loud in the quiet room.

"Do what?" His gut twisted, and he held his breath. The reason he'd pursued work as a U.S. Marshal rather than take a lawman's job in Denver was because every time he came home late, it was to a worried family. Life with a lawman meant that any day could be the one he didn't come home. It was his mother screaming those very words at him which sent him in pursuit of a career further from home.

"This," she said, not elaborating.

"Summer, tell me what you can't do? Why are you crying?" He wouldn't have thought his choice of work would have bothered her at all. She was familiar with it, knew that the risks could be minimized with skill and good sense.

She rolled to her back and looked at him. "Why are you sleeping on the floor again?"

"You left the pallet."

"No, I didn't." She sniffed and rolled toward him, looking

over the edge of the bed at the pile he slept on. "They must have just fallen off me."

"You didn't want me out of our bed?" He was already getting up and lifting the blankets off her.

"No." She made room for him. "You didn't want to be out of it?"

He slid in and lay down. "No," he said then chuckled. "Why would I?"

"I don't know," she almost wailed. "I don't know how this is supposed to go. But you came back and just..." She sniffed loud again but turned against him and set her hand on his hip. "Lay down on the floor and went to sleep."

"You don't know how what is supposed to go?" He knew. He knew it right in his heart. But he needed to hear her say it, either with words or with her body.

"I wanted... I thought maybe we could..."

"You want me, too..."

She nodded and slid her hand down his thigh, back up and closer to his groin. "I did, but... you fell asleep... on the floor."

"I'm awake now," he told her and clenched his jaw, and her fingers brushed his hard-as-diamonds prick. "So's that." He took a breath. "So is it you did, or you do?"

"I do," she said a bit hesitantly.

Chase rolled over her and settled down between her legs. Their difference in height made it so his hips were almost at her knees if he lay so their heads were even. "You said that like you weren't sure." She wouldn't meet his eyes in the moonlight. "Summer?" He set a hand on her cheek and waited. When the minutes ticked by with no answer, "You scared?" She nodded but shifted further under him. "What you scared of?"

"The hurt. That's it's going to hurt. Everyone said it's terrible, but I—"

"It's anything but terrible. And it only hurts if the man you're with doesn't know what he's doing or doesn't care. I know, and I care."

"It won't hurt?"

He shrugged. He couldn't say for sure, but given she'd spent her life in a saddle, astride, not cloistered up in some fancy parlor sipping tea. "I think it'll be good for you. I'll do everything I can to make it better than good."

"You can do that?" She raised her arms and put them around his neck.

"I've had some practice." She snorted at that. "What?"

"Some practice? Way every female looked at you, in church, today—"

He chuckled. "Women always look at me; as long as they don't touch…" he said, throwing her words back at her as he dipped his head for a kiss. She smiled against his lips. He touched her lips briefly then pushed off her, kneeling between her legs. "Sit up," he ordered and helped her do so. "We need to get rid of this." He tugged up her chemise, helping her lift so it was out from under her and then waiting for her to lift her arms.

"We do?" she asked but let him pull it free and toss it to the ground.

"Oh, yes," he said, taking in the sight of her naked breasts. They looked warm and delicious even in the cold moonlight streaming through the window. "Nothing between us, when we make love." He felt her jerk a bit, but she said nothing as he eased her back. She folded her hands together and set them between the full globes, making her arms hide them from his view.

"Ahh," he chided and pulled them away. "Don't hide. You're entirely too beautiful to hide." He pushed her arms down and, setting his fingers at her collar, drew downward. Passing her breasts, he came back and slipped his hand beneath them then leaned forward. "Yep, perfection," he breathed before covering one of the taut nipples with his mouth.

Summer's gasp was some mix of fright and pleasure. Her hand came up to grip his forearms, but that was all she did as he eased from just a gentle sucking to more purposeful draws on the flesh. She gasped again, then moaned as he laved at her nipple. "Just as sweet as I knew they'd be," he said before turning to the other and giving it the same attention.

Shaking off her hand, he set his palm at her hip and slowly took a path to her center. She was already wet and hot when he reached it. The petals of her sex opened for him and his fingers quickly went to work on that hard, little bud that was the key to her complete pleasure.

Taking his time, letting her direct him with her little gasps and sighs, her deep moans and whimpers, he worked to memorize what it took to please her like a woman deserved to be pleased. Shifting back, he placed kisses down her torso, across her hips, over the tops of her thighs, and finally settling completely down between her legs, he replaced his fingers with his mouth.

Summer sucked in a loud breath, arched into him, and clutched the sheets. Her feet planted then shuffled as she twisted away then back. Chase stayed on her. Getting bucked off now would disappoint them both. But she became more desperate. Keeping her riding toward the cliffs took focus off the ride itself. He reached back, hooked her knees, and pushed her legs up and out. Summer's cry was fear tinged. "Let go; don't resist. Summer, don't resist," Chase urged then took a long, hard draw on her clit.

She came with a scream. Then a sob. Then she went limp. Chase lapped up the tangy taste of her pleasure before sliding back up her body as she worked to take a deep breath. Sliding his arm under her shoulders, he lifted her, set his lips on hers, and then drove his tongue into her mouth to coat her with her own taste.

"That's what pleasure tastes like," he said when she gave him a confused look. He hooked her knee and pulled it wide again when she moved to close it. Her tongue came out, licked her bottom lip, and when she looked at him again, it was with a soft smile.

"I like it," she said, and if he'd thought he was hard before, he was unbreakable now. "Is that all?"

"No," he said, shaking his head as his hand smoothed down the inside of her thigh, back to that place that had easily welcomed him a moment ago. "That was only how it starts," he told her, turning his hand so his fingers slid down through that valley. She'd given him more than enough wetness to make entry smooth, but she was small and tight, even for just his tongue. "I'm just going to make you a little more ready." He folded back all but his middle finger and dipped it past that threshold. Her startled gasp stilled his hands. "It's all right. It won't hurt. You're ready." He pulled back then entered again a little deeper. She gasped again. "You're so perfectly tight, just needs a little working, a little stretching." Pushing in as deep as he could, he found no resistance. No barrier. He slowly eased in and out, helped her relax into the invasion. She was tight, but that obnoxious little bit of a woman that so often made sex the first time a disaster was missing. He suspected it would be. Life in the saddle was hard, and women past girlhood often lacked it. Why it was even valued, he didn't know. He withdrew almost completely and then added a second finger. Again, she gasped, and this time squirmed away from him. "Easy, Summer, we'll go easy. Let me make you ready."

"It's a little uncomfortable," she muttered but settled down.

"Because you're so small, but you're made to fit me. It's completely normal." He heard her whimper a bit. "Hurt?" She was still dripping, so he didn't think so. She waited a moment before shaking her head. "It shouldn't, just a stretch." He worked her a little more, fighting to resist his own selfish need. Again, she relaxed, allowing his fingers freer movement. "Hmm, yes, that's the way, I think now maybe." Again, he settled between her thighs, lining them up the way he'd need to bring this to its conclusion. "You're gonna stretch more now, a lot more."

"It'll hurt?"

"Sometimes pain is the best part of the pleasure," he said, pushing in. She clenched down. "Let me in, or tell me no, Summer." He waited, felt her relax, easing in more, her body accommodating him with more perfection than he'd ever experienced before.

"Ah," she cried out and spread her knees more as she pushed her hips down into the bed.

"I know," he soothed. "Let me in; it'll get better I promise."

Once more, she relaxed as he put his weight behind his forward motion, gaining the entrance he wanted and seating himself as deep as he could inside her hot little body. Her hands took hold of his upper arms and her back arched up, causing her breasts to brush his chest. He used the opening to slip both his arms under her, one high at her shoulders, the other lower at her hips.

"Chase?"

"I'm in, how does it feel?"

She licked her lips a few times, squeezed her eyes closed. "Full, stuffed."

"The way it should feel." He pulled his hips back. "Move with me Summer. Just like riding a horse. Come up to meet me." He pushed forward and helped her lift by using his arm. "Pull away," he instructed and let her hips drop. "Exactly like that. Perfect," he praised when she lifted mostly on her own to meet him as he came back in. Nothing was worse than a woman just lying there. The very few he'd had like that didn't seem to even know they should move. Summer took his instruction without complaint and as naturally as she sat a horse, she joined in making this ride better and better.

As she put more effort in it, Chase was able to leverage up on his hands and stroke in and out with more force and more of his cock. She couldn't quite take him all, but she took enough. At some point, he realized she'd wrapped her legs around the back of his thighs and was tentatively urging him in and out. "Ah, yes," he said when she moaned and squeezed down. "Take the bit; run with it." She clamped down again but didn't seem quite able to let go. "A little help."

The cry that left her lips when he put his fingers on her clit was followed by a renewed level of hot wetness as he pumped in and out, increasing the pace, and she seemed to hold on to that pleasure.

For his part, the pull in his sac was becoming painful. He wasn't going to last much longer and he needed to make a decision now. At the last possible moment, he pulled out, grabbed his cock, and finished himself off, spraying thick shots of cum across her belly and chest. Even this was better than he'd ever known. And next time, before they shared this, he'd hear her opinion on taking a chance on pregnancy.

Though that might tie her to him permanently, he didn't want her that way, especially if she'd come to resent it. He shook off the last of his seed then guided himself back inside. Summer cried out and shuddered through a tiny climax.

For a while, the only thing he was aware of was the sound of their breathing and the smell of sex. Both, some of the best things he'd known in his life. Unable to hold himself up on his arms, he dropped heavily to the side, sliding free of Summer's heated body, still half hard. He put one leg over both of hers and dropped his arm over her chest, reaching up to rub his knuckles across her jaw and cheek.

Her breathing was still a bit ragged and she kept her eyes closed, but as best he could tell, there were no tears, no want to turn from him in shame or fear. He placed a kiss at her temple and quietly asked, "Are you all right?"

She nodded slowly. "No one ever said it was like that."

"And by 'like that', you mean nice?" Damn, he hoped so, because he was ready to go again already.

"Yes," she said, finally opening her eyes. She looked briefly his way but then lifted her head and looked down her body still exposed in the moonlight. She reached down and dipped her fingers in one of the warm globs of cum he'd left on her belly.

Chase watched, fascinated by how she swirled it around a bit on her belly then rubbed it between her fingers before bringing them to her nose. If he hadn't just left that with her, he'd have fired off again watching her touch it to her tongue. He ground his teeth then managed, "That first was your pleasure. That..." he nodded toward her belly, "that's mine."

"Salty and..." She didn't finish, just licked the rest from her fingers and snuggled closer. "Chase?"

"Yep?"

"It... was nice. I... thank you." Her shy tone made him smile and squeezed his heart just a bit.

"It's supposed to be nice; you don't need to thank me for it. It was my privilege and pleasure."

"No, but, I mean... All right, but that wasn't what I meant. I mean thank you for hushing that sound a little bit for me. It hasn't been quiet for me for a long time."

Chase leaned up on his forearm. "What sound, sweetheart?"

"That sound of Mother screaming when she was dragged out of the room, and the sound of the other girls I left in that saloon. I hear them most nights," she said, turning to look at him. "But they're quiet now. Thank you."

"Ah, gawd," Chase groaned and tried to pull her even closer. He'd certainly had his fair share of painful things in his life. But nothing broke his heart the way her words did. "I'm gonna do my darnedest to make sure you never hear them again, sweetheart. All right? Understand? You don't deserve that. We'll do what we can to silence them for good." She nodded at his words, but this time when he kissed her temple, he tasted tears. Maybe she just needed sleep; it was late. "Stay right here," he told her and rolled back off the bed.

"Where are you going?" she asked, panic in her voice.

"Wait here; I'll only be a second." Stepping back to the stove, he took the rag, damp and warm, and carried it back to her. "Clean you up, and we can get some sleep. I think we could both use it." He carefully wiped away the evidence he'd taken care not to impregnate her this first time. If she didn't know the significance of his act, it didn't matter. That she found something else more important in how he treated her this first time meant more to him. She moaned a little and lifted in to his touch when he wiped between her legs. At least he was assured she'd be willing to repeat the act. He hastily wiped his cock, still not ready to lie down, before tossing the cloth aside, stretching out beside her, and drawing up the covers. "You're perfect, Summer. You're perfect," he said, tucking her in and holding her close.

A little past sunup, Chase woke to find Summer drawing lazy circles on his chest with her fingers. Collecting them in his fist, he lifted it to his lips and kissed each tip. She giggled, not a sound she made often. Placing her hand back on his chest, right over his heart, he lifted her chin so he could see her face when he asked, "No regrets?"

"No regrets," she echoed back in way of confirmation, sliding closer to him.

He felt the heat coming off her as soon as her pussy aligned with his cock. Giving her tits only a bit of attention, he slid his hand down her side, around her ass, and then between her legs from behind. With hardly any encouragement, she shifted and gave him access. But upon hearing her hiss and feeling her stiffen when he placed his fingers at the entrance, he hesitated. "Sore?"

"Yes, but..." She relaxed against him. "I... like it this time. Maybe you should stop making my ass sore and just make my—"

"Pussy," he supplied the word.

"All right, that," she said, maybe not comfortable with the

word yet. "Sore."

With a chuckle, he slid his fingers up inside her, delighted to find her hot, wet, and ready. "It'd be my pleasure to keep this little kitty purring with a nice ache," he said and watched a smile curl her lips. "But…" Her eyes flashed up to meet his. "Naughty little girls get a nasty ache on their asses. And of course, now, if you're especially naughty, you'll get an ache in your ass, too. I might just even spank your kitty sore."

Her mouth had fallen open and color was high in her cheeks, but her arousal was coating his fingers. When he raised a brow at her, she looked away. "I don't care for the sound of that," she grumbled then shuddered a little when his seeking fingers found her clit.

"Well, it's for punishment," he said, making her moan with a pinch. "You're not supposed to enjoy it." And while he knew he'd make sure she didn't in most every way, he rather suspected, if it happened, she'd take at least some pleasure from it. Placing his hand back at her hip, he rolled her face down. "But so far, today…" he rolled over her back, "…you've been an absolute angel."

"What are you doing?" she asked, trying to lift up.

"Making sure this ache you have lasts the whole day," Chase said, shoving her knees forward and putting her ass in the air the way he liked.

"Chase, it's broad daylight. I don't think we can do this."

"If this," he put his hand over her sex, insuring she wasn't actually protesting the act, only the timing. "Is wet." It was. "And this." He took hold of his cock and thumped her ass with it. "Is hard." It was so much it hurt, so he wasn't just having a normal morning rise. "We can do this. Any time of day, any place we are."

"I'm not in the right position," she told him, even as he lined up his cock with her entrance.

"There are hundreds of positions, sweetheart." He entered

her easy, letting her again welcome his length and girth at her pleasure. Given the loud, long moan he heard, she did. Almost completely inside her, but feeling the limits of her body, Chase took hold of her hips and stroked back, pushing her hips forward then flexed forward and pulled her hips back. She caught on much quicker this time. Maybe even too quick as she soon discovered she'd a little more say in this position about the pace and force set.

She would occasionally hold back or away, and while, at first, he thought she'd just missed the rhythm, her giggles and gasps gave it away. He'd get her back rocking with a slap to her ass, which made her clamp down and arch, increasing his pleasure.

Chase reached around, found her clit, and focused on bringing her to climax. It didn't take long; she didn't try to pull back on the reins this time as she had the first. He stayed in almost a little too long, pulling out just as the first shot came off his cock. He coated her ass then grabbed his cock to wring out every last drop of pleasure he could. God help him when he could finally stay inside her body and feel this. He gritted his teeth through the last wave then leaned forward, taking Summer with him back to the bed.

"I might have liked that more," she said rather boldly, causing Chase to turn and look at her.

Her look gave her away, and he returned his gaze to the ceiling. "You can be in control when you're on top, missy." Just the thought made his wilting cock perk up for a moment.

"If you say so," she quipped, and Chase almost groaned. She might have waited for the right time to share her body, but she'd already mastered the deed and was riding toward control. He might have whipped up more of a storm than he could handle. Then again, Summer was almost too much to handle in every aspect. It was why he loved her as hard as he did and why he'd do anything to hold on to her.

Even if she wouldn't make that chore an easy one.

Chapter 18

Summer tucked her chin and pulled the brim of her hat down. Not because of the cold wind that blew through the streets, but because she could again feel the staring. She'd felt it when she had walked down the street to the mercantile, but assumed it was only because she was again dressed in pants. Chase had walked out with her this morning and not voiced any opinion about her dress, other than he thought she had a fine ass.

That thought brought heat to her face. The things he did to her. The things she did to him. Heat rose again, but this time in a much lower place than her face. Never would she have thought what men and women did in the night behind closed doors could be so wickedly enjoyable, though she knew there was more to it than the act.

Really, if she thought about it, and she did often as she reconciled what she'd believed about it before with what she understood about it now, she knew it wasn't just what men and women did. It was what consenting men and women did. It was what couples who had some care about each other did. Chase did his best to help her understand better that despite what anyone told her, they were equals in the bed, and while he did wrench control from her more often than she did from him, she was never left unsatisfied. The only thing she still couldn't allow to take hold was Chase's constant use of the world love. He used the word so often, she rather thought it meaningless. He couldn't really love her, could he? Because they'd only known each other a bit more than a month, marriage wasn't either of their idea, and he knew in September, when he handed over that money, they'd be done. Or they would unless she chose to stay.

And that was the other thing now, too. Could she stay? This little place seemed ideal for planting her dream and seeing if it might take root. But right now, with the weather and the distance from crops and livestock keeping her from testing out her plan, she didn't know. She might have committed enough to the idea to send for her belongings, but...

She came to an abrupt stop in front of the door of the mercantile. The sign still read closed, but through the glass, she could see that the fancy clock on the wall said it was five past nine. Charlie, the clerk she'd come to know, was never late opening up. Setting her hand back on her gun, she carefully walked down the line of windows and peered in. Nothing looked disturbed, and she couldn't see anyone inside. As she listened, she heard nothing.

"Nelson hasn't opened shop on time in ten years."

Summer spun around to see Sheriff Buckley standing behind her. "So they ain't being held up in the back?" she asked and frowned at him when he spit his tobacco into the street.

"Nope," Buckley said again. "Give him a few more minutes, and he'll open the doors." He pointed to the bench against the wall and Summer moved to take a seat. "Been waiting for him to get back all week, ain't ya?"

"Yep," Summer said vaguely. She didn't really get on with this man. But she didn't know if it was him or her. She did her best not to interact with town sheriffs more than necessary. Most didn't approve of her line of work.

"Itchin' to make use of that there line of credit yer man set up for you?" he asked then spit again.

"Hardly," Summer said, crossing her arms over her chest. "And he hasn't set it up yet, so I couldn't make use even if I was 'itchin' to'."

The man snorted. "Your man's rich as all get out."

"So I hear, or at least I hear his family has money. But like me, he's made his own way. Respectable like." What was this man getting at?

"Suppose," Buckley said, maybe grudgingly giving Chase his dues. She couldn't blame him there. Chase did sometimes look more a dandy or city slicker, but his dress and manners were a very small aspect of the complete man he was. "Still, must be nice being with a man who can take care of you."

A noise at the door brought Summer to her feet. "I can take of myself, Sheriff. What Marshal Storm takes care of is outlaws." She left the man standing on the boardwalk and walked into the store, heading straight to the little bulletin board Charlie had shown her. It hadn't been updated yet, which was likely a product of Mr. Nelson's lacking business model. The train stations wired word each night, letting the towns up ahead know any information deemed relevant. Charlie assured her they'd hear the minute the first trains coming in with food products were on the way.

"More tobacco for you, Sheriff?"

Summer stopped by the bin of fabric bolts, fingering some pretty blue gingham and waited for the two men to finish. The bell overhead rung out and two women walked in and straight to the counter. A moment later, a woman, highly over dressed for her position behind the counter of a mercantile stepped up and the three began chatting.

Summer abandoned the fabric. She couldn't sew anyway, so she'd not be making any dress for herself, and wandered over to the shelf of soaps. She'd have to be doing laundry soon and the little broken bits she had left of soap wouldn't get the job done. She selected a bar, held it to her nose, then set it back. Maybe she should ask first if laundry was one of those things that mutually benefited both of them as she'd a few dollars in her right pocket that Chase gave her and a few pennies in her left that were her own.

"Have a good day, Sheriff." Summer heard the man she presumed to be Mr. Nelson call and she looked in time to see the man open the door, give her one more heated glance, and walk out. Mr. Nelson then stepped over to the ladies still gossiping at the counter. That was when she caught their looks. Damn it, she snatched the soap off the shelf again. She'd pay for it and wash her dress and shirtwaist. She was tired of being stared at. As she turned, she headed to where a wall of items like bath brushes and washboards hung. She took one of each and then dropped everything in a large wash tub.

She, in no manner, had brought enough of her money with her to pay for all of this, but she rationalized Chase would make use of the things too, so she'd pay for some and use his money to pay the rest. If he disapproved, she could pay him back, or he could take it out of the money he was holding for her until the end of their bargain.

A commotion at the counter made her look back, in time to catch the woman behind the counter shoving the man and hissing at him to 'go on'. Summer watched the man, clearly nagged and browbeaten, lift the hinged part of the counter and step out. She wasn't surprised when he started toward her, but his abashed expression did give her pause. Clearly, it wasn't his idea to come question her shopping habits or… whatever he was told to come bother her about.

"Is there something I can help you with, miss?"

"Are you Mr. Nelson, proprietor here?" Summer said and saw him jump back at her forward tone.

"Yes, miss, I—"

"Missus," Summer corrected quickly, knocking down any notion she was just some tramp or vagrant. That she was dressed as she was with a husband's approval. Though it galled her to no end, people thought she needed that.

"Oh, yes, how nice," Nelson said, twisting his hands in his apron. "Is there something I can help you with?"

"Well, if everything your clerk Charlie said was true, then, yes, yes, there is," Summer said, smiling at the man, who relaxed a great deal after, and pointed to a far corner of the store and moved away from the group of women to explain to him what she would like that his services could assist with.

Once she started talking business, the man left behind his weak demeanor, and after a good, long talk with much back and forth, they shook hands on a deal, short term, that should allow Summer to start making money without need of trying to catch a bounty to hunt. They stepped back into the main room, only to find Chase standing at the counter with even more women crowding around him.

"Summer," he called with a smile on his face that went straight to her sex and made it pulse. "Mrs. Nelson said she thought you were in the back talking to Mr. Nelson. Did you finish your shopping?" He pointed to the tub she held against her hip.

"I think so," Summer said and narrowed her eyes at the young woman who pretended to trip and fall against Chase.

"Mr. Nelson able to help you sort out what you needed?"

"Indeed," Mr. Nelson said, clapping his hands together. "And If Mrs...." he faded off, maybe realizing Summer only introduced herself with her first name, not giving him a polite way to address her publicly... "I'm sorry, I didn't catch your married name."

"Storm," both she and Chase answered. She turned to frown at him, only to see him frowning at her.

"Summer's my wife," he announced causing any number of the women around him to gasp and even one to sob out loud. "Marshal Storm," he introduced himself as he crossed the floor, hand held out. "Marshal Chase Storm." The two men shook hands, and Chase stepped past the man to stand next to Summer. "So this will be the person I was telling you I'd want added to my accounts."

"Oh, you didn't say it would be a... woman," the woman behind the counter said with as much disapproval as Summer ever heard anyone give her.

"Will that make it some kind of problem?" Chase asked, disapproval of her disapproval clear in his tone.

"No, no," the woman quickly assured when she realized Chase wasn't a man she could bully. "But you'll want to set a limit for her spending."

"No," Chase said so casually, Summer had to bite her lip not to laugh. "You'll be paying cash for your other purchases, right, sweetheart?"

The question caught her off guard for a moment, more because he was in a stare down with the woman when he said it. "I plan to, for now. But Mr. Nelson and I already discussed the matter and have settled on our terms."

"So we did; so we did," Nelson said, again clapping his hands together. "And what prosperous terms they should be if they work out just so. Yes, indeed."

"I'm rather confident if Mrs. Storm is behind it, it'll get done to everyone's liking," Chase said, endorsing her in the face of the complete censure she was getting from the other woman in the shop. The woman huffed, and when Mr. Nelson made his way back behind the counter, she all but dragged him by the collar over somewhere she could whisper in his ear out of sight.

The loud exclamation of, "You just mind that counter, Mrs. Nelson," again had Summer biting her lip not to laugh.

"Guess he's not as lily-livered as he looked," Chase

commented, taking the wash tub from her. "Did you get every-thing you needed?" he asked, leaving her side to search the shelves and pull items he wanted down. He dropped them in the tub with hers.

"I don't suppose I really need the brush," Summer said, adding up the cost of the items he was pulling down over her head. He dug around in the tub and came up with the item. He took a moment to look it over then slapped it down on his thigh. A slight hiss escaped his lips as he turned and looked straight at her.

"Yep, you really do need it," he said, and Summer's ass clenched the same time her stomach dropped and her pussy throbbed. He dropped it casually back in the tub and continued selecting items until he'd satisfied himself and joined her at the counter.

What a madding combination of things he could make her feel. A look, a touch, both, neither all made her dizzy and off balance. She knew he could do it to her even before they started having sex. She didn't know, though, it would get worse once she was spreading her legs for him.

"And this will be all for today?" Mrs. Nelson's sharp voice brought Summer back from her thoughts.

"You want some candy?" Chase asked, lifting the lid of the jar with the licorice inside.

"No, and you shouldn't eat any either, ruin your supper," Summer said, only half teasing. She hated licorice herself.

"As long as you're cooking, I'm eating. And by the way," he said as he watched the woman take note of what was bought. "There's only one loaf of bread left. I told you if you didn't make more, none of it would ever go stale. And we need stale bread, you said."

"Chase," Summer admonished with a laugh. "I made four loaves on Wednesday. Have you eaten all of them already?" If she thought he gobbled up her bread the first time, as soon as she found a farmer who was willing to sell milk, eggs, and butter to her directly, and he was able to lather butter on the slices...

"There's one left," he said with a grin. "Well, a half one." He turned away, but she didn't miss his smile.

"Lord help me," Summer muttered under her breath. "Oh," she cried out when Mrs. Nelson reached for the soap and started to write it on the same list she'd made of Chase's things. "I'll pay for the soap and the..." Damn, about all she'd brought with her was enough to pay for the soap.

"What you gonna do with the soap?" Chase asked, sticking some of the candy in his mouth.

"Wash clothes, first," Summer said.

"Just yours?"

"Well, I—"

"I mean if you're gonna make me keep washing my own, I can, I just thought..." he pouted at her, actually pouted, and she covered her mouth not to laugh. "Unless you were only trying to save time so you can do more cooking. If that's the case, I can do all the wash. I mean, I don't mind putting my hands on all your frilly dah—"

"I'll do all the wash, thank you, Marshal," Summer shouted, tossing her hands in the air. "Lord knows I don't want your hands on anything of mine that's frilly."

"That's not what you said—"

"Stop," Summer shouted and slapped his arm. "You fool." She had to try hard not to fan herself with her hand for all the heat she felt in her face. If her head didn't burst into flames, she'd be shocked.

"Charge it all together, today, please, Mrs. Nelson," Chase said and pulled Summer into his arms, kissing the top of her head.

"On your account, then?" the old biddy asked.

"No," Chase said, letting Summer go to reach in his pocket.

"I'm here, so I'll pay cash. The account is for Summer, if I'm not here."

"Chase?" Summer started but, at his look, dropped it. Remembering he'd given her a few dollars, though, she reached in her pocket. "I still have—"

"Hang on to it, for next time." He winked at her, then hearing his total, he counted out the money while Summer tried not to cringe at the expense.

Everything was dropped back in the tub and Chase lifted it down, setting it at his hip. He lifted his hat from the counter as well and touched it to his forehead, in a way of a departing gesture, then put it in the small of Summer's back and ushered her toward the door, which he opened and stepped aside so she could go out first. He waited until he was on the boardwalk before putting it on his head. He did have impeccable manners; she could see why the sheriff might worry he was a dandy just playing at lawman.

"I'll carry that home if you need to get back to something," Summer offered.

"Nope, I'll carry it." He looked up and down the street then back at her. "Were you needing to see about anything else?"

"I was going to see if that man Mr. Anders said makes furniture was in town today," Summer said, worried if she couldn't get a bench like she needed, Chase would start hanging shelving all around and she'd lay awake every night waiting to hear her supplies falling to the floor.

"If he's not, I will hang a few shelves," Chase said then stopped dead at her look. "What?"

"Marshal you're awful good at a lot of things; carpentry isn't one of them." He glared at her. "Three of the five nails you put in the wall fell out already," she said, trying not to laugh at the color rising in his neck.

"Maybe pounding nails isn't my forte, but I think I pound something else rather well," he said with a smirk.

"You need to quit." She laughed and slapped his arm. Chase could turn anything into some reference to what they did in each other's arms. Most of the time, like now, it made her eager to do it more.

"Quit? That's not what you said—"

"Chase," Summer cried, hoping the men standing on the boardwalk didn't hear. "You're terrible, and you're gonna ruin your fine, upstanding reputation if you keep it up."

"Sweetheart, there is no way on this green earth that could ruin my reputation," he said with a chuckle then stopped walking. "I need to stop over at the bank, before we head up to Joshua's." He took her elbow as they stepped off into the muddy street and crossed to the bank. As soon as they entered, Summer could see something wasn't right.

Several people stood around grumbling, one old woman at the counter was sobbing uncontrollably as the bank clerk continued to berate her for being careless with the money her late husband had left her. Chase set the tub down in the corner, and Summer followed him up to the window.

"What seems to be the problem here?" Chased asked the clerk, and Summer put her focus on the old woman.

"What happened?" she said in a much softer tone

"How is it any of your business?" she heard someone say from the back of the bank. From the corner of her eye, she watched Chase push back the left side of his coat. "Marshal?"

"Marshal Storm, so I'm asking again. What's the problem here?"

"He said I'm out of money," the old woman cried. "But I can't be. Edgar said there was enough to pay the loan. He said it was there, all I had to do was come in once a month and take out the money and pay it. If I can't pay it, I'll lose the house."

Summer caught the woman's flapping hands and guided her over to the bench. "You haven't taken out any of the money for anything else?" Summer asked as Chase continued talking with the clerk and an older man she assumed was the manager or maybe even the owner.

"Not a penny; Edgar said come once a month, take out exactly fourteen dollars, and take it straight to Mr. Si. And that's what I've done. Every month for the last three years, on the third day of the month, unless that's a Sunday, I've come and taken out just fourteen dollars and… there was enough money. Edgar said so; he said so." She held out the little bank book she carried and tapped with her finger. "He said so. Said I would be taken care of."

"Edgar is your—"

"My late husband. Married fifty-seven years. He ain't never said one untrue thing to me in all that time."

"May I see your book?" Summer asked and pulled it from her fingers. "I'm Summer Ra… Storm," she corrected.

"Edith Miller."

"Well, Mrs. Miller, let's see what might have happened."

"Can you do numbers?" Edith asked.

"I can, pretty well too," Summer said, noting how the first pages of the book were written in a neat, bold hand, all the numbers lining up perfectly and the math done correctly. It was a repeating cycle of every ten months equaling one hundred and forty dollars from a starting amount. But then the last several pages were a mess. Numbers barely legible, nothing lined up, and the math… Even if the numbers were what she was guessing they were, the math was completely wrong. "Did you write these?"

"No, dear, I can't write none, neither. I can read the Bible, though, real good." Edith said with pride.

Summer smiled and touched her shoulder. "I'm sure you can." Though she probably mostly just had it memorized. "Who has been keeping your book for you since Mr. Miller passed?" The old woman pointed a shaking finger at the clerk.

Summer flipped back the pages to the last neat entry. Taking that amount and quickly subtracting the amount that should be missing, the discrepancy was large. She again checked several of the entries made by the people working at the bank, and each one shorted the end total.

"Wait here," Summer said then carried the book to the window and slapped it down. "You make it a habit of cheating old ladies out of their life savings?"

Her statement left the clerk and the older man behind him sputtering in outrage. Chase, not so much, as he grabbed her arm and turned at least her body toward him. "Mrs. Storm," he ground out, trying to make her break eye contact with the men in control of the people's money. "Don't slander people without evidence."

"Of course, Marshal," Summer said but continued to stare down the men. "Maybe they didn't cheat Mrs. Miller, maybe they're just incompetent and can't do simple math."

"Summer," Chase snarled. "Enough. Hold your tongue."

"After they give Edith back the money they stole," Summer said, poking at the book on the counter, and for the first time noticed the loud rumbling from the crowd behind her.

Chase leaned down and whispered in her ear, "Be quiet."

As warning went, his was clear, but Summer wasn't having it. Men always cheated women out of what was rightfully theirs if they thought they'd get away with it. She pushed the book toward Chase. "Not that it's better than your chicken scratch, but each time the balance is written, it's short by anywhere between four and seven dollars. Not only should Mrs. Miller still have money in the bank," she opened the book and pointed out where the late Mr. Miller had made a note of the total deposit, the payment amount, and how many in total there would be, "she should have enough to complete the mortgage and have a small amount left over."

"Nine dollars," Edith piped up. "Edgar said there'd be nine

dollars at the end, and I should buy me some nice shoes to get buried in."

"They've been skimming off her account since her husband's death, and because she can't read or write," Summer said as she watched Chase examine the book, "it's either theft or stupidity, either way, don't put your money in this establishment."

"Go wait outside please," Chase said, and his tone made her skin prickle. But she was right. Why would he not be happy she'd found the mistake, that she had just saved Mrs. Miller from eviction?

"Marshal?"

"Go," he ordered then leaned in close again. "Before you really wish you had."

Summer gave him a hard look then turned on her heels and marched out. She did stop to assure Edith that Chase would see to the matter from here. But if he didn't, she could come find her. She left the bank, closing the door a little too hard behind her, then pulled her coat around her and leaned up against the wall.

She was starting to shiver in the cold when the bank door opened and Mrs. Miller came out with a smile on her face, singing Chase's praises, thanking him profusely. When she spotted Summer, she smiled and said, "Thank you too, dear," before heading off down the walk.

Thank me, too? That was all she was going to get? With a sigh, she pushed off the wall and stepped up next to Chase, who set his hat on his head and shifted the tub to his other side so he could take her by the elbow. "Well?"

"The matter's been fixed," he said, his voice clipped.

"Hope you didn't start an account there. Safer to keep money buried under a house." She felt his hand tighten on her arm.

"I did; you're on it. And you will go back in and apologize for making accusations like that, first chance you get," he said.

Summer stopped dead and pulled out of his grasp. "No, I won't.

I didn't say anything untrue. They were cheating her. The whole lot of them should have been arrested. Why didn't you do your job back there? Or is it fine to cheat and steal because she's just a woman?"

Chase came back, took her by the arm again, and continued walking. "You handled it the wrong way, Summer. You say things like that, with a crowd of people around, you start a panic. People need the bank. They have to trust the bank to keep their money safe and have money to loan. Mrs. Miller's problem was handled. You didn't have any call to make the scene that you made, and you'll go in and tell Mr. Codwells you're sorry for your choice of words."

"The hell I will." Summer again tried to pull her arm free, but Chase held on, kept her walking toward the blacksmith's shop. "Who's Codwells?"

"Bank owner," he supplied but said nothing else about making apologies.

An hour later, they were back home watching Mr. Limus measure out the space they had open, Chase saying the small ready-made table that was exactly what Summer needed wasn't adequate. And though he bought it so she'd have it to use, he ordered a much larger version made. She was grateful as the work space would come in handy as she started the first part of her plan to earn the last of the money she'd need to open her eatery. But as she showed the carpenter out and turned back to face the husband who, twice today, had spoiled her with far more than she needed, her gut cramped and a cold chill made her skin prickle.

Marshal Chase Storm was mad as hell.

Chapter 19

Chase carried the chair from the table to the spot next to the stove and started rolling up his sleeve as soon as Summer showed the man to the door. He'd warned her not to be argumentative in public, and given her outright defiance over his request to make amends at the bank, he didn't think she'd heed his warning not to stir up trouble.

He knew her response was born out of defensiveness. She didn't like to be judged weaker for her sex, and she extended that to other females. And some of what made her able to earn her way as a bounty hunter, a career few women would ever be given a chance to try their hand at, factored in. Her deep-seated sense of right and wrong mandated swift action be taken. Only that kind of stance didn't work well if one was planning to stick around. She, they both, needed to have backing and support from every member of the community. Her, if she didn't want her business to fail before it started, and him, if he was going to keep the respect of the folks he was sworn to protect. And he would have explained all of this to her if she'd heeded him and hushed, rather than try to argue the matter publicly.

Chase wasn't a man who typically cared what people thought

of his personal life. It wasn't their business, and he worked hard not to put it in front of anyone. But it wouldn't serve him to have a wife nobody could tolerate. And he wouldn't have her stepping in to do his job for him. She might have spotted the inconsistency, and, yes, he'd agree that there was a basis for calling it theft, but her responsibly ended when she pointed it out to him. And she should have pointed it out to him before she started calling names and slandering people, before she had the rest of the customers grumbling about pulling out their money. Chase might have thought twice about depositing his money there had she let it go, but as a show of confidence in Mr. Codwells, even a shaky showing, he'd opened his account and was a bit louder than he would have been announcing the amount he would have transferred.

It quickly quieted the grumbling, set things right for the time, but Chase didn't even get a look of gratitude from the banker. And if something illegal was happening at the bank, he wouldn't be able to have it investigated as quietly as he'd like to.

He waited for Summer to close the door and turn around. "Get over here," he ordered.

Her eyes flashed from him to the chair and back to him. "Why?"

"Get over here," he told her again with no further explanation.

"Chase?" She started for him but then stopped. "No," she said, coming to a stop and shaking her head. "No, I was right. I was right, and you can't say I wasn't."

"If I have to come get you, it will be worse for you," he said. He'd address her concerns and her lack of understanding before he punished her, but he was done with the defiance. She didn't move. With a sigh, he crossed over to her and, before she could think to run, wrapped his arm around her back, lifted her from her feet, bent her in half, and brought his hand down, hard.

He continued to bring it down until the fight was all but out of her. Setting her on her feet, he turned, walked back to his original place, pointed to the floor, and ground out, "Get over here."

"Chase?" she whined, but with just one step by him, she was standing in front of him sniffing and rubbing her ass.

Taking her arm, he pulled her over to the chair and took a seat, putting Summer between his knees. "I'm not saying, in any way, you were wrong," he started. "Someone intentionally tried to cheat that lady out of her money. But we don't know who or why. And now, because you were so loud about it, I can't quietly look into the matter without any suspect thinking I am. More than that, if I make a request by wire for someone to come to audit the bank now, people will panic; there'll be a run and everyone will lose. And the thief will likely be able to slip away."

"I..." she started then lifted her arm and wiped her nose on her sleeve. "I didn't—"

"No, you didn't look that far out. You only looked at what was right in front of you. And that's the difference between what you did as a bounty hunter and what I do as a marshal. You also didn't consider once what impact your words are going to have on how people see you in this town. If they feel you're just out to ruin everyone, disrupt their safe little haven, make life harder, they will shun you. You can't be a business owner if you're still behaving like a bounty hunter. People won't accept that. Make your choice now, which you want more."

"I don't like outlaws," Summer said with a last sniff.

"No one does, and even if Mrs. Miller wasn't taken advantage of by an outlaw, no one likes to see an old woman taken advantage of."

"But whoever did it is going to get away with it."

"Did you miss me telling you I'll be looking into it more?" She shook her head. "Thought not, but I will look into it my way, Summer, and you'll not stick your nose in it."

"Fine," she said with a sigh then tried to step back.

"We're not done," he said, holding her behind her legs.

"What?" her voice pitched up a notch.

"I warned you not to argue with me in public. It reflects poorly on both of us. And, though I don't plan on doing it often, when I tell you to do something, you'll do it. If you need a reason, if you can't see the reason for yourself, I'll give you one. But I will not have blatant defiance from you." He waited, watched her react to those words, waited to see if she could recall what he had told her to do. When all she did was shift uncomfortably before him, he gave her the order again. "You'll apologize to Mr. Codwells, and you will be pointedly polite anytime you're in his bank."

"Gawd, fine," she snapped and stomped her foot. "I don't see why—"

"Because, like him or not, trust him or not, you, for now, need him. You need the bank to help with your business as much as you need the mercantile, and you've already made an enemy of Mrs. Nelson."

"I didn't do anything to that old biddy; I didn't even speak to her, not a damn word."

"Hardly matters, she's taken a dislike toward you and if you don't hold the reins, she'll ride rough shod over you every chance she gets."

"Gawd," she said with a long, heavy sigh.

"I'm not going to tell you be her friend, but you'll be polite. Because if you're here for the long term, that is the only way to get along." He watched carefully. That she was weighing it out meant her resolve to remain here, with him, past September, was gaining strength. A moment later, she nodded. It was a bit of having to swallow her pride. She didn't find it easy to walk away from a challenge. "All right," he said, taking her arm and moving her from between his knees to his right side. "Get them britches down, and we'll get this over with."

"What?" she screeched, clearly surprised by his intent. "No, Chase. Why?"

"This is why," he said, looking at her. "I won't have this defiance from you. I gave you a warning about arguing with me in public; that's all you'll get, a warning. And when I tell you to do or don't do something, you'll do as I say. Now, get them jeans down before I fetch up that bath brush."

"I said I'd tell that stupid banker I'm sorry. I did. I will," she whined and stomped her feet beside him.

"Yes, you will, and you'll get them pants off and get over my knee now, or you'll do it with a better than tanned hide."

"Chase," her soft plea was followed up by a tear splashing down on her cheek.

"Now, or I get the brush," he said, refusing to be swayed by her pathetic expression. She bit down on her lip, but then her hands went to her belt and then the buttons. He'd come to really enjoy the way she wiggled out her pants, left hip, right hip, left hip then down her thighs to her knees. Normally, she'd reach down and pull them the rest of the way from the bottom, but she still had her boots on, and clearly, she wasn't sure what to do about that.

Chase took pity and, taking her arm, guided her down across his lap. He adjusted her forward more to his liking, noting she still had quite the blush from the last time he'd laid down his hand. He'd make this lesson a good one, but it wouldn't take too long to do that.

"Chase, please. No," she cried and put her hand back as she tried to squirm off his lap. "Please. I'll do like you say. Please. You already spanked me."

"Because you didn't do what I said." He caught her wrist and pinned it at the small of her back.

Her legs kicked, fluttering more as they were trapped by the pants around her knees.

"Chase," her squeal ending on a cry when he brought his hand down.

He followed it up quickly with three more, each right on top of the last. "Arguing in public makes us look weak. We will not put anything but a united front to anyone." He lifted his hand again and cracked down on her flesh, opposite the spot he'd just battered. Red bloomed, but he didn't give her any chance to catch her breath from that, again adding three more spanks. "You will do what I tell you, when I tell you. I won't ever ask you do something morally corrupt or that goes against your personal principles. And..." He delivered four more swats to the area he first targeted. "I will always explain if you need me to and give you the chance to state your side." He took aim and brought his hand down at the spot that was both ass and thigh. "But I will not," he delivered two forceful blows to either side, "stand for..." Left, then right, he put his arm into each swing. "Blatant," side to side, high, low and middle, "defiance." He finished off with four more smacks to the center of her ass.

The severity did as he intended. Her ass was a deep shade of red and she'd feel it for a few days. And his timing in bring the spanking to an end matched with the end of her will to fight. She'd gone limp across his knees just before the last two blows. When he let go of her wrist, her hand slipped down to his leg and took hold. Sobs racked her body, and she didn't seem aware he'd stopped.

An awkward struggle ensued as he worked to get her rolled over and sitting up in his lap, but as soon as he leaned her against his chest, Summer wrapped her arms around him and pushed her face against the crook of his neck. Her hot tears soaking his collar didn't dry up for a good while. Chase was left holding her, stroking her head, back, and that tender ass until she cried herself to sleep.

He did want to talk with her more, make sure she did under-stand he didn't want to run stampede over her, but he could tell her so when she was better settled. Right now, she probably didn't want or need to hear any more from him. Certainly couldn't be an easy adjustment in any aspect of her life. She went from a fully independent, self-reliant, very alone woman to married, needing to coordinate movement, and navigate through crowds of people. And she'd done it all against her will.

Managing to pull her boots off, he finished relieving her of her pants then carried her to the bed. He was careful to set her down so her ass didn't hit, letting her continue to sleep, and drew up the quilt. Still early in the day, he collected his hat and coat from the pegs by the door and went to see if there was anything more to Mrs. Miller's situation to be investigated. Before he returned, he stopped by the train station to send a wire to his brother. Something was going on at the bank, but without the specific knowledge of banking, he didn't know what or how to proceed. He returned to the house to find Summer at the stove, still sniffing and rubbing her ass in between flipping those pieces of soggy bread in the pan. It might have been an unnecessary peace offering, but Chase wasn't ever going to turn down a chance to eat her cooking.

CHASE LOOKED up as Wickfield ushered Summer to another group of people. He could see she was growing steadily more uncomfortable with the introductions to the women of the area. He also noted the groups of women, most broken up by age, were having very mixed reactions to her.

As they moved toward the last group of ladies, the one that Mrs. Nelson stood with, the hairs on the back of his neck stood up. None of these women were in town when they'd first arrived, and Summer's interaction with at least Nelson had been tense.

"Are you planning to ride out tomorrow Marshal Storm?"

Chase turned back to the men he stood with. "First light,"

Chase confirmed. The increase in missing cattle had surpassed what most every rancher said could be accounted for with natural predators and the weather. And though it wasn't really his job to catch rustlers, no one really had confidence in Sheriff Buckley. "The melt off should allow for good tracking."

"You don't think it is some of them Musgrove boys, done set up again, do ya?"

Chase worked not to laugh at the old man. He likely had some deep seated disgust of that outlaw gang given his age and Chase's understanding he had once lived in Denver. "The last of the Musgroves were taken out almost twenty years ago," Chase said, setting his hand on the old miner's shoulder. "And it wasn't cattle stolen, but horses, remember?" Chase waited to see if the old man could recall the crimes for which Lee Musgrove was charged. The man wasn't given a trial; Marshal Cook had done his best, but when a mob was out to lynch someone, they usually succeeded.

"That man had a bad temper."

"Yes, he did, but he's long buried," Chase assured him. "There are a good number of gangs running up this way out of Arizona and New Mexico. The hard country here gives them access to easy hideouts."

"That's why you been sent up, right, Marshal?" Mr. Winter asked, though his doubt and contempt showed through. Not that Chase would blame the man. According to him, he'd lost some fifty head. That kind of loss would hurt any small rancher. And seeing as the cattlemen were already dealing with the tensions of the long-standing feud between sheep herders and cattlemen, the additional stress of rustlers was going to make tempers short and drawdowns quick.

"I'm sure it's one of the reasons," Chase said with a soft chuckle.

It looked like one of the other men was about to speak on the matter, but as he opened his mouth, Summer stomped past. "I'm leaving," she snarled and didn't pause to explain or to wait for Chase to say his good-byes. A minute later, Mrs. Wickfield stepped up.

"I'm sorry Marshal, I might have not tried to introduce your lovely wife to the town's society ladies."

Chase looked over his shoulder to see Mrs. Nelson and three others all looking at him. Their expression looked to be ones of smug victory. And Chase knew it was because they had managed to run Summer off. Clearly, there was a pecking order in this town, and Summer was low in status.

"Them nasty old biddies," Mr. Winter grumbled. "Do the lot of them some good to have a strap applied to their asses. Pardon me, Mrs. Wickfield."

"What happened?" Chase asked, knowing it would help when he spoke with Summer to have some idea of what might have transpired.

"Seems they didn't take too kindly to Summer not having any kin to speak of. They put so much false worth in blood lines."

"Your wife ain't got no other kin but you?" the old miner asked.

"No, she lost everyone in the raid on Highfield," Chase said absently.

"Lordy, your woman survived Highfield?"

"Yes, she did," Chase said, relieved that at least the men around here could appreciate what it took for someone to fight their way through life after such a thing. Again, Chase looked back over his shoulder. Reverend Wickfield was now with those ladies and it looked like their husbands. Mr. Nelson, Mr. Codwells, and a man he knew owned one of the small silver mines, Mr. Jakes. It did seem the reverend might be doing his best to smooth things out between the group and Summer, but given he'd not seen Summer approach Codwells to give her apology, he'd doubt it would go well. "Was that all they took offense to?"

"I fear not," Mrs. Wickfield said with a sigh. "Seems they know a bit about your family and…"

Chase's stomach dropped. "And have decided I married beneath myself."

"More, that you were taken advantage of by a gold digger." She sighed. "I am sorry, Marshal. Your wife truly is a sweet woman, even if she's a bit reserved."

"She is sweet and reserved, and she's justified in that last one," Chase managed to not let his words be biting. "If you'll pardon me, I'm sure by now my wife is putting some of her bread in the oven, and I don't want to miss it coming out." He nodded at everyone then turned and all but ran home.

He found Summer at the stove, and given the smell, she was frying chicken. "That smells wonderful," he said, hoping to elicit a smile, maybe just get her to relax her posture a bit, take her fist off her hip. She didn't. Hanging his hat and coat on the pegs, he sat on the stool and removed his Sunday shoes. "Not everyone is going to like you right away. Those ladies…" he heard her snort at the word. "Those ladies, are used to being in charge. I'm sure they don't know what to do with someone they can't bully."

Summer blew a strand of hair from her face and remained silent. Chase moved behind the curtain to remove his Sunday clothes. "I didn't even know you had money," Summer said, a good deal of heat in her voice. "And I didn't want to marry you."

"Summer, I know that, honey," Chase said, carrying his shirt with him when he stepped up behind her and wrapped an arm around her.

"What did you tell those people?"

"Tell those people, when?"

"When they asked how we even met?" She shoved him back and pried his arm from her waist. "Did you tell them you found me in a prison? I'm not a damn criminal." He didn't mistake the break in her voice.

"I told them the truth." Chase said, jumping aside when she needed to move to pull the chicken out of the pan.

"And exactly what's your version of the truth?"

"There is only one version of the truth, Summer," Chase said, taking a moment to put his shirt on and button it up. "I told them that we met when we went after the same outlaw, that at my insistence, we ended up in a place where the judge and sheriff were corrupt, the deputy was at the very least a despot, and when they refused you due process over a very minor civil offense, I offered to wed you. That's what I told them."

"You should have told them something else," Summer snapped.

"Like what?"

'I don't know," she said, dropping the plate of crispy chicken on the table and turning to reach for the oven door. "Something respectable, something that people might accept."

"Hey, slow that pony, miss," Chase warned, stepping back up to her as soon as the bread was safely in the oven. Taking her arm, he forced her to face him. "There is nothing unacceptable about how we ended up hitched. Nothing that isn't good and respectable about any of our pasts." He put his fingers under her chin and lifted her head so he could look her in the eye. "I'm not ashamed of it. Not ashamed of you in any way. I still think I'm pretty damn lucky things turned out the way they have. And I don't want you to ever be ashamed of anything, either. Not your past, not how we became husband and wife, not any of it. You hold your head up." He lifted her chin a bit more. "Because no matter what anyone says, I'm proud to be your husband." Still holding her chin up, he raised his other hand and brushed the stray copper-gold strand from her face and tucked it behind her ear. "I'm proud, even if you are a bit stubborn and ornery," he said and saw her almost smile.

"You just say that because you want that bread I just put in the oven," she told him with a pout that wasn't really a pout.

"Naw." Chase chuckled. "I say it because it's true..." He pulled her close then reached past her for the chicken.

"You touch that chicken, Chase Storm, and you'll see ornery," Summer warned, grabbing his arm and pulling it back so it held her.

"You're about the meanest woman I've ever known," he said, letting her push him down into the chair. He watched in amazement as she leaned over and set her hands on his thighs, smoothing upward to where his britches opened. She slipped to her knees as she freed him from the restrictive material. He was hardening fast, but when she wrapped her hand around the base of his shaft, the rush of blood was so much, his head felt a bit light. It only took a few strokes and he was ready for what she might have planned next.

That she was a quick study at such things benefited him immensely. That she realized rather quickly she could control most everything they shared this way, not so much. He certainly didn't mind her doing as she pleased, and it was always his intent that she should be pleased, but he preferred to be master in the bed. Today, though, they were in her kitchen, and when she leaned in and flicked her tongue over his cock, he handed the reins to her completely.

With a moan, Chase tipped his head back and spread his legs a bit more as she swallowed him. That she had the ability to take him so deep in her mouth, amazed. He'd not known that with any other woman. Not even ones he paid top dollar for. Everything about his wife pleased him. Having her was a humbling experience.

He let his hands drift to her head then tangled his fingers in her hair, urging her to take more and take it faster. Her head bobbing up and down in his lap as her fist stroked in time took him further than he thought he could go and still hold back. When she cupped his sac and carefully squeezed him, he knew he wasn't going to last much longer. Even when she used one of his tricks and slowed down what she did, he couldn't whoa this horse. Still, he tried and as soon as she felt he was, she made the push to bring him to his end.

His cum shot down the back of her throat, his cock jerking hard with each subsequent firing. Summer kept her lips wrapped firmly around him. Her head continued to dip down and lift up and her fist tightened, wringing every last drop from him. He shuddered through the last of it then looked down to find her looking up at him with an expression that told him she'd out gunned him this time.

"So how mean am I?" she asked, rocking back on her haunches.

"Meanest woman this side of the Mississippi," Chase managed to get out. "But I know just how to soften you up." Standing, he grabbed her up then swung around enough he could set her on the table. Forcing her to her back and shoving her knees back, he retook his seat, flipped her skirts aside and leaned in. "I think you make the best meal," he said before covering her sex with his mouth.

Summer's giggle ended on a cry as she reached around her dress to take fistfuls of his hair. Lifting her hips, she pushed into his mouth even as she pulled him down more.

Chase put a bit more effort into what he did. Taking the swelling nub in his mouth, he sucked hard, making her cry out again. He stayed there as he added two fingers to her pussy and stroked deep. Already, he could feel himself hardening again and Summer winding up like a rattler ready to strike any moment. One more hard draw on her clit and she released.

"Chase." His name on her lips as she panted through the sensation gave him the last of what he needed to restore life fully to his cock. He stood and pulled her ass to the very edge of the table and slammed his rod deep inside her.

Her legs wrapped around his back as he leaned over her and pumped in and out like a man trying to pull water from a dry well. He was determined to have her soak his cock with her juices.

"Chase," she called, urging him on, trying to take him deeper, moaning harshly when he hit the back of her tunnel, "Chase." Her legs pulled him in, not giving him as much freedom to withdraw. Again, she was trying to control it.

Reaching back, he grabbed her left calf, pulling it and then lifting it high in the air. This opened her up to him in a whole different way, and as he returned to the hard, long, deep undulations, he again felt her tightening.

"Come on, Summer, rain on me. Give it to me. Spill it out." He leaned back and put his fingers on her clit. Two strokes and she came apart, not only coating his shaft but the entire front of his pants. "My turn," he told her, and dropping her leg, he took hold of her waist and rode hard.

"Yes, Chase," she panted, urging him on.

Having just come, it took him a while and Summer took advantage, claiming one more for herself before he pulled out and sent his seed splattering against the inside of her thigh. Breathless, he again leaned forward, settling all his weight on top of her. His head resting over her heart, he could hear the way it thumped in her breast as she too tried to catch her breath.

He didn't know how long they lay there, not long enough as far as he was concerned. But Summer started to squirm under him, and when he wouldn't lift, she thumped him on the shoulder. "You're gonna make me burn the bread," she complained.

"Well, can't have that now," Chase grumbled but gave her a teasing smile. Lifting off, he helped her sit up. Her skirts piled at her waist, leaving her leg with his cum still on it exposed. "You made a mess in your kitchen, missy," he said, ducking back when she took a swing at his head.

"Not me," she told him, using two fingers to scrape some of the thick white cream from her soft flesh. "You," she accused then stuck those fingers in her mouth and sucked them clean.

It was almost enough to turn him for a third time, but while the spirit was willing, the body was not. "Well, I'll help you clean," he said, tucking his cock back in his pants and closing them up before he gave in and let the bread burn.

"I think I can manage," Summer told him as she worked herself off the table. "Besides, don't you want to eat some chicken?"

"I've become rather fond of eating pussy," he said as she made her way to the oven and peeked in on the bread. The fresh aroma wafted through the air, making his stomach rumble. "But man can't dine on his wife alone."

He heard her giggle as he took a rag, wet it, and wiped the table for her before taking his normal seat and letting her serve him supper. He never missed how she'd select carefully which pieces of meat to give him or how he was always given the larger portions of what she made to go with it. And he always smiled when he'd see her smile as she watched him clean every crumb.

More than telling her she was the finest cook, showing her he appreciated her skill and efforts made her happy. He'd no doubt that she'd be giddy every day all day once she started serving up her cooking to others. How could anyone not like even these simple meals?

Surely, if the way she looked when he left her the next morning was any indication, even the group of old biddies wouldn't be able to tear her down. After all, when Deputy Zander arrived just in time for breakfast and very much looked like a man about to come in his chair as he sat eating Chase's favorite meal of fried soggy bread, Summer heard so much praise she actually blushed.

She'd sent them both out the door with a meal wrapped in linen and assured Chase she'd packed him an entire loaf of bread. She made sure he had everything he'd need to see him through the next several days, including a long sweet kiss that left him aching to return to her every day he was away.

Chapter 20

S ummer made her way down the boardwalk toward the bank, the basket on her arm still sending up the tangy scent of the baked goods she'd made just for this chore.

Apologizing to the fat banker wasn't her idea, but Chase had warned her to have it done with before he returned, and while she didn't expect him for a week or more, she'd managed to get the starter for her sourdough finished just after he departed, and the first thing she'd decided to make were pretzels.

Her mother and aunt used to make huge batches and sell them throughout the year for a penny a piece. The old recipe was easy and quick because it required less rising time. She'd started them last night and finished them off as she made herself ready to go out in public again for the first time since she'd been shunned by the town's most prominent women.

She'd taken care with her hair and dress, and just as Chase had told her, she held her head high when she stepped out. Not too high, though. She didn't want to be seen as snooty. It did seem that was one reason Mrs. Lafter wasn't very well liked, though Summer did have a chance to hear what she'd been told about the woman who ran the boarding house's cooking ability confirmed. The old spinster thought herself even too good for Mrs. Nelson and her gang.

With a deep, calming breath, Summer opened the door to the bank, rather surprised to see it packed full of dirty, stinking men. Judging by the dirt that clung in clumps to their skin and clothes, she guessed this was the first herd of miners come to town. Their loud, forceful presence clearly unnerved the clerks, and even Mr. Codwells was staying well back behind the counter, though the bars running up a few feet prevented pretty much any possibility he might be reached.

A few loud catcalls and lude remarks had Summer gripping the rifle she carried in her other hand. Though mostly concealed by her skirts, she'd not left without it. She made her way up to the front, more on the side as her business here wasn't banking, but one of the men in line took exception and, grabbing her by the arm holding the basket, pulled her over and pinned her between his body and the counter.

"Now see here," Mr. Codwells shouted but remained at the back of the bank. "That's the marshal's wife. You'd do well to leave her be."

"Marshal's wife?" the man who held her asked, leaning in to sniff her hair. "Well, how'd a lazy slob, like marshals are, get such a fine filly like yourself."

"He asked nice," Summer said, lifting the rifle so the barrel rested under the man's chin. "Like I will now." The man froze as soon as the cold steel touched his skin, and the rest of the room went still and silent. "Please, let go my arm and step back."

She kept a smile on her lips, but the glare she gave didn't match, and the man, keeping his hands up, took a step backward. "Pardon, Missus, don't mean no harm."

"I'm sure," Summer said, keeping her barrel on him as he took another step backward. "I'm sure none of you mean any harm. I'm sure all you want is to do a little honest business with the fine people at this bank. But I think you fail to understand how rather overwhelming such a huge group of you all can be. There are, after all, only so many clerks and so many windows." She waved the barrel of the Yellow Boy past the crowd. "So how about you all step outside, line up nicely out there, and when one of you has been served and steps out, the next might come in and get the same wonderful treatment." Before she even finished the suggestion, one she really had no authority to make, the door was opened and men all but stampeded out. Only about five remained, and with a sigh of relief, the clerks again took up their windows and helped with their transactions.

Summer turned back around and, lifting her basket and rifle to the counter, called for the bank manager to come speak with her. Codwells came, if for no other reason than he didn't want to be seen as someone intimidated by the woman who'd just cleared his bank for him.

"How might I help you, Mrs. Storm?" he asked, his tone gruff, but his nose sniffing the air.

"Well, it seems I might have taken the bit and ridden a little too hard the other day, and I've come to apologize, make peace if you will."

"That's quite amenable of you," he said, and Summer frowned but refrained from telling him the word was amiable.

"Well, yes, I know I do get a bit…" Summer went on, putting some coyness in her tone, "… emotional, when I see some poor woman in such desperate ways." She managed not to choke on the words, and Codwells appeared to be a sucker for them. "Not every woman is as capable as I of taking care of herself in the face of…" she looked back over her shoulder as one man went out and another came in, "… unscrupulous characters. So I do apologize."

"Of course, I understand. My own wife tells me often that women must band together as it takes quite of few of them to do all a man can. Apology quite accepted," he finished, and Summer managed to keep her finger off the trigger. Codwells stepped a little closer and took a deep breath. "What is that fine aroma, Mrs. Storm?"

"Oh, yes, I nearly forgot, how silly of me," she cooed as she lifted back the towel and showed the man the basket of fresh, warm, golden pretzels. "A gesture, to show you I mean everything I say." She lifted one from the basket, not missing how the miners were now creeping closer to smell the air and see what she had. "I think you might enjoy these. My mother never had one left when she made them."

"May I?" Codwells asked, reaching out even as he asked.

"I brought them for you, and of course, for your wonderful, hardworking tellers." She watched as he lifted one, shuffled it from hand to hand as he blew on his fingers and then took a bite.

Much like Chase did with anything she made, Codwells closed his eyes as he chewed. "This is delicious," he breathed.

"Well, take another; I made plenty."

The man did, and then one of the tellers stepped up and Summer held the basket out to him. Before Summer had finished seeing everyone working at the bank had at least two pretzels, the building was filled with the sound of people enjoying their eats.

"Ma'am?" one of the miners called. Summer turned to find him giving her a pleading look.

"Want to try some?" she asked as he nodded enthusiastically. Summer took one of the three left and broke it in half. She handed half to the man who asked and half to the man standing next to him. "If you like them, I will have some for sale later today. A penny a piece, if you can afford it."

"Oh, yes, ma'am," the man said, chewing and swallowing hard. "Yes, ma'am, I can afford it. This is pure heaven, ma'am."

Summer broke another and handed some to two more miners who also agreed they'd be willing to spend a penny on a whole one. As she lifted out the last, Summer took a bite, chewed, and swallowed. "Well then, I should have plenty more ready by four o'clock. Just come down to the jail and have your money ready," Summer said, collecting her basket and her rifle. "And tell your friends to come as well."

"Yes, ma'am. Yes, sir-ee."

Summer left the bank with a smile. She might not yet be able to really give these people a product they'd pay good money for, but if she could make a few cents selling simple bread goods, it was at least a certain way to help add to her account and make her dream happen sooner.

She sold every single pretzel she made that day and already had men asking if they could pay her to make a dozen or more they could take back with them. She'd never made so many pretzels in her life as that week, but as she sat counting the money on the table in front of her, she could only see good things riding her way.

By the time Chase came home, Summer had established a most regular customer base, and by chance, she'd taken up feeding men who landed in the jailhouse below her for some minor offense. The town paid her to do that, and everyone had a good laugh when it was discovered a few men were getting themselves arrested on purpose just to eat her cooking. Of course, that didn't make her a friend of the old spinster running the boarding house as it was something she had been getting paid to do. But after a few days, the slight tension vanished and the woman remarked she was glad to not have to give her good vittles to such sinners and louts.

Several times, though, through the waves of miners coming to town, Chase had to run her out of the jail, telling her to stop trying to look through all the wanted notices. She could still bribe the sheriff and deputies to let her look through them with whatever baked good or canned goods she made. The arrival of the first fruits of the season added more to her stockpile of money as she solidified the arrangement she made with Mr. Nelson and, using the supplies he ordered just for her, started cooking up jams and sauces that she then placed in his store for purchase. Even at the higher prices Nelson chose to sell her creations at, they still couldn't keep stock for long.

Summer would continue to go through Nelson's suppliers for now, but she started making herself known at the train station when produce was brought in. Knowing, too, with the last of the snows melting off and the nights warming above freezing each day, local farmers would also have things to sell, she took careful note of what she would have to use and what was most popular. Once her belongings arrived, she'd start right away making everything else she could. But even with the additional work space created by the long bench Chase had made, she continued to run out of space to work and store things. She needed her own building, and the one she had her eye on was only a few more dollars out of reach. She also needed it so she could stop hearing Chase complain about how hard she was working and that she needed to hire help. Twice already, he'd woke her up from where she'd fallen asleep canning, and the second time, he bent her in half and made it hard to sit the next day. Now she was forbidden from working on anything past nine o'clock.

Frustrating as it was, it did give her time to both enjoy the benefits of being a married woman with a capable husband and still get some rest. Days that Chase was called out overnight, Summer made up for time lost submitting to what she now mockingly called her bedtime. Still, if she could just get enough together to put a deposit down, she'd feel much better.

And perhaps if she'd have stuck to earning money through her cooking talents, things with Chase would have stayed on track. But she wasn't very good at ignoring temptation when the payout had the potential to be huge. And overhearing the sheriff mention one of the farmers reported seeing smoke coming from Nearfall Bluff and that it could be the three men they'd just been sent bills on... each one was a ten-dollar bounty. If she could take those men, she'd have enough to buy the building by mid-June.

"WHERE YA' headed?"

Summer jumped and spun, her hand going right to the pistol at her hip. "Damn, Chase, you startled me," she complained then finished bridling her mare.

"Sorry," he said, stepping up to press against her back. His lips settled on her neck and worked their way under the collar of her shirt.

"Marshal," Summer chided, but her moan followed when his hand settled on her ribs, just under her breast. She leaned back against him. "Didn't you have enough this morning?"

His chest shook with his soft laughter. "That was only breakfast. I will need a few more... feedings," he said, and Summer burst out laughing. "I'm a big man. I need to eat a lot."

Turning in his arms, she set her hand on his crotch and pressed. He was already stiffening. "You are a big man," she teased. "But you do know you're risking getting fat." Summer slid her hand up past his gun belt where his flat, hard muscled stomach lay. "You don't want to be struggling to get... mounted... you know, like the sheriff and all."

"That's not nice, missy," Chase said, only half-heartedly chiding her. "I'm sure Miss Lyn was only speaking out of jealousy."

She looked up and saw Chase pressing his lips together and trying not to smile. The poor sheriff's prowess as a man was put in question when the woman he normally visited in the saloon in Creed got in a snit over him turning his head toward some new woman who had started there. "I'm sure," Summer agreed as she ran her hand over the defined stomach muscles, up his chest and across his broad shoulders. "And you'll never have his problem when it comes to getting mounted, right?" It might have been a more pointed question than he cared for. For while Chase had no aversion to hard physical labor and often pitched in with any work that needed doing, more than once, she'd caught him with Angelica Codwells or her cousin Stephanie Porter on his arm.

The young ladies had taken to trying to prove Summer wasn't a suitable match for a Storm. And Summer had to concede they could talk to him about things Summer didn't have any knowledge on, like the layout of the governor's mansion in Denver or the dealings of the new state's politically powerful. Chase might have chosen a lawman's career, but his family was high society, influential and, given the steadily arriving furnishings and housewares Chase was sent to help settle him into his new home, very, very wealthy.

The fact that this town's high society was not giving disapproval for the way the two girls threw themselves at a married man grated. If Chase even knew how they spoke about different ways he could rid himself of Summer and select a more suitable wife, she didn't know. He never commented on it. And it left Summer torn, because as much as she wanted her freedom to start and run the eatery as she wanted, the idea of walking away from Chase at the end of September and leaving him to pursue one of those ladies chafed.

She could tell herself all day long she'd walk away at the start of fall, start the life she'd dreamed of even before she'd lost everything, but when the sun set behind the peaks and stars filled the night sky in abundance, Chase took her in his arms and made her reconsider every plan she made.

He sighed before stepping back a bit and grabbing her chin to make her look right at him. "I should have his problem." It was more a warning, she knew. He'd already said he didn't like jealous women. And he'd complained it was a show of distrust that she'd be concerned he escorted any woman down the boardwalk when she was alone and so many miners, ranch hands, and drifters were passing through. "Because I'm a married man, with a willing wife."

Summer nodded, stepped back, then turned and reached for

the saddle. Chase beat her to it and lifted it easily over the animal. She stood aside and let him secure it in place, warmed by how he always took the time to make sure it was in good enough condition, or at least good enough for her standards. He'd offered to buy her a new one; hers once belonged to Sergeant Dexter, and he'd spent years in it before her. But she wasn't ready to let that mean old cavalry man's prized possession go. Like the Yellow Boy he'd sold her for half the amount of her second bounty, it was more than a useful tool; it was a reminder that she'd survived everything life threw at her.

"You didn't say where you were going?" Chase reminded her as he made a final check of the cinch.

Summer started; she'd not really been prepared to explain her dealings today. And although he'd mostly done so with a teasing tone, Chase warning her off going after outlaws was true. Nearfall was out near enough to the Sheffield place where she got her dairy goods. "I need buttermilk." It was out of her mouth before she could stop it, and she looked away so he didn't see the lie.

"Mmm," Chase said, putting his arms around her and squeezing, "you gonna make another one of those cakes?"

"Maybe." Summer giggled. It wouldn't hurt to ride out and pick up some buttermilk, Maybe a cake would be how she soothed him after she brought in those outlaws.

"Maybe I should come with you and make sure you get enough," Chase said, and Summer's stomach cramped. If he went, she'd have no choice but to make that her only errand of the day. She'd not even be able to do some scouting.

"Well..." Trying to think of how to put him off without drawing suspicion, she was saved when Deputy Brown appeared at the livery doors.

"Marshal, The Dark Boys and the Wet Walls are at it again and they're standing on the tracks this time," Brown said. The two rival groups of miners sure had it out for each other, and any time they could start a fight, they did.

"I'm coming," Chase grumbled then took the time to lift her into the saddle. He set his hand on her thigh and squeezed. "Bring back enough for at least two cakes."

"Oh, so I can actually sell one this time, before you eat it?" she teased as she leaned down to kiss him.

"No, so I can eat them both after I'm done eating you," he said, lifting his hand to set it on her arm, the way he did when he silently conveyed his want for her to stay safe.

If she'd perhaps heeded the warning and just got the damn buttermilk, but the next hand that grabbed her arm wasn't conveying that message, and the one it did convey wasn't going to be nearly as bad as the message Chase would send her.

Chapter 21

C hase shoved the last of the rowdy miners into the overcrowded cell. The decision to keep all the working men apart from the three rustlers brought in only an hour ago by Buckley and Winter was more for the safety of the rustlers than anything. Miners liked beef too, and rustlers cutting into a rancher's profits drove up the costs and often decreased the quality. Those men would face trial and likely a long prison term, but Chase wasn't going to let anyone either beat them to death or hang them without due process.

When he returned to the front office, he again tilted his head and listened for any sound from above telling him Summer was back and busy in the kitchen. Her errand to fetch back milk should have been rather fast, but it wasn't unusual for her to stay and chat with the Sheffield sisters. They were good woman, all working like Summer to be independent. Summer considered them friends, and he was thankful because, so far, she'd not really made any in town.

He'd otherwise be amused at how much sway that small group of females had over everyone—no one wanted to cross them—except for the fact they used their sway to keep Summer isolated from those she might make friends with. He did hope, when she finally moved her business out of their home and into a separate building and she started to need to hire people, loyalties would turn. People always put their pockets ahead of fear, especially fear that some spoiled girls and their mothers might not like them anymore.

He wasn't sure why she'd not already taken over the building she'd been eyeing for almost two months. It was a good location, close to the train station but not so close the train would be rattling windows as it made its way past. He knew there were other recently arrived business folks looking at the same property, and he worried if she hesitated and didn't place a deposit soon, she'd lose it to another.

"...and thirty," Sheriff Buckley finished and slid the cash toward Mr. Winter.

"That should take some of the pain off from the head you lost," Chase said and smiled at the man who never smiled.

"It's a start," Winter grumbled as he folded the cash and stuck it in his shirt pocket.

The man wasn't the most pleasant person to deal with. He was, like most, just trying to keep his ranch going through the adversities thrown at him. He worked hard, he helped his neighbors, and he kept to himself. No wife or kids, likely because of how bitter he was that he was forced to yield over a large section of his land for the train to come through. When he spoke to anyone at all, it was all he spoke about, and he lit into anyone who said anything positive about the damn tracks.

"Well, let's hope we catch up to the rest of these men stealing livestock. No one wants to see hard working folks robbed of their livelihood," Chase said, again trying to convey to the man he wasn't alone in any of this.

"Your gal put any more of her goods up in the store?" he asked, setting his hat on his head as he headed for the door.

"I believe she made up something with the berries she picked, but she wouldn't even let me taste any," Chase told him, knowing Summer turned her buckets of red elderberries and strawberries into jams. His comment, though, caused laughter among the lawmen as it'd been reported on several occasions everyone could hear Summer yelling at him to get his fingers out of her pot or bowl.

"Did it stop you?" Winter asked, and Chase felt his brows draw together. "Her not letting you? Did it stop you?"

Chase laughed and shook his head. "No," he admitted. "She sent over elderberry and strawberry preserves." More laughter as the man gave him a nod and maybe a smile and reached for the door.

He was nearly hit in the face when Charlie from the mercantile rushed in. "Marshal, you need get over to Doc Riot," he said, panting.

"What happened?" Chase asked, already lifting his hat and heading for the door.

"I think Mrs. Storm fell or something. Doc sent me for you," Charlie said, stepping out of the way so Chase didn't trample him as he was almost running before he was out of the office.

The doctor's building was at the other end of town, like most of the important things, close to the train, and Chase was running full speed before he was more than a few streets down. He headed around back, as that was where the exam rooms and beds were. Climbing the steps, he tried the door, and finding it locked, he began to pound on it. Mrs. Bleese answered, and Chase pushed in.

"What happened?"

"She's all right, Marshal," Mrs. Bleese told him with that calm demeanor that made her such a good doctor's assistant. "She fell, took a lump on her head and some scratches."

"Can I see her?" Chase asked and felt everything in him uncoil.

"Back here, Marshal," Doc called, stepping out of the room

to grab a bottle from the shelf opposite the door. He stepped back in and Chase followed.

"You didn't need to call him," Summer griped then hissed and whined when the doctor used the cloth, soaked in whatever was in the bottle to clean the large cut on her hand. "I'm fine."

"She is," Doc confirmed, turning to look at Chase. "But the man's your husband, and he should know if you're here."

Chase saw her glare at the man, but her heated look was broken by her cry and pulling away as he pushed back the shirt sleeve, rewet the cloth, and wiped at her arm. "What happened?" He took a moment to look her over. Dirty and disheveled, her hands and knuckles scraped, he might guess maybe she was thrown from her horse, got caught in the stirrup and dragged, but her clothes weren't torn that he could tell and no broken bones.

"I fell, I slipped and fell," Summer snapped and put up a bit of a fight when the doctor tried to take a second pass at her arm with the cloth.

"Down a mine shaft," Doc added dryly as he held the cloth against her elbow for a minute. When he pulled back, it was bloody, and he tossed it aside and wet a new one and again held it against her elbow. He pulled it back again. "I don't know, might need stitches, but it's right above the bend, could heal fine on its own."

Chase heard the man, but he wasn't really listening past the announcement Summer fell down a shaft. These hills and mountains were littered with them, but none that he knew of lay on the road between town and the Sheffield place. She'd have had to go clear back to at least Nearfall and...

"Tell me you didn't go out looking for those rustlers," Chase said and watched her look away. "Summer," he yelled then bit his tongue. He wouldn't do this in public, but damn, if the doctor left him alone and the door had a lock. "They've been caught and the bounty paid," Chase said, doing his best to sound calm even though rage was brewing in his gut. She swung back toward him then, disappointment and maybe shame on her face. Didn't matter, she could regret this bit of recklessness every day for the next year and it wouldn't get her out of what he had planned, and what he planned would have her regretting her actions for the next year. "I'll be out front." He turned on his heels and stepped out of the room.

He was a little surprised to find Sam Black waiting there. Man hated town, never came in but to get supplies, and he always went straight to the mercantile then straight back out of town.

"Marshal," he greeted. "How's the missus?"

"She'll mend," Chase said.

"Yeah, she didn't look too much worse for wear, but her arm bleed pretty good, and she was wobbly as a new colt when I pulled her out."

"I'm sorry? *You* pulled her out?"

"Yes, sir, lucky I heard her. She'd not have ever climbed out on her own, and she had her horse a good bit hidden."

"Well then, I guess I owe you my deepest thanks and much more," Chase said and held out his hand.

"We can call it good if you can get Mrs. Storm to make me one of those fine batches of cookies she made a while back."

"I'll have her make you two," Chase assured. Wasn't like she'd be sitting down resting for a good while. She always cooked standing up, only sitting to eat. He shook the man's hand again and nodded back when he turned to leave.

It was a slightly longer wait than he might have thought, given Summer didn't look beaten down, but almost an hour later, voices drifted out and Chase turned to find Summer headed for him, Mrs. Bleese on her heels.

"Now you come back if you start to feel sick and dizzy again," the woman was saying. "And you clean those cuts good;

you can't make your fine creations with a hand and arm all rotted off."

Chase looked past Summer, who refused to take her eyes off the ground, to see the doctor coming out drying his hands on a towel. He nodded toward Chase. "She'll be fine. Just watch to see if she becomes unsteady on her feet again or has trouble staying awake." Chase's confusion must have shown; how would a few scrapes and cuts cause those problems? Doc chuckled. "I suspect she's hard headed enough not be to be taken out by a rock falling on her head."

"I'll keep my eye on her, Doctor, thank you," Chase said, feeling his gut roll a bit. Exactly how close had he just come to losing this woman? He stepped close and pulled her against him. She resisted but then leaned in.

"Maybe this will convince her to stick to baking. Lord help us all if we had to go without her pretzels. Whole county might revolt," Doc said then turned back for the office he kept next to patient rooms.

"This might not have, but I have something that will," he said so only Summer heard. Her gasp and sniff said she knew exactly what he meant, and as he forced a smile to his lips to pass on to Mrs. Bleese, he tucked Summer under his arm and started back up the street.

"Chase," she called softly.

"You all right, or did you bribe the doctor to say you were?" he asked. No reason to add to her current misery. Not when he'd be adding to it plenty as soon as she was fit enough.

"I'm fine, my arm hurts, but that's it. Really, it wasn't as much as it might be made out to be."

"Well, I suppose when we get around to talking about it, I can decide that for myself." He stopped speaking to tip his hat at a few of the ladies passing on the walk. "What I do know is you now owe Mr. Black a few batches of your cookies, at least. Did you even go to the dairy and get milk?"

"Yes, Chase, I did. And I'm sorry. I only wanted to have a look. I thought if I found something—"

"Did you?" he asked, leading her up the steps and opening the door to the apartment.

"Nothing suggesting anyone had been around the area in a while." She waited while he hung his hat on the peg.

"They were probably never there," Chase said, taking a deep breath before turning to face her. "Go get undressed, put on your nightgown."

"My night… Chase?"

"Don't make me tell you again, missy," he said, using the sternest tone he could muster.

"Chase, I have supper to make and…" He shook his head at her. "I at least need to take care of Shilo. The buttermilk's in my packs—"

"You get undressed, you wash your face, and you get in the bed," he said, turning back to pull his hat off the peg. "I'll take care of your horse and bring in your packs. We'll eat whatever I can mix together when I get back. Do what I tell you and have it done before I get back."

He pulled open the door and stepped out without looking to see if she was already doing it. Shutting the door tightly, he made his way down the steps then entered the jail from the back. When he passed the four cells that lined both walls to the side, he wasn't surprised when one of the men asked what Summer was fixing for supper.

"Sorry, fellas, you're stuck eating Miss Lofter's cooking tonight."

"Why? What happened?" someone asked, and a number of men stepped up to the bars.

"Mrs. Storm took a little fall; she's not cooking for anyone tonight."

"But she'll be good as new by tomorrow. Won't she be able to cook then?"

"I'm not promising nothing," Chase said then felt a real smile when he heard one of the Black Boys cuss and accuse another one of being the reason they was locked up with no chance of getting some of that fine cooking. Damn, if men were brawling in the streets, hoping to get Summer to feed them, he may just have to buy her that damn building himself as a means to preserve the peace in this town.

"How's the missus, Marshal?" Sheriff asked.

"Good as anyone who fell down a mine shaft can be," Chase said and checked the wall for the calendar of events. The town council would be meeting to plan the July celebrations, and he wanted a chance to ask about funding to seal off some of the more dangerous mines in the area.

"Town gonna have to be willing to do something about those open shafts now," Buckley said. "Mrs. Storm gettin' swallowed up by one, and we all go back to starving."

Chase shook his head. Even this man, who'd had a pretty rocky start with her, was now mostly supportive. When she finally opened those doors, she'd be as successful as anyone might be. And he might hope too busy to keep trying her hand at bounty hunting. "Well, I'm gonna do my darnedest to keep that from happening, but at least for tonight and tomorrow, I'll be sticking close to my wife. Doc was worried the knock she took on the head might cause some more trouble."

"Shouldn't be no worry. Brown is walking tonight, and until Zander finds more trail, ain't no catching the rest of them responsible for all the missing livestock."

"Right, then," Chase said. "Well, I need to get a horse put up. Think it too much to ask for you to keep an ear open." He pointed to the ceiling. "If you hear any thumps or bangs—"

"Naw, not a worry. Go on, and if we don't see you in the next few days, we know where to find you."

"Hopefully not in Summer's stew pot," Chase said with a chuckle.

"Well, you still have all your fingers, so I can't see her chopping you to bits soon," Buckley said, also laughing.

Chase nodded and, leaving the building, headed to the livery where he assumed the little red mare waited. This would be a good chance for him to cool his temper before trying to deal with his wayward wife. He already knew he'd need to let her heal before he tanned her hide. And he knew he needed to learn why she'd take such a risk. She was making great money with what she did now, and every time the train pulled in without her belongs onboard, she cussed about how much money she wasn't making without whatever she waited for to make it to her. She shouldn't have to wait too much more. So why she was so impatient now, he wasn't sure. Though thirty dollars would probably go a long way for her. Even with the building secured, she'd need to order the equipment needed to outfit it. She'd every item marked out of the mail order catalog and Mr. Nelson was ready to place it on her say so. Maybe she just needed to swallow her pride and go see Mr. Codwells at the bank for a loan. Her business plan was certainly more well thought out and reasonable than most that got approved by the bank, and she'd proven a hundred times over, she had a product people would pay top money for. There was no reason she couldn't get a loan, and if she couldn't get it on her own, he could put his name on it as a backer.

Chase finished with Shilo and took some time to give some attention to Summer's ornery little mule. Sir was becoming as well-known as she was. But not in a good way with his penchant for biting and his ability to escape and turn up in the saloon in Creed or at some farmer's place mixing with the mares. He'd even shown up at the top of the steps at home, braying for Summer to let him in. He was only tolerated because Summer always compensated any injured party with some special baked good. And maybe a little because everyone knew she had some odd fondness for the animal.

His temper much dissipated, Chase headed home. He'd a few different ideas on how he'd handle this matter, insure it never happened again, but he needed to also sit and talk with Summer. Really talk with her. Find out what was behind this sudden ride into recklessness and, moreover, why she'd lied. Having thought about their exchange this morning, he knew now she had. Worse, he knew if he hadn't seen her head into the livery when he did and she'd ridden off not saying anything to him, if Sam Black hadn't come across her, he'd have had no idea where to look for her.

Pushing through the door, he hung his hat on the peg, set the packs on the floor, then sat on the stool to remove his boots. No sound came from behind the curtain so he pulled out the two jugs of buttermilk, ducked back out to set them in the bottom of the water barrel Summer used to keep things cool until she used them and stepped back in. Still no sound. For a minute, he wondered if maybe she'd hightailed it.

Carrying her packs to where she stored her things, he crossed to the curtain keeping their bed concealed. He drew it back, relieved to see a pair of bare feet and the frilly hem of her chemise. Stepping around, he got a good look at her. Asleep on her side, the sunlight adding to the transparency of the thread-bare dress. She really needed new clothes, but she refused to buy material or go into the dress shop with its readymade ladies' things.

He stepped a little closer, trying to discern if she was asleep or just not wanting to engage him. Steady, even breathing and those sweet soft snores she also made when she was especially tired said she was sound asleep. It wasn't likely a wild stampede down Main Street would wake her.

Chase stepped closer. When he noticed a dark mark at her ankle, he carefully pulled up the hem. Her calf was deeply bruised. Raising the gown more, he could see her thigh was as well. Further inspection showed the other leg to be equally banged up. She looked like she had gone bronc riding and after getting tossed, got stomped. Her knees were scraped, not deep, but he guessed the denim she wore protected her from those kinds of injuries. Lifting her hand made her moan and tug away. The cut on her palm was wrapped, but a bit of blood stained the bandage. Her nails were broken and chipped, she'd scrapes and cuts on her fingers and forearms. The gash on her left elbow, also bandaged, looked to still bleed, but it wasn't soaking the wrap.

Chase could guess that she'd tried hard to climb out on her own and probably slipped back down the shaft a few times. The doctor wasn't overly concerned with any of her injuries, save for her head, and Chase looked now to see if he could see where the rock might have hit. He couldn't, not through the thick hair. He'd maybe give her a better inspection when she woke up. For now, he unfolded the quilt and covered her. Of all the thoughts he'd had about how best to deal with this, he was now settled on one. And the minute he put it in effect, he knew it was the correct one.

Chapter 22

Summer overturned the container and banged on the bottom. The very last of the flour barely put a dusting on the table. She couldn't roll out dough without more flour. When she looked up, she found Chase staring at her from his bent position on the chair as he worked at repairing some piece of leather. The sight of his hands holding that thick, dark, worn strip made her ass clench but, also, her pussy.

Damn, it was madness to actually like that Chase held her accountable and that he was quick, direct, and pointed in any criticism he gave. His praise, on the other hand, was constant, real, and warm. He never let her guess how he might feel about anything. Even his skepticism about things she told him, wasn't derived from anything but her not being clear enough for him to understand what she was explaining.

There was something uniquely satisfying in having a man she found reliable. One who didn't treat her like a stupid child simply because she was born female. In fact, the only time he treated her like a fool was when she acted like one.

Could she have been more foolish than stepping out into that canyon, knowing there were dozens of abandoned mines but not knowing where a single one actually was? Not knowing the layout of any of them? And worse, not telling anyone she planned to go there? Even when she was only hunting bounties, she would send a wire to her friends in Missouri letting them know where she was heading, how long she planned to head that way, and who she was hunting so if something happened, she didn't end up in boot hill with no name on her headstone.

If Sam Black hadn't been passing through, who knows how long she'd have been down in that hole? It was stupid. She deserved what Chase might have planned for her. Only her own cowardice kept her from saying so this last week. But maybe he knew he could wait her out. Knew she had more desire to earn money than to forego getting a lickin'. She couldn't earn anything if she wasn't allowed to leave the house. She needed supplies and she needed to take what she'd already made to the mercantile. But she wasn't allowed to leave until she asked him to spank her. Maybe not even just spank her, as if that wasn't bad enough. She had to ask him specifically to 'punish her as he saw fit'.

The dough she worked again stuck to the table, and dropping her eyes a moment, she met his again. "I can't do this, Chase. I need supplies, and I need to get my things to the store so they can sell."

He sat back in the chair and stared at her. "You know what you have to do. I'm not holding you back from doing anything."

"Chase." She hated that she whined, but damn, who in their right mind asked to be made to not be able to sit for a month? He just stared at her. "Gawd," she said, stomping her feet. "Fine, fine, let's get it done. Punish me, do it. I'm ready."

"I don't think so. You didn't ask right," Chase said, leaning back over and working on the leather.

Was he actually going to make her say it exactly? Well, of course, he was. She knew that. And she'd said half of it, so why was the rest so hard? Because it made her question exactly what he'd do. More dough sticking to the table pushed past the resistance. "Chase, please punish me in the manner you see fit."

He leaned back in the chair again, pulled his watch from his pocket, and checked the time. "All right," he said, standing and laying the leather over the back of the chair. "We don't have a lot of time." He crossed to where she stood. His nearness made her heart pound and her stomach clench. But if it was out of fear or lust, she wasn't sure. The rush of wetness pooling between her legs when he set his hand on her cheek and smiled said lust. "I'm proud of you; you should know that." Her knees weakened a bit. "You're no coward, and you own your mistakes. I couldn't ask for more; I wouldn't ask for more." He leaned in and pressed his lips to hers briefly. "Get cleaned up, and I'll walk you to the mercantile so you can get what you need, place orders if you want. But it's nearing one o'clock, so best hurry."

"What?" Summer queried, already removing the apron she wore and striding to the bucket to wash her hands. "Ain't you gonna—"

"When we get back," he said, moving to the door to sit and put on his boots. "Hurry up, or you'll have to wait until Monday."

Summer wiped off the flour and sticky dough, careful not to scrub open the cut on her hand again, then she took a minute to wrap her long braid around her head and pin it. No one really gave her a second look anymore when she wore pants, but on days when she'd a wilder appearance, she got a few raised brows. Most seemed to know she was just haggard, trying to work hard, but a few, like Mrs. Nelson, still made it a point to be critical.

Turned out, the woman wasn't even in the shop today. Only Charlie, who put together her supplies with polite conversation and honest concern for how she was healing. Summer was almost done and ready to pay, when Chase stepped up and placed a small tin on the counter. "Add this too," he said, and Summer picked it up to see what he thought she needed.

"Chase, I don't need this," she said, handing him back the tin containing some concoction that helps heal dryness of hands or feet.

"Trust me, you do need it, and you'll be the one to pay for it," Chase said, and his tone said, 'don't argue'.

"Three cents," she muttered but nodded for Charlie to add it to her bill.

"You'll be willing to pay five, when you learn how it's gonna be used," Chase whispered in her ear before kissing her temple.

Summer only shrugged, and getting Charlie to promise to deliver the missing supplies as soon as they came in, she picked up her flour, salt, and sugar, while Chase collected the other things. She was so happy by the time she had everything put away, she'd almost forgotten she still had to face Chase. When she turned to locate him, it was clear he'd not forgotten.

He was already sitting in that chair and had already collected the bath brush. It rested on his thighs like a threat, daring her to back out, warning her if she thought what was coming was bad, what would come if she balked now wouldn't even compare.

"Go get undressed," Chase told her and tossed his hand toward the curtain.

"Undressed?"

"Yes, out of everything."

"Naked? In the middle of the day? Chase, that's not natural."

He actually laughed, threw his head back and laughed. "Get," he said, once he could.

Summer complied then used the curtain to conceal herself, though she couldn't say why. It wasn't like this man hadn't seen every inch of her. Hell, he'd kissed, licked, or bitten every inch of her. "Now what?"

"Come over here," he said and pointed to the floor in front of him

"Over there? Naked?" Was he out of his mind? Even when she bathed, she didn't prance around the room naked.

He chuckled, shook his head, and crooked his finger at her. She hesitated but let go the curtain and stepped out and over to him. For a long while, he just looked her over, his intense gaze making her nipples stiffen and her pussy drip. A hand on her hip, and she was turned facing away, but she could still feel his eyes roaming over her body. Her shirt hadn't done much to protect her skin, and for a few days, she'd suffered the itchy sting of those scrapes she had gotten when she first slid down the mine shaft walls. It made sleeping with Chase at her back difficult, and for a few days, he'd slept on top of the blankets, giving her some padding. Again, he turned her and then guided her to his right side.

"I'm gonna punish you in a way I haven't done before, you understand?" She couldn't swallow the lump, so she nodded. "I'm gonna do it my way and until I'm satisfied it's well done." She nodded again and squeezed her thighs together. "When it's over, if you want, we can talk about it, but once I start, you don't get to say stop." She nodded again because there was nothing new about that. Taking her elbow, he guided her over and she did wonder where the brush went, but as she tipped over, she got that answer. "Do you know why you're getting this punishment?"

"I was reckless. Really reckless." Damn, saying that out loud brought tears of shame to her eyes and he'd not even landed one spank. "I'm sorry."

"I could have lost you this time," Chase said, and Summer watched a tear fall to the floor. "I don't want to lose you, Summer. I do everything I can to keep you with me. I always will. I can't control everything, but I can at least corral this reckless streak you have." His palm settled on the high part of her ass. "This isn't something I enjoy, and I don't want to see you broken. But if I have to choose, I will have you broken over having you dead."

Summer sniffed and nodded. She'd no care to be dead, either. And while she might disagree, she needed to endure this to remind her not to be so daw-gum stupid again; it wasn't likely to be wasted.

Without warning, Chase lifted his hand and cracked it down on her ass. Summer gasped and reached down to clutch the chair leg. A second blow of equal force fell, and then it became a steady rhythm. Unlike when he spanked her before, he didn't stop every four or six blows to lecture. Rather, he continued to rain spanks down on her until she was gasping and yelling.

Then he stopped. And Summer sobbed out in relief. It was short lived, though, when Chase reached down and picked up the bath brush.

"Chase," she wailed as he used the smooth, cool wood base to rub her heated ass.

"We're a very long way from done, Summer," he said, and before the words registered in her head, that brush slammed down on her right ass cheek and sent a fiery pain throughout her flanks. It hadn't even ebbed and a second pain blasted through on the other side.

She couldn't so much as catch her breath, and as it fell again for the third time, the little air she'd taken in came out on a scream. One more, and all she could do was sob and whine.

"Don't clench," Chase told her. With blurred vision, she saw the brush set on the floor on the other side. Chase was doing something over her back, but she didn't know what. She continued to cry, but the worst seemed to be passing. At least until she felt Chase's knuckles at her ass crack.

Before she could even consider what he might be about, she felt something greasy spread over her hole. It was a shocking sensation. More so, when Chase added enough pressure, his finger actually went in a little.

"Don't clench," he warned. But when his finger went in again, despite the pain it caused in her cheeks, she squeezed to keep him out. She heard him sigh, felt him shift, and then felt the searing burn of the brush as it fell four times in quick secession. Summer cried out and tried to kick up, but he knocked her legs back down. "You make me pin you and you'll be sorry, missy."

"Chase, please," she begged, dropping her legs. Again, he set aside the brush and his finger returned to her ass hole. "What are you doing? Please?"

"Naughty girls get their ass punished on the outside. Very naughty girls get their ass punished inside too," he said and pushed his finger in deep.

Summer squealed at the invasion. Hadn't he said that to her once before? He went in deeper, and she was utterly torn on how she felt about it. It didn't actually hurt, but his touching her in such an intimate place, it wasn't natural. And why in the hell did it feel like he was also touching her pussy? Because she was certainly feeling something there as well.

He pulled his finger out then pushed it back in, and Summer did all she could not to clench. It wasn't enough because Chase again picked up the brush and delivered four more blows. This time when his finger returned, it wasn't alone and she screeched through clenched teeth as he pushed inside with that second greasy finger then almost died when a familiar ripple of pleasure flashed up her spine.

"Yep," was all Chase said before he started pumping his fingers in and out, every so often slapping his other hand down on her ass. As much as it hurt, she couldn't deny the corresponding pleasure building. Her ass was on fire from the spanking and growing increasingly tender inside as well, but if he didn't stop, she swore he'd take her to orgasm.

And then he did. He stopped. "You're getting twelve more with the brush, and then you're going to let me finish you," Chase said, and again, before she could wonder what he meant, the thick wood of the wicked brush cracked down on her ass. Like when he'd used his hand, he didn't stop until he'd reached his goal. If it was twelve or twelve hundred, Summer couldn't have said. At some point, the individual smacks blurred into a single, unrelenting pain.

And then she was on her feet and Chase moved to stand behind her. He pushed down between her shoulder blades so she bent forward over the seat, palms flat to keep her up. Once more, she felt him spreading the greasy unguent over her asshole and then push some up inside. But for all the choking sobs and the blistering pain, she couldn't have protested what she knew was coming when she felt the head of his cock press up against that entrance. If this was a punishment, why the hell was her pussy dripping so much, it ran down her thigh in rivulets as far as her knees?

The stretch was almost unbearable right up until it wasn't. At some point, he'd pushed in past the resistance, and now all she could feel was his cock sawing in and out with hard, powerful strokes, and much like when he rode her pussy hard, his every pistoning motion sent hot bolts flashing along her spine. The friction caused sparks to tingle over her skin. The repeated battering of her very painful cheeks, every time he thrust in, had her crying out, though she couldn't say if it was in pain or pleasure. And when his fingers gripped harder, his thumbs pressing in, she couldn't have stopped it if she'd wanted.

Her entire body went rigid, and though it seemed impossible there was any room to, given his size barely left room in her pussy, Summer clenched down. The act drove her past any ability to recognize pain for what it was, and like the bison being driven, Summer plunged over the cliffs. She'd a moment of falling with nothing at all to grab onto, and right before she thought she'd hit bottom, Chase drove in hard and she was given a new sensation. His cock firing off inside her picked her up once more, and before she could start down again, he wrapped an arm around her waist, pulled back, forced her foot onto the chair, and brought his hand down hard against her pussy.

The sharp bite of that slap rolled over her like thunder. The next struck like lightening; one more, and she came again. So hard, she felt the release stream down her legs.

"Are you going to be naughty like this again, missy?" Chase asked next to her ear before his teeth sunk into her lobe.

Damn, how did she answer him? No would be the logical answer, the correct answer, but the way she felt at this moment, yes felt like the fitting answer.

"This is what I'll do to you every time you're very naughty," he said as his tongue laved her ear. "This is how you'll be punished. Are you going to be naughty like that again? Are you going to be reckless like that again?"

"Chase," she pleaded. Lord help her, she was going to say yes.

Thankfully, Chase spared her, forcing her around and covering her lips with his as he kissed her until the air ran out in her lungs. When she was ready to rip her mouth free of his, he grabbed her hair and pulled her head back. Staring down at her with something she'd have likened to hate if she saw it in anyone else's eyes, Chase's look made her knees weaken and her body flame to life again.

"I won't lose you, Summer. Whatever I have to do to keep you, I'll do that." This time when his lips took control of hers, it was the way it was most times. Soft, warm, and invoking something she couldn't remember ever feeling, love.

Did she actually love this man? And if she did, how exactly was she going to leave him come September? Did she really have to? She was, after all, already doing exactly what she needed, wanted to do, to fulfill that dream. Would it matter at all if she achieved it alone verses with Chase beside her?

She just couldn't think. It was all too much right now. It was a runaway stage, a stampede, a saddle up on a wild mustang. She was beyond exhausted now, beyond crying about the pain in her ass. But not beyond crying about the frustrating confusion as she continued to try to reason with herself. Reason had always stood with her before. Why was it gone now?

"Shh, sweetheart. Shh. I've got you. Nothing's gonna happen to you now. Shh," Chase said. When had he lifted her and taken a seat with her in his lap? When had he leaned her against his solid frame and wrapped her in his strong, warm embrace? When had it started to feel like she belonged right here? When in the hell had she fallen in love with Marshal Chase Storm?

Chapter 23

"**M**arshal?"

Chase halted in his tracks at the call. The train platform was crowded as it was the monthly major delivery of farming products. While most folks here grew much of what they needed with a little bit to spare and sell off, it wasn't enough to also supply the large mining community. He'd come down to see if he could find Summer. She was usually on the platform when the train pulled in, insuring the produce she specifically ordered for her own needs wasn't sold to someone else. She'd gotten in a few tiffs with Mrs. Nelson already over what they both laid claim to. Chase really did need to go speak with Mr. Nelson about the matter. For while the man had the good sense to want to keep Summer's business, even as she diverted some of it more directly to suppliers on her own, Mrs. Nelson seemed hell bent to do anything she could to make sure Summer had to fight for everything she earned.

Things between Summer and that group of women heated up like a branding iron in a fire pit when the seven members of the ladies' auxiliary voted five to two to ask Summer to provide a large portion of baked goods for the Fourth of July celebrations.

The event would consist of several types of races and games, a large barn dance, and then a display of fireworks.

Personally, he couldn't wait for the dance. Summer admitted a few days ago she couldn't dance, so Chase took her in his arms and started teaching her. It was a wonderful excuse to hold her in his arms, though he didn't need one.

Ever since he had paddled her hide and fucked her ass, she'd been different. More open, more often the one to initiate sex. It actually came as a bit of a surprise how she responded to what he knew now couldn't be used as punishment. Not when she enjoyed it so much. But she'd not indicated yet she was ready to try it as something they did for the pleasure of doing it. It did, however, leave open the opportunity to rough up the sex a bit more.

They'd had a few more spirited nights since she'd fallen down the mine shaft, including the one when he woke to find her sitting in the corner of her kitchen bawling. She'd been near inconsolable, and it had taken a long while to settle her enough she could explain.

Turned out, as he suspected, the building she'd her heart set on was being looked at by another, and while that man didn't yet have a payment together to take possession, the owner wasn't willing to let Summer put the down payment, which she had in full, on the building. From a man, he was willing to accept payment in part; from a woman, he wanted the total upfront.

Summer had herself in a lather, because without the building, she couldn't increase her profits enough to buy it outright, but she couldn't get the building without having all the money upfront. He'd suggested several things, including him buying it and her buying from him, but she rejected every suggestion that even hinted she wouldn't remain independent in the venture.

It came down to Chase going to speak with the man, with Summer. Together, they struck a deal whereas Summer would give the man a deposit and should she fail to be able to take possession of the building within two months' time, he could keep the deposit along with any payments she made. The man took the offer on the spot, but for a few days, Summer made herself sick thinking she'd bitten off more than she could chew. Chase was simply happy she was starting to allow him to help, even if all he did was stand there with her.

However, it seemed word of her fine breads, jams, and confections had spread a bit, and by the end of the week, she was making food that was then taken to the neighboring counties and sold in other mercantiles. And while she still complained about the way selling through a middleman cut into her profits, she was complaining less. Chase, though, knew he was going to have to demand she open an account at the bank. He wasn't comfortable with the amounts of money she sometimes kept in the house. The three different pouches with her profits split for how they were used, were well hidden, but still, someone with enough time to look would find them. He didn't care to invite that kind of trouble. He would get a personal safe made when the house was finished.

That house, too, was coming along as nicely as his relationship with his wife. They'd picked the lot together, a nice, mostly sunny spot so Summer could have a garden to grow whatever pleased her. And as they were talking with a man over the design, they found they'd very similar ideas on most every aspect. He couldn't wait to move in, settle down, and start a family. And given Summer had on a few occasions prevented him from pulling out and not spilling inside her, he thought perhaps a family might be on her mind too. She wasn't going anywhere come the end of summer.

"Marshal?"

Someone calling had him turning back and looking down the track again. He spied one of the rail workers waving at him from a boxcar. So he headed that way. Where Summer was today, he wasn't sure.

"Marshal Storm?"

"That's me," Chase said as he stepped up.

"I have several trunks for you, and..." he reached into his shirt and withdrew a letter "... a note that came with them." He wasn't expecting anything, but taking the note, he saw it was addressed to him, only not in any familiar handwriting. "A few of these are extremely heavy, Marshal, you gonna need a lot of help and a wagon if you have to go more than a few feet." Chase looked up from the letter he was opening to see four grown men lift one of the trunks, with some struggle, and carry it to the edge of the doorway.

"Must be my wife's belongings," Chase mused, though what she could have that could weigh that much, he could only guess. He stepped back, getting out of the way as the workers unloaded the trunks. They knew what they were doing and didn't care to be interfered with. Once on the platform, though, it would be all up to Chase to take them anyplace else.

He went back to the letter, which turned out to basically be a threat. If he wasn't who he said he was, if Summer wasn't happy with him, and if he did anything to hurt her, he'd be finding himself at the end of a short rope. It was the first confirmation he'd had Summer might not be as alone in the world as he thought. Though he'd no plans ever to leave her and his own family would always back her, if something did happen, it was good to know she had others. People she likely trusted well enough, just in case.

The last trunk, a rather small one, was taken off the train and the men all looked at him like he was somehow responsible for their labor. Again, what Summer could possibly own that weighed so much, he couldn't figure, given she'd packed out everything when her home was burned. Still, he reached into his pocket and removed a silver piece, handing it over with his thanks.

"Howdy, Marshal."

Chase felt the smile spread across his face at the sound of that sultry voice. "Howdy, Mrs. Storm," he returned, looking back over his shoulder as she stepped up behind him and put her arms around his waist. "Where you been?"

"Trying to get free of those ladies," she said as she stepped to his side. "I don't need to be told fifty times what I will need to bring to the celebration." She looked up and rolled her eyes.

"I'm sure you have it under control, and I'm sure that as many extra people as are expected for the week, you'll have more business than you can handle," Chase said, giving her a bit of praise and support. Like it always did, it made her smile, a smile that reached her pretty blue eyes.

"What you doing down here?"

"I was looking for you, but then…" he waved his hand at the stack of trunks she'd not seemed to take notice of yet. His chest swelled a bit knowing he could keep her attention more easily now, that she wasn't always on alert, ready to grab her gun. Hell, most days, she didn't carry it.

He gritted his teeth at the high pitched, happy squeal she emitted when she did finally spot them. "My things, they finally came." She all but danced over to the stack. "What perfect timing."

"Been waiting on some of this?" Chase asked casually, only to laugh when she turned and glared at him.

"You know it, and with what I will be able to do now, you'll be cussing the delay as much as I was."

"What's in them that will make me cuss?" Chase asked, trying to lift one of the larger trunks, just to see if he could.

"All my cookware and equipment, and…" she reached for the smallest box and hugged it to her chest, "…all of Ma's recipes."

"Then I guess we better get these trunks over to the house, so you can start cooking for me," Chase teased.

It took six men to get the three largest trunks onto the small wagon then up the stairs over the jail. Summer did offer to unload them on the street and carry things up individually, but the men used their labor to get her to promise them something out of her kitchen, and she agreed with a good laugh. Chase kicked the door closed with his heel as he brought in the last small one on his own and set it down.

Summer was already opening each one and searching through them. "What all is in these?" he asked again, because cookware could mean anything.

Summer held up some odd device. "My apple peeler." She set it aside and lifted another. "My grinder." She moved to another trunk and reached in. "My pie and cake tins, my rolling pins."

"Wait?" Chase stopped her and came around to take one of the dozen or so pie tins she held up. "You can make pies?"

"Well, I can now. I needed my tins."

"Good Lord," Chase cried and slapped his hand on his forehead. "I'd have bought you a hundred tins if I knew that was all you needed to make me a pie." He glared on her, but she only smiled back, clearly trying not to laugh. "You are the meanest woman ever born. I could have been eating pies all this time?" He tossed his hands up. "You're more than mean," he grumbled, and that was all it took to send her into a fit of laugher.

"You think? Because pies aren't like bread. I don't have to make them for everyday an—"

"Oh yes, you do," Chase countered, getting down on the floor beside her.

"I don't," she said. "Way I see it, I only have to make them if you're nice to me." She failed to hide the smirk.

"Woman," Chase said, grabbing her and pulling her over into his lap. "I am always nice to you."

"You could be nicer," she said, putting her arms around his neck and pressing her tits against his chest.

Chase wrapped his arms around her and let his hands drop low enough to cup her ass. "You want me to be nicer to you?" he asked and watched her nod and her eyes drift closed as she leaned in for a kiss. "I might be able to do that. When would you like me to saddle up?"

"Now," she said without hesitation.

"Now?" He chuckled. "I'm on duty, it's the middle of the day... is that natural?" Her fist hit him in the gut. What he might have said next, though, was lost when several shots rang out and Chase flipped her to the floor and covered her body as one of the front windows shattered. "Stay down," he ordered then scrambled up enough, he could make it to the window without being hit by any of the bullets still flying. When he peeked over the sill, he quickly located the source of the commotion and, with a groan, headed back across the room toward the door.

From her place on the floor, Summer rolled to her back and gave him such a look as he almost laughed. "Butte Head?" she asked, referring to a group of troublemaker coal miners who came to town too often for anyone's liking.

"Yep," Chase said and, pulling his hat from the peg, grabbed for the door. "You stay here, and stay away from the windows until I round them all up."

"Chase," she whined but didn't even sit up. He gave her nothing more than a look, and she returned that then sighed. "Well, you tell them I'm not cooking for them since they busted out my window."

Chase smiled at her. "The Constitution forbids cruel punishment," he said before shutting the door and hurrying down to the street. Two hours later, as he and Buckley disarmed and started the last two toward the jailhouse, the sheriff echoed the same sentiment about cruel punishment, and when Chase mentioned Summer was going to start baking pies now, the group of miners almost sounded like they'd cry. There were lots of promises to never come into town like that again if only she'd feed them.

Chase could hardly blame these men. They worked hard,

they often weren't paid well, most of what they did earn was in company credit and couldn't buy anything without going into debt at the company store. Their rations were either old, dry beef, or some scrawny bit of game they managed to catch. One good meal, like they got from Summer, was rare and coveted.

"Stop your griping," Chase heard Deputy Zander say as he grabbed the man Chase was holding. "Mrs. Storm is yelling it up so loud right now, the whole town can hear her. You got glass in her flour."

"Weren't me," one of the miners quickly denied. "I didn't fire a shot; you tell her that."

"Won't matter; she's gonna put holes in all of you," Buckley said, giving Chase a wink before continuing back up the street.

"Marshal? Marshal?"

Chase turned around and tried to find the source of the whispered call. He swallowed the groan when he spotted Miss Angelica Codwells and her cousin Stephanie Porter. They were hiding in the dress shop. Chase stepped closer but not so close, either of them could start touching him as they often did, looping their arms through his, leaning in to speak, like anything they said was confidential or half intelligent. It made him plumb crazy how they behaved. It made him angry, no one, not even their fathers, put a stop to it, and it broke his heart to see the look on Summer's face when she'd watched them do it.

It was a sore spot with her, and even though he believed she knew he wasn't encouraging it and he did try to avoid both young women, it caused the air to chill around her every time. "How can I help you, Miss Codwells?"

"Is it safe now, Marshal?" she asked.

"It's safe now," Chase answered without adding it'd been safe for over an hour already and the answer to her question could have been found just by looking up and down the street as everyone else had already resumed their normal activities.

"Oh, thank heavens," the woman cried and stepped from the

shop. Chase wasn't quite fast enough to avoid getting looped by her arms, and once she had him, she set her head on his chest and sniffed. "I was just so frightened," she cooed. "I don't know at all what we'd do without you, Marshal. So many ruffians and outlaws." She stepped closer and leaned more heavily against him.

"I think you'd do just fine, Miss Codwells," Chase said, taking her arms and setting her back. "Sheriff Buckley and his deputies are very capable men. It's not even part of my job. I'm only helping out when I can."

"You're being modest, Marshal," the girl persisted, taking hold of his arm with both hands and forcing him to turn in the direction of the mercantile. "Before you arrived," she said and started them walking as Miss Porter fell in behind them. "Our poor little home was being shot up and stampeded every week."

Chase tried not to roll his eyes and lengthened his stride so he could more quickly deposit her someplace else. "Well, I think things have settled down greatly, so you have nothing to fear." He nodded his head at two older women coming at him on the boardwalk, grinding his teeth as he knew they were gossips who'd be squawking about how they say him walking 'indecently close, for a married man, with an unwed girl'. And he knew that would get back to Summer.

Chase picked up the pace as much as he could as Angelica took every opportunity to press closer and smile up at him. She wasn't some nag faced, bowlegged, cow. She was actually rather beautiful, in that hot blooded kind of way. But Chase didn't want a woman only good for looking at. He never found use in prancing ponies. He wanted to ride with someone who had endurance and strength. Summer was as hot blooded as a woman might come, but she had an unending willingness to work, to learn, and to adapt to her situation. His wife was the most perfectly balanced, warm blooded creature he'd ever had.

He almost laughed at himself when he finished that thought.

There was no way Summer wouldn't have gelded him if she knew the comparisons he was using. But they simply fit. He had a woman whom he knew and trusted would always rise to the challenge, always have a wild streak, but also always allow the reins to guide her.

Chase brought them to a stop right in front of the mercantile. Opening the door, he stepped aside and let the women pass. "Have a good day, ladies," he said before pulling the door shut, cutting off any attempt to invite him in or continue the foolish games they played.

He crossed the street before heading back toward the jail, just to ensure the females wouldn't follow. But when he spied Reverend Wickfield sweeping off the steps to the church, he crossed back and made his way over to the man. Perhaps if he could get the town's spiritual leader to speak with those girls or their parents, he could stop having to fend them off like a pit of vipers. He left rather hopeful the strikes would end. He might have thought more about where that venom would be used if it wasn't used on him.

Chapter 24

S ummer shifted the crate to her hip and reached for the
door. The rain was still coming down in hard torrents,
and the delay crossing the creek put her even further
behind than Chase's morning lovemaking. The memory of that,
though, kept her warm even as the rain soaked her through.

What she saw when she pushed open the door and stepped in
froze her heart like the January winds.

"Summer," Chase shouted as he worked to pull the arms of
Stephanie Porter from around his neck.

Summer carefully took in the scene. Chase was hardly
dressed. His shirt on the floor next to his feet, his pants still
partially open the way he left them until he tucked in his shirt
and made sure there were no wrinkles. For everything she could
see, he looked exactly as he did every morning before he left the
house to start his rounds. Only the woman in his arms
wasn't her.

For her part, Stephanie Porter didn't even try to look
abashed. She had yet to release her hold on Chase's neck. And
while she couldn't quite understand why Chase was here, in the

middle of the day, it was less understandable why Miss Porter was. And without a chaperone.

She was well aware both the Porter and Codwells women were trying to tangle Chase, and that neither woman's mother seemed to think anything unseemly about their daughters chasing after a married man. But she'd always assumed, always been witness to Chase rebuffing them, at least publicly. How often, though, was this the way things were? As regularly as Summer made her trips out to the various farms for things she wanted to use in her cooking and as often as she often didn't hurry in those errands, was it possible Chase was spending time with them on the side? Was he actually two timing her?

She slowly set the crate with the goat cheese and milk on the floor and took her first step toward the couple.

"Summer," Chase said, his voice tight, maybe with anger, maybe with annoyance as he finally managed to break Stephanie's hold and set her away from him.

"Oh, Marshal, please," Stephanie pleaded as she reached for him again. "You know I'm the right woman, the better woman for you. Please, don't send me away again."

"I never invited you here in the first place," Chase snarled. "I'm married, and you and your cousin need to stop this foolishness before your reputations are completely ruined."

"My reputation will be fine as long as you do right by me," Stephanie insisted.

"I am married," Chase shouted just as Summer reached them.

"He wants me," Stephanie said, turning to glare at Summer. "He wants a woman who can shine on his arm at the governor's ball, not one who is only good for cooking in the servant quarters."

"Well, he got himself the cook," Summer snarled, grabbing the woman at the back of her head and tightening her fist until she felt hairs tearing out. Stephanie screamed and struggled, but

Summer held on. They were about the same height, but Stephanie was heavier. Still, Summer managed to bend her backward then force her to step toward the door. "He got the cook, but I'll let you know when he wants the bitch." Summer shoved the woman out the still open door and watched as the rain quickly gave her the appearance of a drowned cat. "Step back in my home again, and I'll put a nice bullet right down that pretty throat you have." With that, she slammed the door shut in her face.

"Summer," Chase called, but she needed a few deep breaths before she could turn and face him. "Summer, she just showed up. It wasn't what you think. I—"

"Of course not." Summer turned, finally facing the man she was wed to. "Of course not, because the great Marshal Chase Storm wouldn't ever be so reckless with his own reputation as to engage in any indiscretions in broad daylight. That wouldn't be natural at all, would it?"

"Summer, there was no indiscretion. There's hasn't been any," he said, pausing in his dress to reach for her as she passed by to set the crate on the table.

"Of course not," she ground out.

"Summer," Chase called as he stepped up and set his hands on her shoulders. "Nothing happened."

"I have work to do," Summer said, shrugging off his hands. "Are you back for the day or are you… going out again?"

She heard him sigh, felt him step back. "I only came home to change clothes. There was a brawl at the Dark Lady…. with the rain… well, it got muddy."

Summer glanced at the far corner where she washed clothes. Already, there was a large pot on that stove and she could see Chase's shirt and pants hanging over the edge of the tub. Any other day, that might have brought her a bit of joy, knowing her husband wasn't a man who just left his messes for her to clean up. Today, it only made her realize that other than his money, which she was sure was the reason the other women in town tried to pursue him, she did have a good man. Unless, of course, she didn't.

"Summer, I'm sorry." Chase stepped up once more, this time taking her by the arms and turning her to face him. "I will speak with her father, tell him to put a stop to this. But nothing happened; nothing will happen."

She could only nod for the lump in her throat. She held still for the kiss he placed on her cheek, but she couldn't look at him as he left. And with the soft click of the door closing, tears fell.

She'd never questioned her own worth before. She'd never had reason to. But Chase was so above her. Not just as a sworn lawman, but in social status as well. The governor's ball? Did he attend those? Did he want or need to? And what then? He couldn't take her. She couldn't even dance. Even with Chase trying to teach her, she could hardly make it through one turn without stepping on his feet. Her eyes went again to the corner where she did wash.

She'd taken the best dress she had, one that had belonged to her mother, from the trunks, and having washed and pressed it, it now hung waiting for her to put it on in three days so she'd look like a lady when she walked on Chase's arm through the celebration activities.

But it was only a simple blue dress. No lace at the cuff or collar, no embroidery, and she didn't have slippers. She'd have to either wear her boots or go barefoot. All of that might be fine for what was expected here in Willow Creek, but what about in Denver, what about if she went to meet his family? What if she had to be beside him and meet the governor?

She knew without a doubt she could hold her own against outlaws and bread that refused to rise, but was that enough for a man like Chase Storm, whose family was prominent and powerful?

And if it wasn't, and Chase knew that, had he been thinking

about another woman? Didn't he still expect her to leave him in September? Maybe it wasn't right she should be hurt by any flirtations he might make. She'd not told him she thought maybe she'd stay on with him. He'd come here to settle down, start a family, have a home. That he had her tagging along...

A bright flash, followed by a boom of thunder so loud the windows rattled shook her from the thoughts. She couldn't stand there all day and wallow. She had pies to bake and preserves to can. If Chase was looking for her replacement already, that was fine. She could still go in September. It might be harder than she'd first thought it'd be, but she could still do it.

Of course, she didn't know Chase would be the one to make it easy after all.

SUMMER RUSHED down the boardwalk toward the mercantile. She needed more baking soda and salt if she was going to finish the last of the baked goods she intended to send over for the Fourth of July celebrations.

A good amount had already been carried over, and the ladies' auxiliary actually was standing guard to keep anyone from slipping off with a pie or biscuit. A long table was set up inside the large barn and smith shop to hold her canned goods and baskets of pretzels and sweets she'd made over the last three days. Most of those would be sold, but some would be auctioned off to help fund projects in the town and surrounding area, the main goal being to expand Doc Riot's office. The growth of the town had people speaking about building a hospital and bringing in a second doctor.

Most of the businesses in town were still open but planned to close at noon when the games, races, and even a bull ride contest started. Summer was already dressed, her hair braided and twisted up around her head. Chase complemented her on it, but things were still tense between them. It seemed like the more he denied he was casting looks at other women, the more she would find him with one of them in his arms or at his side.

She knew that most of the folks around didn't approve, but none of them spoke up. She didn't even think the Reverend Wickfield had disapproved strongly enough when Chase had the man accompany him to the Porters' big house at the farthest side of town to demand their child stop throwing herself at a married man. Chase came back to her grumbling about it himself. But she couldn't tell if he grumbled because he was happy he was married to Summer, if he was unhappy the woman was marking up his perfect reputation, or he'd already chosen Codwells' daughter over Porter's. Chase kept saying they needed to talk, but every time a moment started to rise up, it was shot down either by a call for him to attend something as marshal or for her to attend something having to do with today's events. She at least could look forward to tonight, after the whirlwinds blew out. Maybe once they spoke, she could make her final plans. If Chase really was already looking to saddle up with someone new, she could officially take up the small room over the eatery. Right now, she just had it holding everything she couldn't fit into the small kitchen space in the house. Once the eatery was fully ready, that room would be empty again. She'd just shift to living there... at least for a while. At least until she could sell out and leave. She already knew, just from the way it hurt now to witness it, she'd not be able to live long watching Chase give his attentions to another woman. Knowing for sure he was doing to that one what he did to her most nights.

Loving someone certainly gave her many wonderful surprises, but there seemed to be a few more heartaches to add to her pile. Pushing into the mercantile, Summer came face to face with every last one of those pains.

She tried to make her way to the counter and ignore the old

biddies and their chicks standing around the fabrics. She managed to smile at Charlie as he stepped up.

"What ya out of now, Mrs. Storm?" he asked with a bit of a laugh.

"Soda and salt," Summer said and bit her tongue when she heard Mrs. Codwells loudly say, "grace and beauty."

"Sure can't wait to try those pies," Charlie said, talking over the woman who now openly disparaged Summer. "Been listening to Sheriff B and the deputies talk about how good they were smelling last night."

"They came out very nice," Summer said as she reached into the little purse she carried. Dresses were not at all practical, no pockets for necessities, and no matter how she tried to set it, the skirts always tangled her hand if she wore her guns. Today, she wasn't even carrying her Yellow Boy as she was only intending to be out of the house these few minutes. She regretted it now, being as how few approached her when she was armed, or at least these women didn't. She could feel them walking up on her now. Charlie was hurrying as fast as he could. Who didn't know that Summer and these women couldn't hardly be in church together without something starting.

Right on the mark, Mrs. Codwells pushed past Summer to the counter and dropped the bolt of cloth, the same pretty blue gingham Summer had admired a few weeks ago. "We'd like a full-dress length of this, Mr. Howard," Mrs. Codwells announced.

"I'll be right with you, ma'am," Charlie said and reached for the ladder that would get him to the top shelves that held the baking soda canisters.

"We were here first," Angelica Codwells whined. "How dare you see to her before us."

"I'm sure Mrs. Nelson will be having to instruct you on which customers deserve your attentions... again," Mrs. Porter said with a sneer.

"Charlie, I'm not in a hurry," Summer said, hoping to keep the poor young man from getting pecked by the old biddy who usually ran the shop. "Cut these... ladies' fabric. I'm sure they are impatient to get something made up that will help them find a single man to pant after."

"Yes, ma'am, Mrs. Storm," Charlie said with a poorly hidden chuckle.

Summer's allies in this town were solid. But then, so were her enemies, and they had far more say in what happened. Summer pushed away from the counter to give the others room.

"The only one panting around here is you. But then most bitches pant when in heat," Stephanie said.

"Do they? I didn't hear you panting very hard when you threw yourself at my husband like the tramp you are. Oh, but then you said bitches pant... what do tramps do?"

"You'd better watch your mouth," Mrs. Codwells snarled. "You might think you can go around impugning the honor of good honest folks, but you're mistaken."

"One would have to be honorable to have their honor impugned, madam. That little whore..." she tossed her hand in Stephanie's direction. "Hell, both these *ladies* you've supposedly raised like a good Christian mother should hardly have the same amount of honor as a pile of horse shit has."

"Why, you little—" Summer turned to see Mrs. Nelson had stepped out of the back room.

"Neither of you good folks," Summer went on despite knowing she should just walk out now and leave it, "has the decency to leave a married man who doesn't want your attentions alone."

"That man is only married to you because he was forced into it. But it don't have to stay that way. As soon as he sees the better choice is me—" Angelica stopped when Stephanie gasped and gave her a shove.

"Marshal Storm comes from good blood, his family is nearly

royalty in Colorado. He certainly deserves better than someone like you," Mrs. Porter stated, though Summer wasn't sure who the comment was directed at.

"Well, Marshal Storm married me, so all of you are out of luck if you're hoping to get that invite to the governor's mansion. And given your lewd behavior, I'm sure no one in Denver would invite you anyway."

"Why, you—" Stephanie stepped up and raised her hand.

"I don't need a gun to set you down," Summer threatened.

"Get out of my shop," Mrs. Nelson yelled, slamming her fists on the counter. "And don't come back. You can find another place to try to peddle your… wares."

"I'm sure I can, but I have a contract with Mr. Nelson, and if you break it, I'll see you before a judge." Summer turned to catch Charlie's eye. "Charlie, my salt if you will."

"Right here, Mrs. Storm," he said, stepping up and putting both her requested items on the counter. Before Summer could set her money down and take what she needed, Nelson snatched them back.

"I just told you, you can't buy things here anymore."

"You better say that in front of your husband," Summer said, hoping the man would remain strong in the face of the nag he was wed to.

"I don't have to," Mrs. Nelson snapped.

"Yeah, so get out," Angelica yelled and shoved Summer, who tripped back,

She grabbed for the counter but only managed to drag the bolt of material with her as she lost her balance and almost went to the ground. The bolt unraveled and spilled out over the floor.

"Look what you did," Mrs. Codwells yelled.

"She ruined my dress material, Mama," Stephanie cried.

"You're a little animal. Why don't you run back out to the range, where you belong?" Angelica said.

Summer got to her feet, but no sooner had she stood upright,

Stephanie took her shot. Summer was shoved hard back into the counter; two jars of hard candies fell and shattered on the floor behind the counter, the edge digging into her back causing her to lose her breath for a second. In that second, Angelica came at her again. This time, though, Summer was able to block her and, hitting her shoulder, spun her away, which allowed Summer to shove her hard from behind.

Angelica stumbled forward, hitting a stack of corn sacks. They toppled over, at least one spilling open. With a growl, she turned and came back at Summer.

Summer sidestepped her, but when she used the counter to push off, she was able to knock Summer backward into the wall of shelving, and several items crashed to the ground.

The space around Summer was open, and she gained her footing as Angelica charged her again. Summer shoved her off once, sending her into a display of fresh eggs and peaches, before she charged a second time. Both women tripped sideways then backward, and Summer let go just as her ass hit the floor. Angelica fell sideways into a display of honey and Summer's own preserves.

The distinct sound of glass shattering and then the full weight of Angelica on top of her were all Summer could discern for a moment. But the fight hadn't left the other girl and when she reached up and grabbed a fist full of hair, Summer reacted instinctively and sent her fist right into the woman's face. Something to her left crashed to the floor.

Angelica began to scream and flay, and the gooey mess of smashed fruit and sticky honey that spread around them from the broken jars made grabbing ahold and keeping it hard. Leveraging her weight, Summer managed to roll Angelica to her back under her. She pulled her fist back and was about to blacken her other eye when someone grabbed her wrist and yanked her backward.

"What is going on?" Chase snarled as he wrapped his arm

around Summer's waist to prevent her from taking her last shot at Angelica Codwells.

"Look at what you've done," Mrs. Nelson yelled. "Who is going to pay for all this?"

"Marshal Storm?" Mr. Nelson fretted.

"Summer, what is going on? What do you think you are doing?"

"Me?" Summer almost shrieked. Why the hell was he blaming her? She didn't start this.

"That... woman is no longer welcome in this store," Mrs. Nelson shouted. "Look at what she's done in here."

"I didn't start this, you old nag," Summer started, only to be jerked back and silenced by Chase.

"Frank," Chase called, stepping toward Mr. Nelson who was wringing his hands over the lost merchandise. Summer saw the man look up then look around the group before looking back at her. "You were just about to close shop?"

"I was, will now for sure, to get this cleaned up."

"Mrs. Storm will be cleaning this up, and she'll pay for the damages," Chase said, and his look dared her to argue the matter.

"Mama," Angelica wailed. "My dress, it's ruined."

Before Summer could even form a thought, Chase was already making his known. "Summer will pay to clean or replace that as well, Miss Codwells."

"I won't," Summer snapped, only to get jerked back again. She bit her tongue for now, but there was no way in hell she was going to pay for that dress.

"Get a bill for the damages and get it to my wife," Chase said to Mr. Nelson. "Add the expense of the dress to that," he told Mrs. Codwells. "You better get a bucket and water and get this cleaned up," he said to Summer before he leaned in. "And not a word out of your mouth about it. I'm not going to garner a reputation for having a wild hooligan for a wife. Take responsibility for this, or I'll make you wish you had."

With that, he turned, opened the door, gestured for the other women in the shop to go ahead of him and followed without so much as a glance backward. Summer could only stand there and stare. What the Sam Hill? How did all this become her fault?

"Water's out back," Mrs. Nelson snarled, practically throwing the bucket at Summer. "And my feet better not stick to the floors when I come back."

Summer watched her open the door, step out, popping her parasol open and then walking away, leaving the door open in her wake.

"Mrs. Storm?" Charlie called, stepping up. "Want that I should go tell the marshal this wasn't your fault? That you didn't start nothing?"

"What happened?" Mr. Nelson asked as he carried over a broom and dust pan.

"Mrs. Storm?"

Summer heard the name but could hardly connect it to herself. Her own husband just shot her in the back. He didn't even hear her side. He didn't so much as frown at the real perpetrators in this.

"Mrs. Storm?"

Damn, she wasn't going to cry; she wasn't. If that was the trail he wanted to take, she'd let him and tip her hat at his departure. Why she was even surprised after the other day, she didn't know. Hell, he was probably counting the days now until September. It was her own fault for thinking maybe she could hitch up for the long ride.

"Mrs. Storm, I'll help you," Charlie said, but when he reached for the bucket, she snatched it back.

"No," she snapped, then amended, as this man had nothing to do with the fact she was married to a snake. "No, I'll clean it up. That's what the marshal wants, that's what he'll get." She turned to look at Mr. Nelson then. "And you can cancel all my orders. I'll take my business over to Creed, as that's what your wife wants."

"Mrs. Storm," Mr. Nelson sputtered, but Summer just turned her back and walked toward the back of the store where she knew she'd be able to use the door to access the well.

It took more than two hours, using only cold water to scrub up all the honey and jam, and then maybe two more to sweep up the glass and candy, stack the remaining jars of honey and the bags of grain, and replace what had fallen from the shelves. She put it all back far more neatly than it'd been, but she didn't want to hear even one complaint from anyone, especially that pole cat she was married to. She left the jars of her jams and preserves to the side, planning on fetching them back after she grabbed her basket. She, at least, could be assured no one would see the dirty, sticky mess she was as the whole town was over in the stockyards. The loud cheering told that the bull and bronc riding events were well on their way. The races would happen after that and would cut through town, but as long as she made it home before then, she could at least avoid the embarrassment of having her hair pasted to her face with strawberry jam. She closed the door to the mercantile then noticed Mr. Codwells coming out of the bank with another man she didn't recognize. It was odd he'd be conducting business now. Not only because of the celebration, but it was Saturday and well past two. Something didn't look right, but it wasn't going to be her concern. But for the fact Chase had forced her to put her money in that establishment for 'safekeeping', she'd almost wished a bank robbery to befall the man. She didn't like banks, and more than ever. she didn't like the man who ran it as he let his wife and daughter act like hussies with her husband. How could such a man even be trusted?

A loud roar from the crowd went up, maybe signaling the end of the rodeo. Summer didn't wait to find out. Ducking around the corner of the building, she used the alley to reach the jail and hurried up the steps. Opening the door, she was instantly reminded why she'd even gone to the shop in the first place.

The last of the goods she was going to take to the barn for the dance were ruined. The time and supplies used to create them wasted. More damn money lost, and now she was left with very little in the way of what she might take over to complete the order. Giving in to both her temper and the hurt, she used the privacy she still had to throw a small fit then regretted it as it only added to the mess she'd have to clean up. Still, as she wiped her face on her sleeve, she had to admit she wanted to throw a much larger one.

She wasn't in the wrong back at the store, and she didn't start the fight. Chase shouldn't have put it all on her. He shouldn't have been so fast to accuse her of trying to ruin his reputation. Especially, given it wasn't her the town whispered about, it was him and those two bitches. Even before he'd walked in, Mrs. Nelson assured her life was going to be more difficult for a time. Having to go all the way to Creed for her supplies until she could establish direct delivery for herself was going to mean she lost an entire day of work. More money lost. If this kept up, she'd not be able to pay off the note on the building in the limited time she had to do so, and she still needed to buy the rest of the equipment she needed if she was going to have more than an empty building. The only thing she'd going for her at the moment was this celebration. All the surrounding towns were consolidated in Willow Springs. They'd all have the chance to sample her wares and perhaps want to take orders. But if she didn't saddle up now and get the last dish over there, all she'd have would be a reputation for not being able to deliver.

It took far too long for her to find a recipe she'd all the ingredients for and could feed the crowd she was assuming would be there tonight, and only after she got the last of it in her oven was she able to start trying to clean herself up. At least she'd started water heating. As dried on as the honey and jams were, they'd never come off with only cold water. And she'd be lucky if the stains would ever come out of her dress. If she'd any thought about still trying to attend the last half of the celebration, those fled with the wind.

She wouldn't show up in the same dress she wore every Sunday to church, and other than that dress, all she had were her pants and flannel shirts. She'd gotten behind on wash trying to keep up with her cooking. As she was scrubbing the fabric over the washboard, a bit of doubt crept in. Could she really do this on her own? Even her mother had needed her aunt, and Summer had done a lot of work, too. She had no one at all helping her run a home and a business. And with the complications added on today...

"Damn," she almost shouted to the empty room. Damn, she wasn't going to start wallowing in pity, but damn it, at the moment, it was all she was feeling. Money wasted, time wasted, business contracts broken, stable supplies lost. What else could go wrong?

"There you are," Chase called out as he pushed open the door and destroyed her sanctuary. At least he was able to give her something else to feel for a moment. Rage welled up when he causally crossed the room to stand over her as she went back to scrubbing her dress clean. "You missed the whole rodeo and the race." His stupid smile made her want to draw on him, but her holster was by the door. "Better get moving, or we'll be late for the food and the dance," he said as he pulled off the shirt he'd worn for the dirty part of the day. She'd never been annoyed before by the amount of clothes he owned as it meant less days of having to do his wash. But as he so easily changed into something clean and fresh, she almost hated him. He was fast cleaning himself up, even using the water she'd heated for her own use to wash his face and neck before picking up the clothes brush and brushing off his denim pants.

Summer did her best to ignore him, taking time to wring out

the dress and inspect it for any more stains. The dark color hid them well enough, but it'd never be her 'best' dress again. Something else lost today. Again, she gave in to the frustration and flung the gown back into the tub. Chase stepped up and loomed over her. Blinking back the tears, she dared to look up and glare at him.

"You have something," he started then reached down and drew his thumb across her cheek. She knocked it away only to watch him lift his thumb to his mouth and suck off the red goo. "Raspberry," he muttered as he made sure to get every bit into his mouth. "I like your apple better." Even more this time, his stupid smile made her want to blow a hole in him. "Giddy up, or there won't be any pie left at all."

"I'm not going," Summer said and managed to resist grabbing her gun as she went to the door intending to get more water to heat so she could finally bathe.

"What do you mean, you're not going?"

"Do you need me to say it in Apache? I'm not going. So feel free to go choke on pie." She pushed the bucket down into the barrel that held water just outside the door and pulled it up. Before she could carry it inside, Chase pulled it from her hands and set it down.

"What bee's in your bonnet now?"

It was on the tip of her tongue to tell him exactly what bee was buzzing her, but the knot she felt growing in her stomach and the lump in her throat prevented it. She wasn't going to cry in front of this man again. She wasn't going to give him the satisfaction of knowing he'd hurt her. "Just leave," she said and, picking up the bucket, made her way inside.

"I thought you wanted to go," Chase said, following her back inside as she added water to the pot on the stove. "I thought you learned to dance just so you could dance with me tonight."

"Well, now you can dance with someone who knows how to and won't step on your feet," Summer said and hated that her voice cracked. "I'm sure the lovely Miss Angelica knows how to waltz perfectly."

"Summer," Chase snarled and grabbed her arm, causing water to spill out across the floor. "I don't want to dance with her."

"Well, I don't want to dance with you," she yelled, rounding on him so she could keep him in front of her. She did her best to ignore his hurt look. "Just leave; I want to bathe, and I don't want you here."

"Summer, I'll wait until you've cleaned up," Chase said, sounding a bit pleading. "I'll wait and we can go together, there's still the fireworks and—"

"I'm not going," Summer all but screamed. Why couldn't he just walk away?

"Summer?"

"I'm not going, Chase, I'm not going." Maybe he just needed a better reason from her other than she really didn't like him at the moment. "I don't have anything to wear now," she said and pointed at the dress floating in the wash tub. "That is my only dress, and it's ruined. It's sticky, and it's stained and—" she stopped before she really did start to cry.

"Wear that one," Chase said, pointing to her Sunday skirt. She shook her head at him, and given the look she saw on his face, she didn't need to explain why she couldn't. "Then just wear what you have on."

She almost laughed. What she had on was the clothes she'd been wearing for the last four days as she baked and cooked. She wasn't even planning on putting these clothes back on after she washed, though she might as well as she still had some cleaning up to do before she could put out the lights and go to bed. "Just go," she said and grabbed a cloth from the pile so she could at least wash her face.

"Not without you," Chase snapped, grabbing her arm and heading toward the door.

"Chase," Summer cried and set back on her heels. "I'm not going. I'm not going at all, let alone dressed like Jane Canary. Half or better of the population of Colorado are going to be at that dance. I'm not going to show up in front of potential customers looking like I just survived a damn stampede. That's not the reputation I want." She jerked her arm free. "You need to leave. You have a reputation to uphold, and seeing as how it's always me who seems to put it in jeopardy, it's better that you go without me."

"Summer," he started, and once again, that look of hurt that crossed his face might as well have been the bullet to her heart.

"Damn it, leave," she yelled. "Leave. Give me some damn peace."

For just a moment, he looked undecided. Marshal Chase Storm looked like he didn't know what he was supposed to do... She'd laugh, maybe, someday in the future, over that, because it was the biggest part of his reputation. He always knew exactly what to do. But the look passed, and without a word, he turned and walked out the door, closing it softly behind him.

She held her breath a moment, willing him to come back. Praying he'd come back and take her in his arms and simply refuse to go to the dance, too. He didn't, and when it became obvious he wouldn't, she let go of what she'd held onto the entire time she faced him.

By the time the tears stopped pouring out and she could take a breath, the water on the stove was near boiling. Mixing it with cold water, she went through the motions of washing. First, herself, then the clothes she'd been wearing and, finally, the space she'd been calling home for the last two months. Collecting the food meant for the dance, she headed out the door. She'd just drop it off and go home. No one would even see her. Too bad she couldn't have been given the same blessing.

Chapter 25

"**M**arshal Storm, you dance so well. Much better than any of the other boys around these parts."

Chase ground his teeth and turned Miss Porter again, doing his best to keep them to the outside of the dance floor. Even knowing he wouldn't see her, he looked around again for Summer, still hoping she'd change her mind.

She was right, in that a great number of people were asking about her baked goods, jams, and sweets, many of them also business owners who'd benefit from keeping a supply of each on hand. It might not have been good for her professional reputation to show up covered in flour with her hair in a tangled mess. He knew that she did her best to always present as professional as she could, no matter what she did. Denim pants that clung to her curves and a flannel shirt that stretched tight over her breasts was the look of a gunslinger, not a baker. But not showing up at all was equally detrimental to her. These people wanted to meet the woman behind the pies with the flakiest crust ever tasted. They wanted to ask where she learned to make pretzels that melted on their tongues. She should be here.

He wanted her here. And he wanted the chance to ask her

who had run her off so easily. For while he hoped it was just the woman currently clinging to him inappropriately, or her cohort, he had to grudgingly admit it was likely his own words and actions that had her pushing him away.

Learning from Charlie, Summer hadn't done anything to start the fight and was only defending herself when he walked in meant he had a lot to apologize for. He'd not handled that well, putting it all on her. He almost wished Summer was here just to see Angelica's black eye. Though she was taking advantage of the sympathy it gained her, few were, in that crowd.

As much as he hated to have to walk back his word, in this case, he couldn't see any other option. He'd made Summer do the labor, but he wouldn't make her pay for the damages. And seeing as her dress was just as ruined as Angelica's, they could call it even on that one. And Chase would insist Summer buy some more material and have another dress made. One actually made for her, not one that she managed to find when she was scavenging the ruins of her burnt out home for anything useful.

"Marshal?" Stephanie Porter pouted. "You're not being very attentive, what's a lady to think?"

Chase brought them to a stop and stepped back. "Maybe she should think how inappropriate it is to toss a rope at a man already wearing someone's brand."

"Marshal," Stephanie cooed and stepped back into his arms. "Everyone knows you didn't want to marry that girl, and everyone knows you can do so much better."

Chase stepped back again, only to be stalked down. The woman set her palms on his chest and started rubbing. Chase covered her hands with his. "Can I?" he asked and waited while Stephanie stepped closer, and her smile turned from coy to wicked.

"You know you can," she said and rose up on her toes. "You know you want to."

"What I know," Chase said, tightening his grip on her hands.

"Is that I require a woman beside me." He stepped back and tossed her hands back at her. "A faithful woman, not a spoiled, stupid child who doesn't respect herself or anyone else. Not a bratty little girl who'd be best served having a strap taken to her backside. What I know is any woman who can't respect the bonds of marriage from the outside won't respect them from the inside. I couldn't find better than the woman I have now if I looked around the world. I most certainly can't see any way you'd ever be the better wife, when you can't even be a better woman." Chase turned and took a step toward the doors, knowing full well several people had stopped to listen. "And you can tell your cousin I hold the same opinion of her as well." Without pausing to say anything to anyone, he headed straight to where his coat and hat were. The grumbling throughout the barn was quickly covered by music, and Chase did his best to make his escape before anyone could approach him. He was likely to punch anyone who said a damn word to him.

"Oh, Marshal," Mrs. Wickfield said as she stepped up carrying a basket of fresh baked corn bread. "Didn't Summer find you?"

"No." Chase froze. "Is she here?" He looked around.

"She just dropped off the last basket," the old woman said with a smile.

"She just ran out," Buckley said, stepping up to take a piece from the basket. "Said something about if you want better, have it. She didn't care."

"Damn it," Chase swore then muttered an apology to the reverend's wife before pushing through the crowd who'd begun to gather outside to see the fireworks. How much she might have overheard, he couldn't say, but he could guess that she left before he could rebut Stephanie's words. He made his way home as the first burst of saltpeter and sulfur lit the sky and reflected off the jagged peaks surrounding the valley. The boom echoed around, magnified by the shape of the valley. He took the steps two at a time and didn't pause to take off his hat as he came through the door.

"Summer?" No answer from the dark room. He crossed to the bed and shoved back the curtain. "Summer?" The bed was still perfectly made. "Damn it," he swore again, looking around the room. Everything was in its place, the way she always kept their home. Even her dress and a few other clothes were stretched out on a line to dry. She'd likely planned to hang them outside tomorrow. Damn, he wished the house he was having built was done now and not by this time next month. He'd no idea where he might look for her. Where else could she have taken refuge? He turned and headed back outside, his gut twisting a bit as he changed direction and made his way to the stables.

Relief weakened his knees when he saw both her horse and Sir in their stalls. She might have gone inside the jail, but with a few rowdy cowboys still there, he'd have heard something if she'd gone inside. The only other place he could think was the building she'd bought for her eatery. Perhaps she went there. She always seemed to feel more secure in her kitchen. Maybe she needed a bigger one. More fireworks exploded overhead, and the cheers from the crowd nearly drowned out the reverberations. Chase stretched out his stride and was at a near run by the time he reached the corner building with the huge glass windows giving a full view down both Main Street and Second. It was the perfect place for her to have her bakery.

No lights, though Chase tried the door anyway. Locked. Heading over one street, he came back up the backside of the building and tried the door that would lead directly to the kitchen area. It was open, and as he pushed inside, he listened. From the far side, he could hear only what could be crying. Swearing under his breath again, he made his way back to the small room Summer was planning to keep as an office. There was still no light, but the sobbing grew louder.

"Summer?" Chase called and tried to open the door, only to find it locked. He rapped his knuckles lightly on the door and called again. "Summer?"

"Leave me alone, you two timing snake," she hissed through the door.

"Summer, please open the door and talk to me."

"Leave me alone."

"Summer, you misunderstood, I—"

"No, I didn't. No, I didn't. I have understood for a long while. You can have better. But don't worry, in another two months, I'll stop being a burr under your saddle. You can have a wife worthy of your fine reputation."

"I already have that. Summer, open this door," Chase yelled, slamming his fist against the wood.

"Leave me alone. I don't want to speak to you, I don't want to see you. All I want is for it to be September, so we can be done. I'm done. Leave me alone. I hate you."

Chase felt the blood drain from his face at those words. How had it collapsed so fast? Just last night, she'd whispered the exact opposite to him, though she thought he was already asleep. Love didn't die in the space of a single day. It'd certainly take actual death to make him stop loving her. Resting his forehead against the door, he took a breath and tossed his rope at some calm. Summer was mad. She'd a good temper, even if she rarely showed it. And she'd a good reason for showing it now, given everything that had happened. She just needed to calm down enough she'd listen to him. He could fix this. The barn doors were open, but none of the cows were out yet.

"Come home, Summer. I'll wait there for you," he said with every intention of doing exactly that.

CHASE RODE back into town just ahead of the wagon carrying

the three bodies. The would-be claim jumpers had managed to kill one miner before Chase and the sheriff could rout them. And while it would have been better to make them stand trial, several of the other miners thought to take matters into their own hands. Knowing the mines planned to collectively hire some security helped, but it would be a few months yet before anyone actually showed up.

Looking back over his shoulder, he watched the sheriff pull the line of four horses and men past where the wagon stopped in front of the funeral house. It'd be those miners on trial now. But given the circumstances, if they were found guilty of any crimes, it'd be a surprise.

"I'll take these ones over to the jail, if you want to wire out for a judge to head this way," Berkley said.

"Well, I hope a judge comes this way, or else I'm gonna just let 'em go," Chase said, reining his horse in the correct direction. The sheriff nodded in agreement as they'd both been on the trail for more than two weeks escorting another train robber down from Telluride to Durango to stand trial there. The marshal from that area had fallen and broken his leg. Chase was the nearest man with the authority, given it was a crime against the railroads, who could be asked to do it. Buckley tagged along for safety and to ensure he had a witness. Word had reached them of the wrongful imprisonment of a young man in Silverton, some upstart kid named Porter who had a liking for horses that maybe weren't his. More law around these parts wouldn't hurt nothing.

"I agree," Buckley said. "I'll get these ones all set in; you can go on see to that pretty wife of yours. Maybe ask her what's for supper," he said with a wink, making Chase smile a bit.

"I used to not mind campfire food and hard tack," Chase said.

"Woman ruined all of us."

"Yes, she did," Chase agreed. And she'd ruined more than just his belly's ability to eat about anything he found. Never had being on the trail been so lonely and long. Never had he ached so hard to get back home that he'd seriously given thought to running his horse to ground just to cut down the number of days. And never had he been so unable to sleep.

He knew too, sleep eluded him because he'd not gotten his chance to speak to Summer before he'd had to ride out. She'd avoided him so completely, he often had to hear from someone else where she even was. How that was possible, he didn't know. But she'd taken up sleeping in that office, and she kept the doors to the building locked. He hadn't tried to rope her and tie her down because he thought she was still angry and upset, and because he wanted to let her draw first in the showdown that was coming.

But he really needed to see her now. He needed to hold her in his arms and know she was real. If it meant wrangling her into submission, he would. They'd get to mending fences today, because fall was coming up the tracks far too fast.

By the time Chase managed to actually get to that moment of truth between them, he might have thought it was the dead of winter again and the blizzard would bury him completely.

Chapter 26

Summer shifted again and breathed in to try to stop the pain from making her puke. Lifting the small glass on the table before her, she downed the last of the cheap whiskey and let that burn override the burn in her left arm, before she pulled her hat lower and leaned sideways against the wall of the dining car she rode in.

"Another for you?" the car attendant asked. Summer only shook her head. She couldn't afford another. She couldn't afford anything.

She'd only managed to get one of the two bounties she was after down in Pueblo, and she'd not been able to convince the sheriff there to give her another bill. She'd still be more than a hundred dollars short. She'd already sold her horse, saddle, and mule. All she had left was her rifle and her pistol. She might be able to get enough and hope to have money left so she could still leave Willow Creek behind for good.

She'd been a fool for ever believing she might have what she'd dreamed of her whole life. A damn fool for hoping she might have more than just that one dream too. There was nothing left now. She would leave with less than she had when she left Highfield. Nothing and no place she could go to try and start over. Best she could maybe hope for was to take up Miss Dolly's suggestion and come work as one of her girls. Woman promised all the ladies at the Silver Dollar made close to four dollars a week, more during the cattle drives.

How ironic Summer had spent her whole life trying to avoid the fate of Lizbeth and the other girls who'd survived the raid, only to have circled back to that exact outcome. All she could say was at least now she knew what she'd be forced to do to earn a living. She wasn't going in unaware and unwilling. And maybe someday, she could still…

She stopped before she could let that thought finish. It was over. Her life was over. Chase Storm coming into her life had wreaked more havoc than any tornado on the Kansas plains ever could have. Her world wasn't just torn apart and scattered, it was obliterated. There weren't even scraps left to pick up. And she couldn't help but think that was exactly how Chase planned it.

She'd almost been ready to try to talk to him that day she was approached by Mrs. Nelson and Reverend Wickfield. Nelson handed her a folded paper, told her it was the bill for the damages, reminded her she wasn't allowed to protest it and noted the reverend was along only as a witness to the fact it was handed over. Summer simply took it, slipped it in her basket, and went about her business. It was nearly noon before she took it out and almost fainted. The amount was so outrageous as to be sinful. And no matter how many times she counted the little bit of money she kept back for herself, it was never going to equal the seven hundred and thirty-five dollars being demanded.

Summer knew she'd have to take money from her bank account. Knew, too, that would mean delaying buying the second oven she'd need and the rest of the tables and chairs for the eatery. She thought, though, she could make up the difference within a few months because she'd found the name of a supplier who would sell directly to her, and once she was open, she could sell her canned goods directly from the eatery and not have to give a percentage to any shop owner. If she was frugal in how she operated, it would still be all right. And she believed that right up until she walked into the bank to get the money she didn't owe but would pay just to end the ride. Of course, it was there she discovered the true depths of Chase's deception.

The huge amount of money she'd saved for the last ten years was no longer in an account held by her, but in her husband's accounts, 'as it should be', according to Mr. Codwells. And also according to that odious man, she wasn't allowed to withdraw more than five dollars a week without her husband making the withdrawal himself. She was effectively ruined. She couldn't operate the eatery without full access to those monies. She wouldn't operate a business if she needed to beg anyone to act so she might.

She walked out of the bank with the five dollars she was allowed and started that very moment ending every association with the town of Willow Creek and the man she thought she loved, Marshal Chase D. Storm.

"Mind if I sit here?" the deep tenor voice broke into her thoughts. "Place is kind of crowded."

Summer only shrugged then regretted it when pain ripped through again. She swallowed, hoping to keep the bile down and then raised her hand to wipe at the sweat beading on the back of her neck. It wasn't the heat; it couldn't be as she actually felt cold.

"Willow Creek, next stop," the conductor called out as he moved through the car.

"Finally," she said under her breath.

"Your stop?" the man sitting across from her now asked.

"Temporarily," Summer said, supporting her left arm now.

He chuckled. "Sounds like you won't be able to get out of there fast enough. Know where you're headed after this?"

"At this moment, where ever the wind blows," Summer said, wondering if she might take this opportunity to try her hand at flirting the way the women in the saloon did. If she was going to get boxed in as to have no other way to earn money, she'd have to learn how it was done. She glanced up, meaning to give the man a bit of a smile, but almost fainted at how very much he looked like her husband.

Was that going to be how it was for her for the rest of her life? Every man would somehow remind her of the man she'd hitched her wagon to only to have the horse run away with it. She wouldn't be able to do it. Trying to live her life constantly reminded of what it was like to be kissed by Chase, touched by him, to have his warm, hard body at her back every night, she'd go mad.

"Are you all right, miss?" the man asked, making Summer shudder with how much his voice sounded like Chase too.

She needed to get away from Chase; maybe she'd start by just finding a place to camp. If she lived off game and lay low, she could then make her way to some town some place and start over. She offered the man a weak smile. "Just tired."

The train began to slow, and Summer slid her Yellow Boy off her lap and bent to grab her one pack from under the seat. "Willow Creek," the conductor called again. Summer took a moment before sitting back straight. It did nothing to keep her head from spinning.

"You wouldn't happen to know where I might find Marshal Chase Strom, would you?" the man asked, setting his hand at her elbow and helping her stand.

"If there was any justice in the world… Hell," Summer said, not able to put any venom in her tone. She was too far past the rage and hurt, and it was almost over, so she wouldn't put any effort in it anymore. "But there isn't any, so I'll guess you'll find him on the north end of town at the sheriff's office. Or maybe you'll find him sipping tea in one Miss Angelica Codwells' parlor. Either way, watch your back around that dirty snake before he takes you for everything you worked for all your life."

The whistle blew overhead and Summer moved to the stair-well of the car. Barely at a full stop, she stepped off and almost fell on her face, but for the conductor's steadying hand. She tried again to offer a smile, but the pain was increasing with every breath.

"Mrs. Storm?"

When she looked up, she found Deputy Zander coming at her. She didn't even try to smile. "What can I do for you, Deputy?"

"Nothing, ma'am, I..." he stammered. "Ma'am, you don't look so good."

"I'm tired, Zander. I'm tired, and I still have things to do."

"Marshal been looking for you; he's about out his mind. He sent wires to every state and territory from Mississippi to California, Texas to Wyoming," Zander went on, tipping his hat back to scratch his head.

"You posted to see if I get off the train?" Summer asked. Why the hell would he even be looking for her? "Is he in town now?" She let the pack slide to the ground as it was just too heavy to stand around with.

"No, him and Winter got on the trail of some rustlers 'bout two days ago. Mrs. Storm, are you all right? You looking mighty pale."

"I'm fine, and maybe I'll be better before too long," Summer told him. If he was chasing thieves, he might be gone a week or more. She could figure out how to make the last hundred dollars and get gone. "You still wanting to buy my rifle?" she asked, holding up the weapon that once belonged to Sgt. Dexter. She'd never thought she'd part with it, but then she'd never thought she'd be parting with the life she'd worked so hard to build.

"You mean it? You willing to sell it now?" Zander's excitement actually hurt.

"If you got cash," Summer said.

"I got ten," Zander told her.

"I can't let it go for that," Summer told him. "This here is a crack shot; you know that." He should; he'd tried to take her on once when she went out target shooting.

"Well, what you want for it?" Zander asked.

Knowing how much a week the man made and knowing how he spent his money, she said, "Twenty."

"Twenty?" Zander groaned. "Mrs. Storm, you know I don't got that kind of loot on me."

"I'll buy it."

Summer turned at the words. "Pardon?"

"I'll buy it," the man from the train stepped up and pulled a roll of cash from his coat. "Hundred dollars. Right now." He began peeling off the amount.

"I…" Summer's stomach knotted. As much as she needed the money, and that was just what she needed, the rifle was precious to her. She'd have sold it to Zander knowing it was in good hands, but a complete stranger? But his offer would allow her to pay the debt, pack her things and be gone when the train came back. Maybe before Chase even returned.

"One fifty," the man said and peeled off a few more bills from his stack.

"Done," she said before she could change her mind. She handed the weapon over and took the cash. "Don't blame me if you end up using it on Marshal Storm."

"Oh, now, Mrs. Storm," Zander whined. "That ain't no kind of nice thing to say."

"I'm not in a nice kind of way," Summer said. Again, bending over and lifting her pack made her head spin and her stomach roll. "The gentleman here was looking for the marshal; make sure you point him out from a vantage point." With that, Summer headed down the platform and straight toward the mercantile. She paused only a moment to see if the new owner had started work, but the building was dark. With a shake of her head, she moved on. How wasteful. She'd been in that building every day trying to set it up. Again, she shook her head. Look what that got her. Nothing.

Pushing through the door, she let her eyes adjust to the dim lighting. The bright July sun outside hardly warmed her, and in here, she shuddered again with the same cold feeling she'd had the last three days. Her arm pulsed and she reached up to cover the wound that still oozed.

The bullets hadn't hit directly, but the ricochet struck home. She was simply grateful it was her left arm hit. The doctor in Pueblo hadn't done much as she couldn't pay him, but he at least assured her it wouldn't kill her. Only now, was she thinking he might be wrong.

"What do you want?"

Summer looked up to find Mrs. Nelson behind the counter. Without a word, she pulled her small leather bag from her pack. The bell ringing over the door didn't distract her for a moment as she pulled out the bill she was handed almost three weeks ago and started counting out the money. Money from the building she no longer owned, from the bank account she no longer had, from the sale of her horse, her mule, and her rifle, everything meaningful in her life, and the bounty she collected, and the money she'd always held back in case... she'd never know what the in case might have been, but as it turned out, it was in case she ever found herself needing to start over with absolutely nothing.

"There's your money, you old biddy. I hope it buys you a nice place in Hell." Summer turned on her toes and stepped forward, only to run straight into the man from the train.

"Good riddance to you," Mrs. Nelson called out as Summer stepped around the man and headed for the door.

Stepping out onto the boardwalk, she ran straight into Mr. Nelson. "Mrs. Storm? You're back. Oh good, the orders are piling up and—"

"What orders?" She'd canceled everything before any could

be shipped, even down at the train station, she was sure to tell everyone to stop shipping supplies.

"What orders? Why, the ones for your canned goods and—"

"You'll have to tell everyone they are out of luck, I'm out of business, and as soon as the train comes back through, I'm out of here. I won't be supplying you canned goods you can profit on anymore," Summer told him as she stepped around and headed toward the jail.

"B-but we had a deal, a contract."

"And your wife broke it. You don't like how she does business, you should speak with her. But we're done." Summer rounded the corner, choosing to once again use the back alley to avoid anyone else who might like to point out she was back. Her only goal now was to pack her things and get out of town before Chase returned.

She did make a stop at the church to ask Mrs. Wickfield if she could store her trunks in the church basement until she knew where she'd be settling. The woman was in tears by the time Summer left. Both for the fact Summer was cutting out and that her marriage was over. Summer listened to the woman tell her that sometimes men needed a second chance to prove themselves. And it wasn't right Summer wasn't willing to take counsel or even hear Marshal Storm out. If listening to the woman tell her divorce was a sin was the price of having her things secured until she could figure out what to do with them, she'd pay it. But the time it took cost in strength and determination, too.

By the time she reached the apartment over the jail, she was soaked in sweat, shaking with pain and hardly able to hold herself up, but she dragged the trunks away from the wall and began storing everything that was hers but that she wouldn't be taking with her. She was still debating on if she should at least pack her camp gear with her even if she did expect to move straight into a saloon somewhere when the door burst open and Chase practically tumbled in.

"Summer?" he shouted. The joy in his tone nearly took her to her knees; she wasn't expecting it. "Where the hell have you been?" That was the tone she had expected. "What are you doing?"

"What does it look like I'm doing?" she ground out, turning so she didn't have to see him standing there, looking so perfect, so open and willing to hold her if she but stepped into his arms. Damn, he was still temptation incarnate.

"It looks like you're packing," he said, moving to one of the trunks and peering inside. "Why are you packing?"

"Because I'm leaving."

"Leaving?" he stepped closer, and Summer moved around the table to keep the distance between them. "Summer, you can't leave."

"Yes, I can, and I am. I'm through with you. Go live your life with someone more to your standards. Someone who won't ruin your damn precious reputation," she said, reaching for the small bundle of clothes she'd carry with her. None of them appropriate for a saloon girl, she was sure, but what did it matter? She'd be naked for the business she'd be conducting.

"It's only July," Chase said and tried to pull her packs out of reach. "We had a bargain. I won't pay you if you leave before September."

"Ha," she snapped and jerked her packs close enough she could stuff the clothes inside. "Like I even believe you ever intended to pay me. And that money will never make up for what you stole from me now, will it? Ten years of my life. Ten years, and you just stole it. But maybe that's what it costs to get trained to be a whore. At least I won't have to walk into some saloon now not knowing what's expected. Still, it's funny that I worked so hard to escape that fate, that I willingly left behind people I knew and cared about, only to end up exactly where I should have ended up ten years ago." She stopped and leveled a look at him she hoped killed him. "Only, it's not funny at all. It's not the least bit funny. I never should have trusted you. I should have shot you dead in the desert in Arizona and went on with my own life. It would have been better. It wouldn't have been this." She waved her arms around, only to have to bite her lip to keep from crying out at the added pain the movement caused.

"Summer, you need to whoa that pony and let me have a say," Chase said, coming around the table before she could make her feet move. "I'm pretty sure, at this moment, what I do know isn't everything that I should know. But if you think I'm gonna let you walk out that door, you're plumb loco." He stepped closer.

Summer stood her ground, waited for him to get so close that there was hardly air between their bodies, then she watched carefully as his expression went from determined to scared. "I still thought I had something to lose last time, Marshal," Summer said, her voice low and hard, the way it was when she drew down on any other man. The barrel of her revolver pushed into his gut, and Chase instinctively raised his hands and stepped back. "I was mistaken then; I won't make the same mistake this time. I have nothing left to lose, and I'll ease into Hell happy for putting a bullet through your middle. At least if you're dead first, I can be assured what you stole won't be used on whoever you planned to trade me for."

"Summer, I swear I haven't stolen anything. If you'd hear me out—" Chase took another step back, keeping his hands up where she could see them. Not that it mattered. Maybe it'd even be better if he drew on her and ended it before she had to know what it was like living life as a whore. Maybe she wouldn't go back to Pueblo, maybe she'd head back to Breaker and see if she could get in with Lizbeth and her crowd.

"You got nothing to say I want to hear," she said, cocking back the hammer, hoping with everything she had that he'd draw and just end it for her now. Why'd she have to live through the raid? Why did she have to run from that first saloon? Why did she have to take that first bounty? Why'd she have to run into

Marshal Storm? Why'd she have to fall so in love with him that even knowing everything he'd done to ruin her dreams, death seemed preferable to leaving him? Why couldn't she hate him enough, this minute, to pull the trigger?

"Summer, come on, sweetheart. Think about what you're doing. You don't want this. This isn't who you are."

"It wasn't, but it's who you made me," she screamed, the effort behind it making her shake.

"Summer," Chase pleaded.

"This is what you made me, and I hope you burn in Hell for it."

"Chase?"

"Marshal?"

The voices calling up from outside were her undoing. She only took her eyes off Chase for a moment, but it was enough he was able to knock the gun aside and topple her to the floor. The echo from the shot fired as her hand hit the floor mixed with the ringing caused by the pain was the last conscious thought, and everything went black.

Chapter 27

Chase gave his head a shake to stop the ringing in his ears. Reaching blindly, he found Summer's hand, now slack and unable to hold the pistol. Still, he grabbed it and tossed it away before he lifted any of his weight from her.

He would have bet the farm she'd have shot him down in the next breath, had she not been distracted by someone calling for him. She'd have shot him down, tears streaming down her pale, sweaty face. And as close as they stood, all the shaking she was doing, she'd still not have missed. And damn it all, he was thinking better he was dead than to live without her.

"Chase?"

Chase looked up briefly to see his oldest brother Adam come through the door, a very familiar looking rifle in his hands. Taking a deep breath, he pushed up off Summer and held up his hand to indicate everything was under control.

"Marshal?" Buckley came in right behind Adam, but he didn't hesitate to cross to where Summer lay, still as death on the floor. "You shot her?"

"No!" Chase said, now feeling a new kind of concern. Summer still hadn't roused herself.

"She shot you?" Buckley asked but without the normal teasing. "Sam Hill, Marshal," Buckley yelled and boldly put his hand on Summer's chest, right where her shirt lay open. "Girl's burning up."

Chase didn't bother to confirm it. Given the way she looked and acted, something was seriously wrong with her. "Doc in town?" he asked, moving to scoop Summer into his arms and get to his feet. He could feel the heat now, and her clothes were soaked through with sweat.

"Should be," Buckley said then went out to the top of the stairs. "Brown, bring that wagon 'round; hurry up."

"You ever going to have a peaceful moment?" Adam asked, stepping aside so Chase could carry Summer down the steps.

"Peace is for the grave," Chase managed to quip. Then he sent a prayer Summer wasn't about to give him any just yet.

"Sheriff went ahead to tell Doc we're coming," Deputy Brown said as he waited for Chase to climb into the wagon and get settled. "You shot her?"

"No," Chase said, trying to adjust them so they weren't bounced out.

"She shot you?" Brown asked, only he did sound a bit light-hearted.

"This a problem you been having, baby brother, with the two of you trying to shoot each other?" Adam asked as he used one hand to hold the wagon and one to hold on to Chase.

"We've had words," Chase said and managed a smile. Summer did like to say she was going to either shoot him or string him up for eating something or another before she was ready to let him. Almost every time, he'd escaped her tirades to walk into a jailhouse full of laughing men all wanting to know what deliciousness she'd whipped up that day.

Damn, life with this woman was better than he'd known it could be. He couldn't lose her. Death would be better than that.

"Love her that much already?" Adam asked. "Never thought I'd see the one who could hogtie you."

Chase didn't bother to respond; Doc Riot was already out on the street waiting for them. "She's got a fever," Chase said as the man put his hand on Summer's forehead then moved down her neck and chest. "I don't know what from or for how long."

"At least two days," Adam said and helped Chase get her out of the wagon and into the building. "Came in on the train with her, noticed her right off." Chase gave him a cutting look. His oldest brother was a female connoisseur. Once he set his eyes on one, she was his. Adam only shrugged. Like all the Storm men, he rarely apologized for how he was. They got Summer up on the table and stepped back so the doctor could look her over. "She's been favoring that left arm, up high, just below her shoulder," Adam said, and the doctor reached for some scissors. The sleeve fell away, and all three men groaned.

The wrap around Summer's upper arm was soaked with blood and puss, the skin above and below, red and swollen. Doc cut away the bandages and turned his head away for the stench.

"Someone stitched her up, but they did about as bad a job as they might have," Doc said, moving to the wall with all the cabinets of bottles and equipment. "That's well infected."

Chase moved so he could see for himself. "Damn it, she going to lose that arm?"

"Not if I can help it. Not after she 'bout singlehandedly raised enough money for the new hospital. You need to get out and let me work."

"Come on, kid," Adam said as he tried to pull Chase out the door. "Come on, you can't help; you'll only get in the way."

Chase hesitated a little longer as the doctor started cutting open the stitches. That he didn't even have to use ether was more unsettling than Chase imagined.

"I'm here; I'm here," Mrs. Bleese called, pushing into the room then pushing Chase out and shutting the door in his face.

He could hear them talking and moving about but couldn't make out the words.

"Chase, come on. Come sit down before you fall down." Adam pulled on his arm again, and this time Chase went.

"Marshal?" Buckley called getting to his feet. "She gonna be all right?"

Chase couldn't answer. The injury had looked pretty bad, and the infection looked to have a good hold on her. He'd seen stronger men die from less. And even if she didn't die, she could still lose her arm. Pressure on his shoulders forced him down into a chair.

"Girl's gonna be fine. Storm men don't hitch themselves to orchids. And that one seemed as prickly as any cactus I've ever seen."

"What happened? She tell you where she's been the last two weeks?"

"She didn't say anything," Chase said, leaning forward to hold his head in his hands.

"She said some rather unflattering things about you," Adam told him.

"I imagine," Chase said. What he already knew was bad enough. He'd maybe underestimated how hurt she'd been when he'd not given her cover from those women. But there had to be more to it. She'd not have backed out of buying that shop because of a tiff between her and them. And he thought he knew her well enough to think she'd rather stand and fight than just let either Miss Porter or Miss Codwells sink their claws into him.

"What'd you do to that girl, then?" Adam asked, sounding way too much like their father at the moment.

"Nothing," Chase said, sitting up then back before slumping down in the chair. "Nothing; it was a misunderstanding."

"Marshal done got himself two little brats that don't mind he's married and won't take go away for an answer," Buckley said, and Chase only barely managed not to groan.

"You encouraging them?" Adam asked.

"No," Chase said, disappointed his own brother would ask. "No, I am not."

"One of 'em ain't that old sow I seen in the mercantile, is it? Cause that'd be a damn shame."

"Mrs. Nelson?" Chase sat up a bit. "God, no, why would you think that?"

"Because your wife got off the train hot to sell off her rifle, and once she was paid, she went straight to the mercantile and paid that woman a handy sum, they had words, and then she stomped out." He reached into his pocket and pulled out a slip of paper. Unfolding it, he scanned the page before holding it out for Chase to take. "Girl in there don't seem the type to ever wear a forty-dollar dress."

"Forty..." Chase snatched the paper away and turned it so he could read it. It was a list of items that included honey, grain, cloth, something listed as shelving, all of it with numbers beside them, all completely overpriced, no matter how it was viewed. The list contained several other smaller items, and sure enough, next to the word dress, the number forty. The total at the bottom was seven hundred thirty-five, seven hundred thirty-five dollars, almost the very amount Chase still held back for the Gracen bounty that first brought them together "What the Sam Hill?" Chase looked over the list again and realized it had to be the bill from the fight Summer had in the store on the Fourth. "There is no way these were the charges for the damages."

"I took that list and did a little shopping on my own," Adam said. "Best I could spend was twenty-two and that was with two bolts of cloth from the dress wares pile."

"She didn't say anything to me..." Chase started then stopped and slapped his hand against his forehead.

"What?"

"I told her to pay what was asked and not to say a word, or

she'd be sorry. It was a few jars of honey. It should have been a few dollars. Not..." he waved the paper around, "...this."

"Could she even pay that?" Adam asked.

"She has an account at the bank; it's got a good amount in it."

"Then why was she looking to sell her rifle?"

"I don't know, but I can guess for the same reason she sold her horse, mule, and the building she was going to start her bakery in," Chase said. He'd already bought back her horse and the building. The mule, Sir, he'd left, because the mean animal actually seemed rather happy where he was.

"Might need to have a talk with the bank and..." Adam waved his hand at the paper Chase still held, "...the woman at the mercantile."

"Marshal," Doc called as he stepped into the parlor holding out a small bowl. Chase got to his feet. "I removed six bits of shrapnel from that wound," he said, shaking the bowl and making the bits of lead rattle around. "Any idea how she might have come by these? You shoot her?"

"Damn it," Chase groaned. "No, I haven't shot my wife... yet." He was sure thinking about doing so now. What the hell was she about that she'd ended up full of lead? And why hadn't she sought treatment?

"I cleaned and dressed the wound. I don't think it's a good idea to stitch it up yet. If the fever breaks, and she wakes up..."

Chase didn't care for the hint of doubt he heard in the man's voice. "Can I see her?"

"Gladis is getting her comfortable; she'll come let you know when you can go in." He pushed the small bowl into Chase's hand. "You might want to do a better job at looking after her. This town needs her, maybe more than they need you."

With that, the man turned and walked away. A moment later, he felt a familiar hand squeeze his shoulder. "Exactly what that girl of yours do that's more important than what you do?"

"She cooks," Buckley said with so much enthusiasm, even Chase chuckled.

"She cooks?" Adam echoed, disbelief in his tone.

"Remember Mrs. Steward?" Chase asked and saw his brother nod. "Summer makes her cooking seem like Pa's."

"No," Adam said, stepping back and leveling a hard look at Chase who only nodded. "Damn, kid, how'd you get so lucky?"

"I do not know," Chase said then followed Mrs. Bleese who was waving at him from the hall.

For three days and two nights, Chase sat up in a chair next to Summer's bed. The number of people who came by to see how she was doing and to ask if he needed anything wasn't as comforting as they must have thought it would be.

Summer's fever would break but then return, her few moments of consciousness so riddled with pain that Doc Riot smothered her with ether just to keep her from thrashing around. They brought in a tub, filled it with ice to try to bring her temperature down, they dribbled broth and water into her mouth, and every day, someone told Chase to go home, get some rest. It was no different tonight, as Doc Riot came in one more time before he turned in.

"You're not doing either of you any good," the man said as he pressed his stethoscope to Summer's chest. "You should at least go get some clean clothes."

Chase leaned forward and sighed. The man was right. He needed to change and wash. And maybe he could go through Summer's packs to see if it held any clues as to how she came to be shot. Though he suspected his brother's pointed questions would eventually bring him the answers. He said he was heading out today to see what Summer had been doing up in Creed days before she left. With another sigh, he pushed up out the chair and grabbed his hat off the table.

"I'll be back by morning," he said and watched the man nod but continue to listen to Summer's heart. He might ask the man if a broken heart sounded the same as a not broken one, but he was afraid the answer would be no, and so he'd still not know if he had a chance with his wife or not.

"YOUR WIFE'S SOME BOUNTY HUNTER?"

Chase sat up from a dead sleep. "Pa?" he called out, rubbing his eyes and feeling the same clench in his gut as he would feel when he was seven.

"No, you ass." Adam's hand landed hard across the back of his head.

"Ow," Chase griped, rubbing the back of his head. He stopped mid rub to look around. The room was filled with daylight. "Damn, what time is it? How long was I asleep?" Chase scrambled from the bed. He'd only sat down intending to pull off his socks.

"Only a few hours," Adam said, not sounding at all sympathetic. "You didn't tell us in your letter you married a bounty hunter."

"Because it wasn't important; she wasn't a bounty hunter after I married her," Chase said, wondering how his family had found out about Summer's activities so fast. It wasn't that he was hiding them. There was nothing wrong with how she earned her living, but Summer herself seemed to want to start over as just a woman who ran an eatery. With the exception of her one little foray that landed her down a mine shaft, she'd not so much as done more than look over the few wanted notices.

"She wasn't, because she said so or because you told her so?"

"Neither," Chase said, pulling off his shirt and crossing over to where he'd set a pot of water to heat. Most of it had cooked away, but there was enough he was able to heat the water in the basin and start washing. "Both, maybe," he said, giving the question a bit more thought. He never outright told her she couldn't chase a bounty, but being as that fell under the reckless category... "Why?"

"Because she went up to Creed to get a bill written up. She told the sheriff there it was for you or at least implied it was. That's what she was doing in Pueblo." He handed Chase a telegram. "Sheriff there said she took both men, but the gun fight left one dead, her hurt, and he only paid half because they were both wanted alive bills."

Chase could well enough read that for himself. "I don't understand."

"She must have wanted to pay that bill awful bad," Adam said, holding out a fresh shirt so Chase could finish dressing and get back to the doctor's.

"But she had money in the bank." Damn it, if Summer had risked her life to pay that erroneous bill from the mercantile, he'd personally see Nelson strung up.

"Are you sure? Could she have spent it all?" Adam asked, following him across the room to the stool by the door.

"Summer is more miserly than Scrooge," Chase said, sitting down and pulling on his boots.

"You and your books." Adam shook his head. "For someone who hated school."

"I didn't hate school," Chase denied. "I hated the teacher."

"You hated the teacher's cane and Pa's belt after that," Adam said with a smirk as he opened the door and preceded Chase outside. Chase could only shrug. His brother knew him well, so why lie?

They made their way down the street, stopped several times by folks wanting to know how Summer was doing. He didn't miss it when Miss Porter crossed the street rather than walk past him, and neither did Adam, but he'd the good sense to not say anything.

They were barely in the door when Doc Riot stepped out and blocked their way. "She's awake, fever looks broke for good.

She doesn't want to see you," he said in that clinical tone he often used.

"She's my wife," Chase snapped and made to push past.

"She doesn't want to see you, and she says she's already written someone about a divorce," Doc said, and being he was no old, frail man, he readily kept Chase from getting past.

"I need to talk to her," Chase stated. "I need to know why she thought she had to go after a bounty when she has money in the bank and when she has full access to our accounts if she wants."

"Doctor Emeute," Adam started in his most formal legal tone. "Wife or not, Mrs. Storm may well be a victim of fraud and possible theft. Marshal Storm has a need to investigate so it can be determined or disproven, and if determined, he might seek out other victims."

Sometimes Chase could really appreciate having family who excelled at law. Now, as Doc stepped aside and let them pass was one of those times. "You're going to anyway, but try not to upset her too much," he said. "She needs to stay still, and getting out of bed to take off your head…"

Chase didn't know who he wanted to punch, Doc for saying that or his brother for chuckling at it. But when Adam, with only a sharp knock, opened the door, his focus went completely on Summer.

She sat in bed, reading a book, and was slow to look up. The first thing he noted was she looked frighteningly pale, then that her eyes were less bright than normal. But a spark certainly tried to put the flame back in them as soon as she spotted him.

"Get out, Marshal," she snapped.

"Mrs. Storm?" Adam started, only to be sharply corrected.

"Miss Rain." Summer closed the book and, struggling, managed to push more upright.

"Rain?" Adam said, more to Chase than to Summer. "Really?"

"What can I say? It was fate," Chase commented with a shrug.

"Did you sign the marriage documents with 'D' or with 'Danials'?" Adam asked, stepping further into the room.

Chase managed a chuckle as it was the exact remark Summer had made about their combined names. Summer shot down his amusement rather abruptly. "Who could even tell what he wrote with that chicken scratch?"

"Your familiarity with Marshal Storm's lacking penmanship tells me you at least saw a recording of your marriage." Summer narrowed her eyes but nodded once. "Then until there is a record of dissolution of that marriage... Mrs. Storm... there are questions you need to answer."

"Who in hell do you think you are?"

"Adam Jefferson, Esquire," Adam introduced himself not adding his last name to the deed.

"What question?" Summer snapped, giving Chase some hope.

"What the hell were you thinking, going after a bounty?" Chase blurted out. He barely managed to duck as the book flew past his head.

"Now stop that," Adam chided.

"Get out, both of you," Summer yelled, reaching for something on the small table beside the bed. Chase tensed, ready to duck that object too, but Adam interfered, grabbing Summer's wrist and pulling the object from her fingers.

"You best pull up on those reins, young lady. Stop behaving like a bratty child," Adam warned, and Chase saw the same expression he was sure all the Storm children wore at some point in their lives. Only Summer wasn't easily bucked off.

"Don't tell me what to do. You don't know me; you don't know anything about the situation," she said, jerking her arm free, the act clearly causing pain.

"Adam…" Chase started. The hard look he got made him falter. "Doc said don't upset her."

"You think I don't know you. I know you well enough. I know you're a strong, independent woman who doesn't abide weakness or stupidity. That you're more than capable of taking care of your affairs and that you do so logically and reasonably. I also know you're as stubborn as the day is long and your temper, along with your mouth, are about to get you bent over for a spanking that will make sitting hard for a good while. So, stop behaving like a bratty child and answer the questions you're being asked."

Summer's eyes flashed to him then back to Adam. Lifting her hand, she covered the bandage wrapped around her upper arm. "I needed the money. I'd already sold everything I could, and it still wasn't enough to pay for those damages."

Her grumbled reply didn't really tell him anything Chase didn't already know, but it gave him an opening. "If you'd have at least spoken to me, I would have told you I'd decided that same day to tell Mr. Nelson you weren't going to be paying for anything." She swung around to stare at him. Stepping closer to the bed, Chase continued. "You were right; you didn't get in a fight by yourself. It took two of you at least. You did the labor, cleaned up the mess. It would have only been right that Stephanie pay for the broken jars."

"I paid for her dress too," Summer reminded him, and he cringed at how her voice cracked. "Better make sure you marry her in that forty-dollar get-up. Though I'm sure she plans to wear it to attend the governor's ball."

"I'm not marrying anyone," Chase almost cried.

"That's not what it sounded like to me."

"Because you set your spurs to soon. If you'd have waited just a second more, you'd have heard me tell her exactly what I thought about her and Angelica. I'm being well enough avoided now by both of them, thank God."

"Marshal Storm says you had sufficient funds in the bank," Adam interrupted. "Why didn't you use them rather than sell your horse and go after a bounty?"

"Because he stole all that money," Summer said, and any ground Chase thought he'd gained was washed out by the thunderclouds brewing in her eyes.

"He stole the money from the bank?"

"I did not," Chase denied. What kind of wives' tale was that?

"He took every cent I had and put it in his account and then made it so I could only get out five dollars a week. I couldn't pay that bill, and I can't run a business like that."

"I didn't take anything and put it anywhere." Chase barely refrained from yelling this time. Why did she think he'd taken her money? Money, damn it, it was the bane of his existence when it came to his wife.

"Yes, you did," Summer shot back.

"No, I didn't," Chase yelled then spun on his heels and paced across the room.

"Who told you, or rather how did you find out your funds were removed from your accounts by your husband?" Adam asked.

"I didn't remove her damn money," Chase yelled, only to again get that look from his brother.

"Mrs. Storm, what circumstance led you to become aware the funds were not available to you?"

"What do you think? I couldn't pay that bill with just what I had. I knew it was going to delay making the few last purchases for my shop, but all I could do was take it out of the bank. I went in, asked for the money, and was told my account had been combined with his, and that he set the limit I could use at five dollars a week." Summer leaned her head back against the headboard and shut her eyes.

"Who told you that?" Adam pressed.

"Mr. Codwells." She was now rubbing her arm just below the bandages.

"The bank owner," Chase said when Adam looked at him expectantly. "But I didn't tell him to do any of that. I certainly didn't tell him to limit how much she could take out of my... our accounts. Why would I?" He looked back at Summer who still had her eyes closed. "Summer, why would I limit what you could use at the bank, when I didn't limit what you could spend at the mercantile, or the dress shop or any place else? I told you if its mine, it's yours."

"How should I know? You did it because you know I can't make purchases at the mercantile anymore. What difference does it make now? Everything's ruined."

"Summer, nothing is ruined." Chase again stepped to the bed, and this time took a seat. "Nothing is ruined. We can fix this."

"No, we can't," she said and wiped at the tears seeping out the corners of her eyes.

"We can straighten it out at the bank, and we can talk to Nelson... Mr. Nelson and you can go back to getting those supplies you can only get through him."

"It's too late," Summer said, a small sob slipping. Chase lifted her hand and gave it a squeeze.

"It's not."

"I already broke the contract on the building. I canceled all the orders from the producers, and I don't have enough money to start over. It's too late. I can't stay. I can't have this one thing. I never should have run when I was taken to Breaker. I can't escape what I was always just meant to be."

"No, Summer, no. I won't accept that," Chase said, taking the chance and hoping she didn't buck him off as he slid closer and put his arm around her. He drew her forward to lean against him. "I won't accept that at all." God help him if she'd actually been considering turning to whoring because of this. "We can fix this. You just need to let me take the reins and do what's in my power to do."

"It can't be fixed," she persisted, but her right hand took a grip on his arm and her left settled down on his thigh. "And I can't stay here. Not after this, not after them…"

"You marry someone so easily run off, kid?" Adam asked, drawing attention to the fact he was still in the room.

"No," Chase told him but then lifted Summer's chin. "But this time, if she wants to walk away from the showdown, I'll walk away with her."

She jerked back from him. "Chase, you can't, this is where you've been assigned."

"So I ask for reassignment, or I resign altogether. I'm not losing you. Not over a misunderstanding, not over a resolvable situation, not because of your recklessness, and not because the seasons will eventually change. I'm not losing you. I love you. I don't want to ride range with anyone else."

"You don't?" Summer asked, a little more spark lighting up her eyes.

"I don't," Chase confirmed. "Are you maybe still willing to partner me?"

"I…" Her uncertainty was unnerving. She always seemed rather able to make quick, sure decisions.

"You might be needing this?" Adam asked, bumping his arm with a small velvet sack.

"Why you always intruding on my best moments?" Chase grumbled as he watched a bit of those clouds retuning to Summer's eyes.

"Because if I didn't, you'd already be hitched to Crazy Lucy and her twenty-seven cats," Adam said, causing Chase to drop his head. "Besides, that's what big brothers are for. You gonna take this, or do I get to give it to her? Because if I get to give it to her, I think that makes it a legal transfer."

"You're a jackass," Chase grumbled but snatched the bag and started pulling open the strings.

"Wait, you're brothers?" Summer asked, sitting back and giving Chase an accusing look.

Chase would let his brother handle that little omission. He busied himself getting the object out of the pouch.

"I'm the oldest," Adam said.

"Brothers," Summer almost sighed the word. "Thank goodness."

"Thank goodness?" Chase asked, getting the proper grip on the beautiful platinum ring. The large diamond surrounded by a wreath of sapphires sparkled in the dappled light coming through the curtains. Lifting her left hand, he waited for her to answer.

"I thought... I mean..." she stammered, looking back and forth between both men. "When I was on the train, I was worried that every man I'd see once I left you would remind me of you. He sat down and opened his mouth, and I thought I was going to lose my mind. He sounded just like you."

"No, he sounds like Pa," Chase grumbled. He was still waiting for Summer to give him an answer.

"We all sound like Pa," Adam grumbled.

"Not Beaker," Chase said and tried to catch Summer's eye so he might direct her without actually saying it, to look down.

"Don't call him Beaker; you know Cass hates that."

"Not as much as she hates you calling her Cass." Summer's eyes finally came back to his, full of questions. Chase sighed. "Cassandra..."

"She's the second oldest," Adam supplied and, as always, sounded like he was insulted. The fact they were twins could well have something to do with it.

"According to you," Chase said and took the time to enjoy his brother's scowl. "They're twins," Chase clarified when Summer again turned her pretty blue eyes back to him. "She done gave birth to the scrawniest young'in. Can't even tell he's got any Storm blood in him."

"Well, I told her not to marry that accountant," Adam said, again distracting Summer from Chase's attempt to get a ring on her finger.

"Yes, well, she always did like the dudes and dandies." This time, he set her hand down and used his free hand to turn her face back to him. "But that's not what you like, right, sweetheart?"

"No, I…" She pulled her head away and turned back to look at Adam. "You have a twin? A girl twin."

Chase barely managed not to burst out laughing; the snort that did escape earned him a smack on the back of the head. "Don't worry; she's much prettier than he is. Way much prettier."

"Why don't you just pay attention to what's happening there?" Adam grumbled and pointed down to where Chase again waited, poised to slide on the ring. "Stop worrying about what I might look like in a dress."

Summer's eyes came back to his, and he didn't miss the bit of sparkle or the smirk in them on her lips, but in the brief moment it took for her to drop her head, spot the ring, and look back up at him, her expression had gone to complete disbelief and her eyes flooded with tears. "Chase?"

"I'd ask you to marry me, but you already did that," Chase told her. "So I'll ask will you stay, past this September? Stay past the next eighty Septembers?" He saw her hesitation and quickly added, "Stay with me, Summer. Wherever I am. If not here, somewhere. I can be happy any place you are. We can weather anything if we stay together through it. Will you stay?"

"Yes," she whispered, and as he slid the ring past her knuckle, she leaned in. "I'll stay, but we might both always chase the summer rain storm."

"Saddle up, sweetheart, I'm ready if you are," Chase said then covered her lips with his.

Epilogue

"Summer, you mean woman."

Summer turned from the stove where she was stirring the warm peach jam to see Chase standing in the doorway of the huge kitchen of their new home.

"You have got to be the meanest daw'gum female alive," he said, making his way over to the table where the jars she'd already filled sat cooling.

"What, now?" Summer laughed then quickly reached out to slap his fingers away from the sweets. "Keep your fingers out of my jam, Marshal."

"Mean," Chase grumbled, rubbing his hand like the smack might have hurt. "How come I have to find out you made peach pies after you let everyone else, including Buckley and his lot, eat them all?"

"You were gone," Summer said, setting her spoon aside and moving to the sideboard.

"I was gone for six hours," Chase almost wailed. "Zander said there were eleven pies. I didn't get a single bite."

Summer chuckled. Life with Marshal Storm was certainly rarely dull. Making the decision to stay in Willow Creek was the second-best decision of her life. Staying married to this man being the first. And she was more than assured it was what he really wanted because she'd seen how he held his breath every day through the entire month of September. Only last week, as they marked the calendar for their fall plans, had he seemed more sure she was staying.

"Get your fingers out of my jam," she scolded again as she lifted the towel covering the deep pan she'd set aside just for him.

"Stop being mean to me, woman," Chase yelled then plopped down in a chair and pouted.

"I'm never mean to you, Marshal," Summer cooed as she carried the fresh, still warm pie over to where he sat.

"Is that for me?"

Summer laughed out loud at that. "Just for you." She set it down and reached for a fork. "Are you gonna bother with a plate?"

"Do I have to?" he asked, already sticking his fork in and working a bite free.

"Not this time, I suppose." Damn, but he was a fine thing to watch enjoying something, be it her cooking or her body. He always showed his love and appreciation, though each in a different way. "But I think by this time next year, you'll not only have to use a plate, you'll have to share."

He chewed then swallowed hard. "Share with who?" She bit her lip not to laugh at how he circled the pie with his arm. He probably didn't even know he did it. "Summer, share with who? Is someone coming?"

"Someone is coming."

"Who? Everyone from my family has already rode in."

It was true. Not even two weeks after Chase put that ring on her finger, the rest of the very large Storm family came for a visit. They packed three whole train cars, every spare bed that could be rented out was taken, and still several of the family members made camp. Summer had been nearly overwhelmed, and if not for Chase's strong hand holding hers tightly, she might have run off to hide in the pine and aspen until they all rode out.

To her complete surprise, his family embraced her. She was welcomed in and made one of them as if she'd been born to them. She'd never felt more love than when James Chase wrapped his arms around her and whispered his gratitude for settling his boy finally. The same was expressed by his mother, though she had a different way of doing so. One that, when it crossed some line, was quickly corralled by her husband.

"Summer?" Chase called, fork poised to go in his mouth. "Who's coming? More family?"

"I don't know who's coming, but it will definitely be family," she said and set a hand over her belly.

Chase's mouth opened and closed a few times before he dropped his fork and scrambled to his feet. "Are you…"

She giggled and nodded. Telling him made her feel even more excited than when Doc Riot had confirmed it for her. "He should be arriving sometime in May."

"Really? Really?" Chase asked, grabbing her around the waist and pulling her hard against him. "You're gonna have a baby?"

"*We're* gonna have one," Summer said then squealed when Chase lifted her and spun her around.

"A baby," he said and leaned in to kiss her. "You mean woman."

"Mean? How am I mean?" Summer asked but tipped her head so he could kiss up along the side of her neck.

"You're trying to kill me with all the happiness you cook up." He nipped her earlobe. "Damn, woman, I love you," he said, and like they so often did, the words made her sex clench. "I love you so damn much." He moved to cover her lips again, but Summer felt when he reached past her.

"Get your fingers out of my jams, Marshal Storm," she

yelled, only to have her home filled with the booming sound of laugher. In the distance, she could hear the whistle of the train.

"Train's coming in, wonder what it's bringing us today?" Chase said as he took a seat and pulled her into his lap. His solid frame warmed like no seasonal sun could.

"Whatever it is, it can't be better than this," Summer said, lifting a bite of the pie to her lips as Chase's hand splayed across her belly.

"Nothing could be better than this."

THE END

Marie Hall

Marie Hall is a romantic with an imagination and she uses those skills to both entertain and inform.

Because of her love for the written word, she spends her days (and a lot of nights too) creating characters in setting and situations the reader will hopefully love and believe in.

Writing erotica, historical and contemporary, allows her to reach a broader audience. Focusing on the complex dynamics of a dominate/submissive relationship, with love and respect as a main theme.

Marie uses her degree in history to add facts about the time periods she writes and blogs about those facts from time to time. When she is not writing or blogging she spends time with her family, her husband of more than twenty years and her adult daughter. Mostly, though, with her little four legged fur-child, Tuck. They spend time enjoying the contrasting landscape of Western Colorado. With his high reaching, jagged and rough peaks and its soft sloping valleys it is the perfect setting to sit back and think up stories to tell.

Please take the time to enjoy a book. Books open doors in life, takes you to places or times you may never have known and lift your spirit.

Be Safe,
    And as always, READ ON!

    Don't miss these exciting titles by Marie Hall and Blushing Books!

Connect with Marie Hall:
www.cynsitywriting.org

Blushing Books

Blushing Books is one of the oldest eBook publishers on the web. We've been running websites that publish spanking and BDSM related romance and erotica since 1999, and we have been selling eBooks since 2003. We hope you'll check out our hundreds of offerings at http://www.blushingbooks.com.

Lightning Source UK Ltd.
Milton Keynes UK
UKHW040612200120
357267UK00001B/40